After the Fact

Red Adept Publishing, LLC

104 Bugenfield Court

Garner, NC 27529

https://RedAdeptPublishing.com/

This is a work of fiction. Names, characters, places, and incidents either are the product of the author's imagination or are used fictitiously, and any resemblance to locales, events, business establishments, or actual persons—living or dead—is entirely coincidental.

---

1.  http://StreetlightGraphics.com

*For Alexandra*

# PROLOGUE

Abigail Walker sat alone at a table large enough for twelve. Her wet hair lapped at the collar of a threadbare bathrobe as she sat in silence and surveyed a plate of pale turkey and even paler rice. Not even two glasses of white Burgundy had made this dinner palatable. Perhaps the third would do the trick. Placing a fine crystal wineglass against her lips, she emptied it halfway with a single swallow. *A few more hours to pass*, she thought. *Just a few more.*

This version of Abigail barely resembled the one who had eaten lunch with the governor of New York just a few hours earlier. At lunch, she had been simply radiant—a middle-aged icon in perfect makeup and a timeless designer suit. She had given her adoring public what they wanted to see: the loyal widow, the generous philanthropist, the steadfast advocate for causes great and small. She had chatted with tourists. She had forced countless smiles for the cameras. She had listened intently to every politician who blathered in her direction.

But mercifully, that was done, at least for today. The admirers and cameras were long gone, and a hot shower had washed away her daytime façade. A stream of makeup swirling into the shower drain had left behind the true widow Walker: a rapidly aging woman wearing her husband's old bathrobe, desperately lonely and spiraling toward her life's last sunset. This was her reality. She deserved no better.

She flicked her fork at a slice of overcooked turkey then turned her attention to the pile of unopened mail. On a good night, she might have found some solace in working through the stack of envelopes. One of her few remaining joys was reading the email and letters from those she had inspired, her spirits buoyed by the public's continuing interest in her and her life. But tonight she wanted none of that. She sighed and slid the pile toward the middle of the table. The staff could deal with it tomorrow.

But as she struggled to return her attention to her dinner plate, something caught her eye. A pristine white envelope sat atop the pile of cream and manila. No postage, no postmark, no return address. So odd—and irresistible. She snatched it from the top of the pile and slit it open with a single pass of her fingernail. *Please be interesting,* she thought as she unfolded the enclosed sheets of paper and began to read.

The writing was cryptic, the words like riddles. "I know what you did," the unnamed writer warned. "I know *everything.*" *Oh, I'm sure you do,* Abigail thought as she grabbed the wineglass and drained it. *I'm sure you know all my darkest secrets.* She scoffed as she read on with morbid curiosity, her heart quickening with the day's first real excitement. *What horrors will you accuse me of?*

She soon had her answer. A chill radiated up her spine and unleashed a stream of tears. She wailed, nearly loud enough to be heard in the apartment next door. "No," she called out to the empty room. "No, no, no."

Despite her wealth and power, Abigail's life had been marked by dreadful moments: the moment her drunken father had stormed out the kitchen door, never to return; the moment she'd first heard the word *myeloma*; the moment her husband, Senator Harold Walker, had died just outside the gates of Harvard Yard. Now another moment, perhaps worse than all that had come before, was added to the list—the moment the blackmail began. She bolted into the kitchen, grabbed her phone off the counter and dialed frantically. Barely able to control her voice, she wasted no time with pleasantries. "I need you," she barked. "I need to see you. Somebody knows..." She took in a gasping breath, struggling to collect enough air to continue. "They know. And they want money."

The man on the other end of the line tried to ask a question, but she had no time for that. "Just get here, Ted. Now." There was no hint of request in her tone. It was pure command, punctuated by the slam of the phone onto the counter.

She stumbled a few feet across the kitchen and filled a glass with ice, her trembling hands scattering half of the cubes onto the travertine floor. She opened a bottle of Grey Goose and a bottle of pills then poured enough liquor to drown seven years of bad dreams.

After downing three Xanax with a full gulp of vodka, she shuffled back through the dining room and into the living room beyond. She slumped into a beige Queen Anne chair and closed her eyes, waiting for the drugs to work their magic. Waiting for the pounding of her pulse to slow. Waiting for her lawyer to arrive and pledge to help her bear this great burden—to promise, even falsely, that everything would be all right.

As a drug-induced fog wrapped around her, she brooded over how completely she had failed Harold Walker during his life. She swore to protect him in his death, to do whatever it took to appease her blackmailers. She would pay for their silence, at any price. She would give all she had to protect her late husband's legacy, to spare him from the consequences of his wife's terrible choices.

Harold Walker would always be Abigail's one true love.

Killing him had been the greatest mistake of her life.

# AUGUST
## Four years later
# CHAPTER 1

J ack Collins bounded up the steps to the train platform and looked at his wristwatch for the fifth time in as many minutes. He had planned his morning brilliantly. Despite a few missed traffic lights and an extra loop around the parking garage, he was still right on time.

Standing on the platform amid the crowd waiting for the 7:55 express from Stamford to New York City, he surveyed the commuters around him. One was working on a crossword puzzle, and another was catching up on the sports pages, occasionally turning to the man next to him to offer a disparaging remark about the Red Sox. In his gray suit and red tie, Jack looked exactly like all the others lined up in the morning light. But he didn't act like them. He didn't read. He didn't chat. He simply waited, alternately staring across the platform and down at his freshly shined wingtips. For the others, this was an ordinary Monday morning. For him, it was so much more.

He was just thirty-one, yet carried the regrets of a man twice his age. And this morning was his chance to finally live the life he should have lived long ago. So he stood on this train platform, trying his best to ignore the subtle trembling of his knees, committed to following through on his plan. *It will all work out*, he reassured himself. *It will all be okay.*

A distant rumble soon interrupted his contemplation. He turned his head toward the sound, hoping to catch a glimpse of the incoming train. He thought of the gleaming skyscraper that awaited him, a glass-and-steel fortress that housed his greatest dream: a job at one of the nation's finest law firms, an office down the hall from the legendary Ted Parker, a chance to begin his adult life anew. All of it was just a train ride away.

The rumbling grew louder. He placed his hand above his eyes to block out the glare as he continued to scan the horizon, desperate to see the first glimpse of headlights. The August sunlight reflected off the endless tracks, its golden rays bathing everything in the glow of summer. Even the plain concrete platform beneath his feet seemed somehow more inviting in this light. In reality, the concrete was dingy and dead, marred by the elements and marked by the battered soles of weary commuters. But in this bright sunshine, this most favorable of light, the platform glistened with the intensity of diamonds.

The blinding reflections scorched his eyes, but he refused to turn away. Finally, a red-and-silver Metro North train emerged into view and rolled into the station, a wave of hot air marking its arrival. As the first car rumbled past, he tightened his grip on a shiny new briefcase, a trickle of sweat forming where his wedding ring pressed against the leather handle. His breath grew shallow. His heart pounded with anticipation, its pace quickening as the vibration of the train echoed through the station.

After the train lurched to a stop, he left the sunlit platform and followed the crowd through a set of stainless-steel doors. He placed his suit jacket and briefcase on the rack above his head and slid into a blue vinyl seat.

He sat back and forced a mouthful of air into his lungs. He looked up at the briefcase and remembered his father's words when he handed it to him the evening before. "You're ready for this," the elder Collins had promised. "You're going to be great." Then, forcing back a tear, "And I'll be just fine."

Jack batted at his eyes with the back of his hand, stifling his own tears just as they had begun to form. Regardless of what his father said, he wasn't ready for this. Not by a long shot. *I should end this folly.* He should bolt back through the open doors and race back to his old office, returning to the comfortable life he knew so well. He could be there in five minutes.

"This is the express train to New York," boomed a raspy voice over the intercom. "If you're heading anyplace else, you need to get off."

So many times in his life, Jack had given up at moments like this. But today he didn't budge. He summoned his courage and settled deeper into his seat. *You're doing this*, he resolved, as he pressed his palms against his quivering legs. *Don't you dare give up.*

A warning bell sounded as the doors shut with a thud. Then the train lurched forward toward New York.

# CHAPTER 2

Ted Parker had arrived at his desk early enough to watch the first rays of sunlight dance across the Manhattan skyline. The solitude of early morning had not yet yielded to the hectic pace of the upcoming day. For at least a few more moments, he would actually be alone—no phone calls, no emails, no other interruptions. The only sound to be heard was one of his favorites: Brahms's Third Symphony, reverberating from the small stereo in the corner of his office.

A partner and head of the private wealth department at the legendary Reynolds & Harris law firm, known to most as simply R&H, Ted had risen to the pinnacle of the legal profession. Though barely past fifty, he was widely regarded as one of the nation's best estate planning attorneys and had come to dominate a field full of far senior lawyers. In firm partnership meetings, his sandy hair stood out among the gray and the bald, a visual testament to a career that had ascended further, and faster, than many of his colleagues could comprehend.

As a result of his concerted efforts and a little good fortune, Ted had come to represent some of America's wealthiest and most newsworthy individuals. In the traditionally understated world of trusts and estates, he had become a rare superstar. Yet there was no doubt who his single most important client was, and always would be: Abigail Walker. The widow of one senator from Massachusetts and the mother of another, she was the guardian of one of America's great family names. She was also the undisputed centerpiece of Ted's legal career. And today, like every day, her life and his were intertwined.

Ted looked at the clock on his desk and sighed. He could feel the muscles of his abdomen tense as he thought about his next task. It had been this way for nearly four years, since the evening Abigail had got-

7

ten the letter that would change both their lives. Staring at Ted across her living room, she had issued simple instructions. "Pay it. Do whatever you have to do." Then she'd risen from her favorite chair and stumbled toward her bedroom, giving her final command. "Never talk to me about it. Just handle it." With that, she was gone.

He and Abigail had never again revisited that moment, never again spoken of the blackmailer's demand. Ted had simply *handled it*, exactly as his client had instructed him to do. Now it was time to handle it again. And so, on this morning, like the first morning of every month, Ted had prepared a letter requesting a series of transfers from Abigail Walker's account at Constitution Trust to various other banks. Buried among the payments of Abigail's bills, gifts to her children, and charitable pledges was a two-hundred-thousand-dollar transfer to account number 402-9620 at Atlantic Coast Bank. Located in the Cayman Islands, the bank was a favorite destination for financial criminals seeking to avoid U.S. banking laws. Included among the unsavory account holders was Abigail's blackmailer.

Ted signed the two-page letter and penned in the date beneath his name. He stood from his plush leather chair, papers in hand, and headed toward his office door. Turning off Brahms as he passed the stereo, he walked into the desolate hallways of R&H to the fax machine that none of the secretaries likely realized he knew how to use. He dialed a number from memory, fed the letter into the machine, and then slid the original into the adjacent shredder.

A hundred miles away, in Hartford, Connecticut, a fax machine would soon purr to life. Per the plan, Ben would be the only custody officer on the third floor of Constitution Trust Company who had arrived for the day. He would handle the fax himself. He would make all the transfers. He would raise no red flags.

Ted was also certain that Ben would never ask why Abigail was funneling money into an offshore account. He wouldn't question what the money was for. And most importantly of all, he would never tell anyone that account 402-9620 was owned by Ted Parker himself.

In the wrong hands, such information could destroy countless lives. But Ben Parker could be trusted with that epic secret. He would never betray a client's confidence. He would never disappoint his father.

# CHAPTER 3

As the elevator made its way skyward from the lobby of 1593 Broadway to its forty-fourth floor, the quivering returned to Jack's knees. He exited the elevator car and headed through the etched glass doors that marked theentrance to Reynolds & Harris.

First impressions often meant everything in life, and R&H made one hell of a first impression. The massive walnut reception desk bore a mirror-like shine. Brass lamps with emerald-green shades radiated a soft glow the color of money. The smell of fresh-cut flowers drifted through the air. The overall message was clear: this was a place of power, a place that mattered.

Jack smiled at the woman sitting behind the desk. "Good morning," he said as clearly as his parched mouth would allow. "I'm Jack Collins. It's my first day."

"Of course, Mr. Collins. Welcome to Reynolds & Harris." The receptionist stood and extended her hand.

"Thank you. It's great to be here."

She motioned toward a sitting area a few feet away. "Please make yourself comfortable. I'll have one of Mr. Parker's assistants come for you."

After settling into an armchair, he surveyed the room. Set out before him was a collection of antiques and artwork worthy of a museum, including a wall of original oil portraits spanning back through the firm's eighty-year history.

Until a few months earlier, he had never even interviewed at a firm like R&H. He had worked at the same small Stamford law firm during both summers at Yale Law and returned there immediately upon graduation. He'd spent the entire time at that firm trying to convince himself that he was happy there—far happier than he could be at an international law firm employing more than a thousand lawyers. He had been so very wrong.

Across an oriental carpet, the skyline beckoned. Pressing his phone against the glass, he sent his wife a photo of the city glistening below. Three letters and an exclamation point were all he needed to fully narrate the moment. *Wow!*

He turned toward the sound of approaching footsteps. A petite woman stepped toward him, a steaming cup of coffee outstretched before her.

"I almost didn't recognize you," he confessed. Unlike the last time they'd met, Claire Reed had her hair pulled back in a ponytail. Her classic blue suit and white silk blouse made her seem more like an executive than the legal secretary he had met just six weeks before.

"A lunch date today—a banker-type. Do you think this is too stuffy?"

"Not at all. You can never go wrong with navy," he replied as Claire turned to share his view of the city.

He'd immediately hit it off with her when they met during his job interview. Although this was just their second meeting, he already liked her immensely and trusted her instinctively, in no small part because she looked and acted like his own sister. As Jack stared at her doppelganger reflected in the window, he remembered Emily Collins. The daredevil of the family. The one who fearlessly skied black diamonds, and drove too fast with music blaring, and broke her curfew every chance she got. The one who pushed the envelope for twenty-one years and four days before death finally responded to her constant flirtation, converting Jack from baby brother to sole survivor.

"Amazing view, huh?" Claire asked, breaking Jack's pensive silence. "We had it brought in just for you."

A broad smile crossed his face as he laughed for the first time since he'd boarded the train that morning. "That was nice of you," he said.

"My old office had a fabulous view of a dying pear tree. This is amazing." As he surveyed the skyline, he took a sip of the French roast, smoky and rich, but also incredibly sweet.

"Wow, you remembered."

"No cream but lots of sugar," she replied. "A good memory comes in handy around here."

"Well, then you'll be my savior."

"I doubt that, Mr. Collins," she teased. "From what I hear, you're smart enough for the both of us." She paused for just a moment before continuing. "But then again, I do know one thing you don't."

"Oh yeah? What's that?"

"I know where your office is. Want to see it?" Without waiting for him to reply, she pivoted away from the windows and began to walk back toward the reception desk.

He followed her for a few steps but then paused and turned back to stare out the massive lobby windows one last time. He took another sip of the coffee as he looked out toward infinity. The sense of power was heady, nearly overwhelming. "Okay. I'm ready," he said as he felt the tremors return to his legs.

# CHAPTER 4

J ack had been working at R&H for less than an hour, and a flood of paperwork had already found him. Two stacks of client files guarded the corners of his massive wood desk, but he hadn't even started to look at those. He first had to work through the pile of documents required by the human resources department—confidentiality agreement, nondisclosure agreement, forms consenting to periodic background and credit checks. He thought he had signed all of these a month earlier, but R&H apparently wanted them again.

He hadn't seen this many employment forms since his senior year in college, when he had applied for a two-month internship with the Honorable Angela Robinson, an associate justice of the Massachusetts Supreme Court. That application process had required even more forms than any paying job he'd ever had, plus a set of fingerprints. Although R&H seemingly wanted every other detail of his financial and personal life, they hadn't inked his fingertips—at least not yet.

As he signed and countersigned the forms on his desk, the sound of knuckles on mahogany snapped him out of his trance.

"How's my newest soldier?"

In his flawlessly tailored pinstripe suit, crisp white shirt, and bright-red tie, Ted Parker defied the stereotype of the tax lawyer wearing oversized eyeglasses and rumpled clothing. Like a seasoned politician, Ted's presence dominated any room from the moment he entered it. Jack's office was no exception.

"Good morning, Mr. Parker." Jack could feel his throat tighten as he stood from his chair. His increasing tension added a squeaky lilt to his voice.

"I hope Claire has everything under control," Ted said.

"Of course. She's great. Everyone has been wonderful."

"That's super. Just super."

Jack had heard mixed reviews of Ted Parker. Some called him a gift-ed tax lawyer, while others dismissed him as a mere self-promoter. But the first time Jack had seen Ted with his own eyes, he realized that nei-ther legal skills nor good marketing alone had made his new boss a leg-end. Rather, Ted's success came from the way he could dominate any encounter by the sheer strength of his charisma. He could look you in the eye and talk to you in a way that only a Southern gentleman could. From a rural town in South Carolina but educated at Exeter, Dartmouth, and Harvard Law School, he could alternately call upon his simple roots or completely conceal them. With subtle adjustments to his wardrobe and his accent, Ted could be all things to all people.

Jack felt nervous sweat forming in his armpits as he stepped for-ward to shake Ted's outstretched hand. "It's a pleasure to see you again, Mr. Parker."

Ted laughed and shook his head sideways. "I'm pretty sure that *Mister* isn't necessary. In fact, at least in the office, Ted will probably do."

"Of course, whatever you prefer," Jack gushed. "I'm excited to get to work."

"Good, because we have plenty of that around here. As soon as she gets to it, Claire will bring you a memo about some clients I saw last week. They need all-new estate-planning documents—wills, a couple of trusts, health care proxies. I'm sure you've done all of that a million times before. Read the files to get up to speed, and then Deb will keep you busy the rest of the week."

Jack had come to R&H to work with Ted, so he didn't like how his new boss had completely omitted his own name from the discussion of Jack's initial assignments. Instead, at least for the moment, he would be relegated to the care of Ted's secretary and his senior associate, Deb

Miller. Jack was likely speaking to his new boss for the only time he would that day—maybe even that week.

"That sounds perfect," he said, forcing an upbeat smile.

"Good. Welcome again, Jack. We're glad to have you here."

From his conversations with friends who worked at other New York law firms, Jack knew that a man like Ted Parker almost never came to your office. If he did, he certainly didn't stay long. In a profession built on protocol and procedure, a senior partner would extend you some rare courtesies on your first few days. Thereafter, he expected you to know your place—and to revere his. And so, after another quick handshake and a pat on the shoulder, Ted made a ghostlike retreat through Jack's office doorway, vanishing as quickly and silently as he had appeared.

# CHAPTER 5

Deb Miller walked slowly toward the West 4th Street subway station. She strolled at a tourist's pace down the sunlit sidewalk, caring little that she was a good forty minutes late. Everyone at R&H knew she was not a morning person, and most certainly not a *Monday* morning person. Still, she had recorded more than twenty-five hundred billable hours last year, way above the target for a senior associate. Nobody was in a position to complain about her work ethic.

Her watch starting vibrating. From the recesses of her handbag, she dug out her phone and answered.

"Are you awake yet?" Ted sounded only mildly annoyed. He periodically chided her about her irregular working hours, usually as part of a melodramatic pep talk about the need for her to "cause less dissension" and be more of a "team player." But, he didn't really mean it. Deep down, he admired her strong personality. She was the best lawyer in the place. Without her, he'd be completely lost.

"Yeah, I'm in the subway. I've been waiting forever for a train. The service sucks today."

"Look, I'm going to be buried all day," he said. "Babysit the new kid for me, okay?"

*Babysit, indeed.* Truth be told, she wanted absolutely nothing to do with *the new kid*. Rather, she fully hated Jack Collins, even though she had barely met him. It was nothing personal. In their first and only meeting, he had been perfectly pleasant, even charming. But despite his best efforts, she loathed the very thought of him.

Ted generated enough legal work to employ a small army of associates. Yet amid that fury of paperwork, it was often hard to find the good work amid the mind-numbing tasks. There were only so many exciting meetings to attend, only so many cutting-edge assignments. And, most importantly, there were only so many available moments of Ted's attention. She wanted all of those gems for herself—the best jobs, the best meetings, and the fullest attention. She deserved all of that. She had earned it.

In her eight years at R&H, she had served as Ted's proverbial right hand and had weathered the challenges of a seemingly relentless stream of potential successors. She was getting better and better at ending their careers. If she stayed true to that form, she would dispose of Jack by Christmas.

"Of course. I'll be glad to do it." She finally reached the subway station and started down the stairs.

"I'm sure you will. You're always so charming with the new associates."

"What's that supposed—"

"Look, I've got a meeting in a minute. You're in charge. Just try to be nice to him. We don't need another Clay Warren."

"Come on. That's so unfair."

"Let's just try to keep this one," he snapped. With that, the line went dead.

Deb tossed her phone back into her handbag. A minute later, a silver D train rumbled into the station and lurched to a halt before her. She strode purposefully through the open doors and secured the last free seat. She reached into her briefcase and pulled out a stick of gum and a dog-eared romance novel. After letting the gum wrapper fall to the floor, she crossed her legs and opened the book. Lost amid the flavor of artificial strawberry and the tale of mindless lust, she forgot all about Jack Collins.

# CHAPTER 6

"**I** didn't forget about you."

Jack looked up from his computer screen to see Deb Miller striding through his doorway. While her wavy brown hair straddled the line between professional and unkempt, her tailored beige suit was all business.

He stood to shake her hand. "I didn't think you'd forgotten. I'm sure you've got a million things to do."

"A few million, to be exact." Without waiting to be invited, she sat in one of the antique chairs across from his desk. "So, are you having fun yet?"

"Absolutely. I'm having a great time."

She tucked her hair behind her ears, leaning slightly toward him. A mischievous smile accentuated her noticeable dimples. "I think it's so awesome that you're here."

"I think it's awesome too."

She inched her chair forward and set her palms on the edge of his desk. She was now sitting close enough that he could smell the faint whiff of lemon and flowers wafting from her neck. Her gaze was intense, her dark-brown eyes locked on his. "You are going to be such a star. Seriously, you're like a young Ted Parker."

Given that she had now seen him exactly twice in her life, he couldn't help but laugh at that suggestion. As he did, he pushed back slightly from his desk, trying to subtly widen the gap between himself and his new supervisor. "Flattery will get you everywhere. Seriously, you missed your calling. You should be a publicist."

She sat back in her chair and crossed her arms over her chest, smiling but saying nothing. He tried to restart the conversation. "Hey, Ted said you'll have some work for me. Just let me know what you need done."

"I will. I've been in client meetings all morning, so let me get settled, and I'll swing by a bit later. Then I'll take you to this great Chinese place for lunch."

"That would be super."

"It will be. How about this for a deal: you buy me lunch, and I'll give you the lay of the land? Try to keep you from screwing up around here."

"That sounds a little ominous."

She stood abruptly from her chair, smoothed the fabric of her skirt with both hands, and picked a piece of lint off the front of her suit jacket. He couldn't help but follow the motion of her hands, following their path up from her toned legs to the spot where the top button of her blouse tugged ever so slightly against her chest.

"It's not ominous," she said, breaking him out of his trance. "But you're a little Connecticut boy. This is the big, tough city."

"Hey—" He tried to protest, but she rolled on.

"Seriously, the Nutmeg State? You're from a state named after a spice. And a pretty lame spice at that." Her mischievous smile was back.

"Now wait a minute. Nutmeg is a perfectly good spice."

"Okay, Spice Boy, whatever you say. In any event, there are really just a few simple rules to know here in the *Empire* State, and you'll be fine. Here's the most important: Ted's very particular, so always let me know what you're working on. Give me a first peek at everything he asks you to do. The guy before you totally messed up a case Ted and I gave him to handle. I tried to help him, but he was too smart for his own good."

"What did he do?" Jack asked as his throat tightened.

"It doesn't really matter. I'm not trying to freak you out. I just want you to go slow and be careful."

"Okay, I've got it."

"Good." She stood up and moved to the office door, turning around as she reached the threshold. "You are going to do great here, Mr. Nutmeg. Just trust me. I won't let you down."

# CHAPTER 7

Ted stepped into his office to find Doug Crabtree waiting for him. A tax lawyer by training, the fifty-something Crabtree had spent much of his career at R&H. He'd left the firm seven years earlier to help found one of New England's most exclusive private banks. Specializing in high-end residential mortgages, Doug and his team now loaned out a billion dollars each year and held the mortgages on some of Massachusetts's most prestigious addresses. Included among those was the oceanfront Nantucket home Ted had purchased with 5.8 million dollars of borrowed money just two years earlier.

"Sorry," Ted said as he closed the door behind him. "It's been a crazy day already. I'm on this task force for Congress, and I've been on a conference call all morning."

"It's no problem," Doug said as he stood from his chair and shook Ted's hand. "I just got here myself. Claire said I could wait."

"You look good, Doug. You've cut some weight."

"I'm trying. Thanks for noticing."

"Twenty pounds?"

"More like ten."

"That's still great. Your family well?"

"They are. How about Suzy and the kids?"

"Everyone is just fine."

Ted sat down across from his guest. "Thanks again for coming over," he said softly as he leaned in toward Doug, trying to direct his voice away from the office walls. "I didn't want to deal with this by phone."

"My pleasure. I'm sorry to have to call on you for this." Doug took an audible breath. He was visibly uncomfortable to be having this meeting with the man who used to be his law partner and had referred countless well-heeled clients to his bank.

Given the circumstances, Doug was surprisingly cordial. Ted hadn't paid his Nantucket mortgage for the past three months. He knew full well that Doug had made the Nantucket loan largely as a favor—a *professional courtesy* that the bank's underwriting department had understandably advised against at the time. The underwriters had since been proven right. The amount past due on Ted's loan approached one hundred thousand dollars, an amount that even Ted's old friend apparently could no longer ignore.

"I'm not trying to pressure you," Doug began, droplets of perspiration beginning to moisten the scalp beneath his thinning hair. "We go way back. I can give you some time. I just need to know where this is heading."

Ted reached across the desk and handed Doug a copy of an updated balance sheet. He watched Doug's face redden as he scanned the figures.

"Jesus, Ted. This is pretty tight. There's a ton of debt here."

"I know," Ted said softly. "And I appreciate your discretion on this so far." He paused to give Doug a moment to read through the entire document. When the banker's eyes finally rose from the paper, Ted pleaded his case. "I do have a plan. I promise you. I just need to give it some more time."

As he took another pass at the balance sheet, Doug's tone became noticeably more strident. "These numbers are just way off. Have you thought about selling the place? The season is coming to a close, but you could probably walk away even."

Ted shook his head. "Not possible. Suzy is way too attached to the house. Off the table."

Doug visibly bristled, and Ted understood exactly why. Mrs. Susan Parker's proclivity for hosting lavish parties on the island was doing nothing to help her husband pay the thirty thousand monthly mortgage. Plus, she'd been impolitic enough to leave the Crabtrees off her guest list more than once. "Off the table," Ted repeated curtly, speaking like a man who had more leverage than he actually did.

"I know it's tough," Doug said sternly, "but I am getting a lot of pressure on this. After three months, we're supposed to begin foreclosure. I can drag it out on my end, but I can't hold it back forever."

"Look, just give me just a bit more time," Ted pleaded. "I've got everything worked out. I really do. I'm close to the biggest payday of my career. I just can't tap it right now. But soon. Very soon."

Doug waited for an awkwardly long time before replying. "I can't promise anything, but I'll do all that I can."

"I appreciate it, my friend," Ted said before exhaling deeply.

"But you need to fix this. Do whatever you have to."

"I will," Ted promised, looking down at his desk as he spoke. "Believe me, I will."

# CHAPTER 8

Jack tried his best to keep pace with Deb as the two walked down Broadway, but she maintained a half-step advantage on him the entire way along the pedestrian-choked sidewalk. Their brisk tempo had a calming effect on Jack, dissipating some of his nervous energy and keeping him from focusing too much on the fact that he was about to have lunch with his new boss and his most important client.

The past week had been far and away the most thrilling of his career. As exciting as it had been back in Stamford to meet his first client or make his first courtroom appearance, nothing from that life compared to the nonstop exhilaration of being in New York City. The throngs of tourists flowing through Times Square took him back to the chaos of Harvard Yard. Once again, he felt like he was at the center of something vital.

As the two lawyers moved onto a slightly less populated section of sidewalk, Deb slowed her pace and drifted back toward Jack. She lit a cigarette and sent a cloud of smoke swirling upward. "I'm so glad you're here," she said as she tucked her arm around his, cozying up against him as if the two were the oldest of friends. He could smell the scent of berries as a few stray strands of her hair tickled the side of his face.

"I'm glad to be here too," he replied as he slipped his arm away from hers. "It's been an incredible first week."

He meant it, mostly. While he was still disappointed that he had spoken to Ted exactly one time since joining R&H, he had found an unexpected pleasure in his new relationship with Deb. He had spent nearly half his waking hours with her, she in the role of master and he her very willing apprentice. She was perhaps the most intense person he had ever met—intense in the way she worked and equally intense in the way she interacted with others. Already twice this week, she had turned a friendly lunch over Chinese food into an opportunity to grill him on every aspect of his personal and professional life. The encounters seemed to be part therapy session and part first date, drawing him far closer to her, far faster, than he'd ever before experienced. Though he was attempting to maintain some professional distance, the task was proving difficult.

Without warning, she tossed her cigarette to the sidewalk and accelerated away, regaining her half-step lead. He followed a step behind as she turned left on 44th Street and headed for number twenty-seven. The stately brick building was nestled amid a row of nondescript office buildings and understated boutique hotels. From the facade flew two flags representing what most of the building's occupants considered to be the two greatest institutions in the history of mankind. Above the left door, the familiar stars and stripes of the United States. Above the right, the banner of a far older world power, a solid maroon flag with a white *H* in the center. The uniformed doorman opened the right-hand door and invited them inside.

"Welcome to the Harvard Club."

Jack felt his face flush as he stepped over the threshold and onto the lobby's parquet floor. *You can do this,* he thought. He forced a deep breath into his tightening chest, his lungs pushing back at only half their usual capacity, as he mentally ticked through the information Claire had dutifully provided that morning.

Abigail Walker hadn't gone to Harvard, Claire had said, but Harold Walker sure had. When the proud alum moved to New York, he became one of the most active members of the Harvard Club and continued as such for some forty years, four of them as club president. Upon the senator's death, his portrait was hung in the dining room, and his widow was named an honorary lifetime member.

Ted Parker was also a member of the Harvard Club and had lunch there nearly every day. As often as he could, he ate at his regular table, "the best seat in the house," as Claire had referred to it in a mock drawl. Four days a week, Ted entertained a rotating assemblage of investment bankers and accountants. But Fridays were reserved for Abigail Walker.

"Come on, Jack. Let's go," Deb sniped as she stepped in front of him and snapped him to attention, her heels clicking on the hardwood as she accelerated away. He assumed pursuit as she wove through a lounge and into the club's dining room, stopping only when she arrived at the table tucked into the far corner. As he stepped up beside her, breathless, Jack immediately recognized the famous portrait hanging on the wall and the equally famous woman sitting below it. His heart raced as she stood from the table to greet them.

"Deborah, it's so nice to see you," Abigail said as she took Deb's hand in hers and squeezed it.

"Thank you, Mrs. Walker. Ted should be here any minute. In addition, we've brought a special guest." Like a game-show hostess showcasing a prize, Deb held both arms out toward him. "Mrs. Walker, may I introduce Jack Collins, a proud alum of Harvard College and my newest colleague at the firm."

Abigail took a step toward him and clutched his right hand in both of hers. "Mr. Collins, it is my sincere pleasure to meet you," she said formally, her careful diction suppressing all but a trace of her Boston accent.

"The pleasure is mine, Mrs. Walker," he replied, exactly as he had rehearsed it all morning. "It's an honor to meet you." Since Claire had warned him about Abigail's frail health, he was surprised by the strength of her grip and the vigor with which she shook his hand. Yet, as he looked at her face, he could see other subtle signs of illness. Brittle gray strands wove through her shoulder-length blond hair. Deep wrinkles and dark patches surrounded her eyes, two vulnerable circles of skin showing through her heavy makeup. Up close, she looked ten years older than she had from just a few paces away.

Abigail withdrew her hand and reclaimed her seat. "Mr. Collins, have you been to the club before?" she asked as she placed her napkin in her lap.

"Yes, Mrs. Walker. I'm actually a brand-new member. C-1919," he recited his membership number with pride and a smile.

"Well, then, welcome to our club."

As Jack took his own seat, he paused to reflect on her brilliantly crafted sentence. With just a few words, she had made clear that, although they were both members of the same club, she was in a position to welcome him, and not the reverse. At the same time, and with the same sentence, she reminded Deb that she was merely a guest inside this privileged bastion—unlike Jack and Abigail and the soon-to-arrive Ted Parker. Neither Deb's father's long tenure on the Harvard Law School faculty nor her own successes at Cornell and NYU Law would enable her to apply for membership.

Just as his lunch companions had settled into their seats, Ted arrived, and another round of handshakes ensued. "I take it you've met Jack," Ted said as he took his seat. "A great hire, if we ignore the whole Yale thing," he added with a chuckle. "You like the table, Jack?" he asked through a broad grin as he grabbed his napkin off the tablecloth. "Best seat in the house."

A bottle of wine appeared without being ordered, a waiter silently filling four glasses.

Abigail turned toward Ted. "Anything I need to know?"

"Not really. Constitution made a bunch of payments on Monday, but nothing we need to talk about."

"Good," she replied before taking an indelicate gulp of wine. "Then we can talk about something more interesting."

That *something* turned out to be an off-Broadway play everyone at the table but Jack had seen and loved. The conversation then jumped effortlessly from topic to topic as the three others chatted about people he had never met and events of which he had never heard. Every once in a while, either Abigail or Ted would direct a random comment or question in his direction, a thoughtful effort to make him feel at least marginally included. But Jack knew that he wasn't part of this group, at least not yet. As the table around him hummed with life, he faded into the background.

———————⧫———————

AS THE CLOCK APPROACHED two, the waiter appeared with four espressos and handed Ted a familiar white card. Ted thanked him and signed the check while Abigail snuck a peek at the ice bucket sitting beside him, sighing when she saw that it was empty. She supposed that, as usual, she had already had far too much to drink. But still, a little more would be better. A few hours of numbness would be worth the vicious headache that would inevitably follow.

She shifted her attention from the ice bucket to the young man sitting across from her. He was so perfectly polite, so very poised. *Yes, Mrs. Walker. Thank you, Mrs. Walker.* He must be bursting with pride at having shared lunch with the famous widow Walker—as proud as he must be to work with the brilliant Ted Parker and his comely lieutenant. *If only he knew the truth. The poor thing has no idea, none at all.*

She forced a smile and placed her napkin on the tablecloth. "Thank you all for lunch. It is always wonderful to see you."

Everyone rose from the table in unison. After kissing Deb on the cheek, Abigail extended her hand in Jack's direction. "I see a bright future for you, Mr. Collins. Stick with Mr. Parker here. He will make you famous."

"Thank you, Mrs. Walker. It was a great pleasure to meet you."

She took Ted's hand in hers and squeezed it affectionately. She could feel the strength in his fingers as they wrapped around the back of her palm. She held onto his hand just a second or two longer than she had the others, trying to enjoy one last moment with him before they parted.

She stepped forward, and the others yielded to her lead. She forced herself perfectly erect as she walked, the alcohol mercifully having masked, at least for now, the knifelike pains in her spine. As she moved away from the table, she looked up at the portrait of her husband.

"Be good, my love," she said and blew him a kiss. "I'll see you next week."

# CHAPTER 9

Jack bounded through the kitchen door, his briefcase in one hand and a dozen pink roses in the other. "Seven thirty on the dot. Just like I promised."

"Hi, sweetheart," Amanda Collins said, peeking up from the piles of paper covering their kitchen table. "I'll finish this report and clean this up soon."

Jack dangled the flowers beneath her nose. "Have someplace to put these?"

"Wow, they smell great! Just set them on the counter. I'll put them in water in a minute."

He slid a dirty plate into the sink, setting the flowers in its place. "You better not have finished all of the lo mein," he warned jokingly.

"I wouldn't dare." She fired a series of staples into a stack of paper. "I even saved you an egg roll."

"Thanks."

For now, that was the extent of their interaction. No clinging embrace, no passionate kiss. She merely turned back to her piles of paperwork as he walked through the kitchen and down the hallway to their bedroom.

Things had not always been this way between them.

Amanda had been a constant in a third of his life. On his brighter days, she was the best thing that had ever happened—or possibly *could* ever happen to him. But in his darkest moments, thoughts of her filled him with doubt.

He loved her. That was certain. He admired her as much as ever. But that didn't mean that the passage of time had been kind to their relationship. Too many Friday nights had been lost to her paperwork,

30

others to his. Bills piled up. Leftovers replaced date nights. Talk of children and buying a house increasingly dominated their rushed conversations. They had a perfectly good life, everything he should have wanted. And yet something had gone missing.

Though their marriage increasingly struggled, their first meeting had seemed an act of destiny. Even though a decade had passed, Jack still considered the day he'd met Amanda to be the single most romantic day of his life.

As is always the case, a million things could have changed just the slightest bit that day, and the two of them never would have met. His two roommates could have let him write an overdue history paper instead of dragging him to a football game. The Holy Cross placekicker could have made a field goal in the final seconds of the game. Jack and his friends could have chosen to celebrate Harvard's victory at any one of a half-dozen bars more convenient than the River House. The list went on and on.

The first round was on Scott—a miracle in itself. When it was time for round two, the overworked waitress was nowhere to be seen. And Jack, for whatever reason, chose not to wait for her return. So he stood from the table, scooped up the roommates' three empty beer mugs, and began to edge toward the bar.

He had long since forgotten what song was playing as he stepped up to the bar that November day. He couldn't say what kind of beer he was drinking or what game was on television. Nor could he recall what the bartender said or did or how he looked, or whether Jack gave him a decent tip. But he still knew everything that mattered about the first moment he saw Amanda Payton. He could recall what she wore and what she said and how she looked and what he thought. Of Amanda, he remembered every detail.

When he first saw her, she was sitting on a barstool, two of her friends between her and him. Facing his way but not seeing him, she talked to the other women, laughing and smiling. Her hair was tucked

under a purple baseball hat, a perfect match to her sweatshirt emblazoned with white block letters. A blue wool overcoat draped over her
shoulders obscured the words, but he knew what they said.

Something happened to Jack in that moment that rarely did. More
precisely, the usual things *didn't* happen. There was no great indecision.
No angst, no rehearsing of lines. He placed the three empty mugs on
the bar, gestured to the bartender to refill them, and moved past the
two other women sitting on barstools. He caught Amanda's eye as he
walked straight up to her.

"Sorry about that field goal."

It was a fairly lame opening line, but apparently it was enough. He
soon wrangled a stool from one of her friends and sat beside her. He
was captivated by her smile, by the way she laughed, by the way she
played with her left pearl earring as she leaned in closer to him.

At some point, her friends dropped out of the conversation. At
some point, his roommates came to retrieve their warm beers from the
top of the bar. At some point, Jack and Amanda began to fall in love.

They sat together at the bar for well over an hour, though at the
time it seemed like just minutes. Their interaction was so easy. Everything he said was funny or charming. Everything she said was endearing, but in her own way—with just a little bit of an edge. He felt lost in
her, with no desire to find his way out.

But reality soon intervened. Time had marched on despite their
oblivion. It had grown dark outside the bar's windows. The crowds had
thinned as thoughts of beer turned to thoughts of dinner. And now,
male hands on his shoulders mirrored the female hands pulling at hers.
Their friends had spoken: it was time to go.

He tried to delay the inevitable. "You should stay for dinner. We'll
show you around campus."

She looked at her friends with wide eyes, but they countered with
downturned lips and rigid posture. Amanda's ignoring them for an
hour had clearly taken its toll.

"I think we need to get back." Her sad eyes made clear that this was not her choice to make. "Don't take that the wrong way," she added for clarity.

After asking for his phone, she tapped at the keypad.

"Call me," she said as she slipped the phone back into his hand.

Staring into her dark-green eyes, his reply came without hesitation. "I will."

Nearly four years later, one late July evening, Jack repeated those same words, and Amanda Payton became his wife.

# CHAPTER 10

Abigail had spent far too much time in Donna Hansen's office. She could practically recite the wording of every diploma and certificate that adorned the oncologist's office walls and had long since stopped finding comfort in her doctor's training and accolades.

Abigail was dying. There was nothing new in that for her—she had been dying for years. But the last few weeks had brought a marked decline. Her energy level was falling every day. New aches and pains arrived with every sunset. She sensed the end hurtling toward her.

Dr. Hansen entered the room and reached her hand out to shake Abigail's. The manila folder tucked under her arm was overflowing with paper, a tribute to the length and intensity of Abigail's illness, a testament to the health battles one can wage when blessed with both fierce determination and endless financial resources.

"How are your children, Abby? Wonderful story in the *Times* about Kate's health care proposals—"

"Dr. Hansen," she interrupted. No matter how many times she had been invited to, she had never been willing to call her oncologist by her first name. "Can we avoid the small talk today?"

"Of course," the doctor said. "Your last blood work was not good. Your calcium—"

Abigail extended a palm in her direction. "How long?"

"Well…" The doctor hesitated. "That question is so difficult to answer. Last time you responded far better to the—"

Abigail flashed the palm of her hand again. "Oh please, spare me. However long I have is not long enough to hear about every test over and over. I see all these diplomas. They tell me one thing—that you can answer my question."

Dr. Hansen closed the manila folder and looked straight into her eyes. "My best guess?"

"Yes."

"Three months."

She had steeled herself in anticipation of the words, but they hit hard nonetheless. Previously, there had always been ranges: five to seven years, twelve to eighteen months. The ranges kept getting shorter and shorter, but they had always included the possibility that her fate was not inevitable, her death not precisely scheduled. But today, it was almost as if the date had been selected. Three months. That was all. After a twenty-year battle, it had come to this.

She swallowed hard, forcing back her emotions. "Thank you for your candor."

The doctor nodded, and Abigail could see the anguish in her downturned eyes.

"I wish I had better news, Abby. I really do."

Abigail nodded her assent as she dabbed her eyes with a tissue. "That makes two of us."

———— ◉ ————

TED'S OFFICE PHONE interrupted the silence of an early morning. Recognizing the number on the display, he picked it up himself.

"Good morning. How'd it go with Hansen?"

"Three months," Abigail reported stoically. "Then I'm gone."

"Look, I'm sure we can figure out—"

"She said three months. Are you now an oncologist?"

"Look, you've fooled them all before. I don't count you out yet."

He meant it. He had seen her on death's doorstep a dozen times over the past twenty years. Every time, she had clawed her way back. But this time seemed different. She sounded tired, defeated—ready to give up the battle. Ready to succumb.

She listened to his pep talk but said little more in response. After a few minutes, she was apparently out of patience. "Thank you for always being there, Ted," she said somewhat brusquely. "I'll call you later."

After setting down the phone, Ted walked over to his office windows, staring out into the morning sunlight. His heart ached for his dear friend. He could hear the fear in her voice. He could feel her sorrow and her loneliness. He had spent so much of his life dealing with her dark emotions.

But staring out into the warm glow of a summer morning, he turned his focus away from her past struggles and toward his own future. He had charted a clear course for his life—a journey that had long ago become intertwined with Abigail's but would continue on without her. Her life was ending. His was not. To the contrary, the macabre truth was that her death would mean his rebirth.

A plan set in motion years ago was unfolding just in time. Soon, his problems would be gone—the mortgages, the money struggles, and the petty politics of R&H all behind him. He could see the end. At last, he'd be able to cash out—to finally get what he wanted, what he deserved.

And no one was going to get in his way.

# CHAPTER 11

I t had taken the regional jet just fourteen minutes to climb to twenty-one thousand feet and level off. Sitting by the window in row six, Federal Agent Joseph Andrews loosened his tie and rolled up the sleeves of his white oxford shirt. It was two weeks until his thirty-second birthday, and his life was on the ascent. He was in his best physical shape ever, running five miles a day and swimming laps at least three times a week. Yet such athletic prowess was not immediately evident to those who met him. At five feet nine and one hundred fifty pounds, his physical stature was far from imposing.

Fortunately, he almost never needed to rely on physical force. Instead, he possessed a keen mind that provided all the strength required to vanquish most opponents. A high school chess champion, Joe was legendary in his ability to foresee how a game would unfold. In his senior year, while playing for the state championship, he had looked at his opponent during the final match and muttered, "You're done." He said nothing else until four moves later, when he slid his queen sideways three spaces and declared the match over. "Checkmate."

Joe leaned forward in his airplane seat and glanced at the older woman beside him. She was about seventy, wearing a set of thick reading glasses, and sufficiently engrossed in a crossword puzzle to be of no further concern. He slid his briefcase out from underneath the seat in front of him, unlocked the two brass latches, and removed a nondescript folder. The tab on the file contained just one word: *Walker*.

As Joe flipped through sheets of paper compiled by the FBI Financial Crimes Task Force, he was transported back to the 1940s, when future senator Harold Walker had been born into a family of overachievers. Walker was not even twenty-two when he jumped straight from college to military service, beginning a journey that would take him from Cambridge to Vietnam. Despite having failed to eradicate communism, he returned triumphant and wearing a bronze star.

But being a war hero was just a start, a tiny taste of all the glory that was to come. He immediately moved to New York City and joined a company called Eastern Telephone, an upstart firm that set out to develop a system for phone communication based on satellites and microwaves. The business model worked. The company grew through merger after merger, making Walker wealthy beyond all expectations. By the time he became CEO, the company was one of the country's largest corporations, and Walker was widely considered one of the most important American businessmen of his generation. Like his father and grandfather before him, Harold Walker had become a household name.

Having been as successful in business as he had been in war, it was time for yet another act. He returned from New York to the state of his birth and launched a successful effort to become the junior senator from Massachusetts. On election night, while Walker addressed his supporters, an ailing former president made a surprise appearance on the stage. While the crowd erupted into frenzied applause and photographers jostled for the perfect shot, father and son silently embraced.

The senator had lived a charmed life, professionally and personally. His relationship with Abigail was yet another part of this fairy tale. Nearly fifteen years his junior, she had joined Eastern Telephone as a marketing consultant and stayed exactly seventeen days. It took seven of those days for her to catch the eye of a senior VP named Harold Walker and just ten more for him to fall in love with her. Her short, albeit successful, tenure at Eastern Telephone thus came to an end. Despite her Barnard education, Harold Walker's future wife didn't need to work for a living. She never would again.

For nearly three decades thereafter, the Walkers lived an idyllic life together. They raised two beautiful children. They owned both an apartment overlooking Central Park and a picture-perfect Cambridge colonial. They attended charity balls and graced magazine covers. It was the stuff of fairy tales. And then it was suddenly all gone, having ended in a way no one could have imagined.

Joe had read the story of that tragic day over and over. He knew it so well that he could repeat it by heart, almost as if he had been there. He closed the folder, and then his eyes, and let the scene play out.

It began as a nondescript October morning. Senator Walker was scheduled to depart from New York City, where he had attended a banquet the evening before, and head back to DC to attend to Senate business. He had showered and shaved. A black sedan stood idling at the curb in front of the Plaza Hotel, ready to whisk him to the airport. But as he stood in his hotel room getting dressed, Walker called in an aide and announced that he had changed his plans. The senator, as was his style, gave no explanation. "Richard, let's head home to Cambridge." That was all he said—and all he needed to. Scarcely an hour later, the senator sat in seat 2A as the Delta Shuttle lifted off runway 04 of New York's LaGuardia airport. At 9:25, they touched down on runway 15R of Logan Airport in Boston and taxied to a waiting gate.

Try as he might, it was hard for Harold Walker to move quickly through an airport, particularly Logan. The well-wishers and autograph seekers treated him like a movie star, shouting greetings and extending hands. The businessmen who wanted to criticize his stand on tax policy or talk *ad nauseam* about government regulations circled him like hungry sharks. Always the gentleman, Senator Walker took time to speak to his constituents as he inched through the terminal, accompanied by a cadre of Massachusetts state troopers. Eventually, he reached the exit. There waited another black sedan, its rear door wide open and its driver standing beside it.

Terry O'Reilly saw the senator the moment he stepped into the morning sunlight and stepped directly toward him. Without a word, Terry removed the bag from the senator's hand and placed it in the sedan's trunk.

As Walker politely thanked his police escorts for their service, Terry returned to his post beside the open car door. "Good morning, Senator."

"How are you, Terry?"

"I'm doing well, sir. Welcome home."

Walker ducked his head as he entered the sedan and planted himself firmly in the rear seat. "Well, we're not home just yet."

Terry closed the car door and quickly returned to his own seat. For the duration of the trip to Cambridge, he would spend more time driving and less time chatting.

After they turned onto Linden Street and arrived at the Walkers' white colonial, Terry turned off the engine and walked around to the passenger side.

"Now, welcome home, Senator," Terry said with a smile as he opened the rear door of the sedan.

"Now, thank you." The senator smiled right back at him. These two men, one of the nation's most powerful political figures and a former Boston cop who often acted as his chauffeur, had developed an unlikely rapport in their years together. The warmth between them was genuine, an unusual bond between men born into very different classes.

"Richard will call you about tomorrow," Walker instructed. "I figure it will be early."

"Whenever you need me, sir."

Terry began to reach for the senator's bag, but Walker waved him off. "Thank you, Terry. I can handle things from here. Until tomorrow, then."

"Absolutely, sir. Have a good day, Senator. My best to Mrs. Walker."

Walker acknowledged Terry's remark with a nod as he made his way along the worn slate path and up the front steps. He unlocked the front door, stepped inside, and slowly shut it behind him.

After he watched the front door shut, Terry O'Reilly drove away without looking back—or so he had insisted countless times under oath. Less than an hour later, a breaking news report interrupted the song playing on his car stereo and almost sent him driving off the road.

The junior senator from Massachusetts was dead.

———————•———————

THE AIRPLANE HIT A patch of minor turbulence, and Joe opened his eyes and looked out at the clouds cascading beneath him. Pitching from side to side in his seat, he wondered what had happened behind the Walkers' front door that fateful morning. While Joe, like much of America, often pondered that question, he held only a passing interest in the senator's cause of death. He cared much more deeply about the senator's money.

For the past eighteen months, he had traced a stream of Walker's money flowing from Hartford to the Cayman Islands. He had analyzed bank records. He had intercepted phone calls and emails. Through diligent study, he had pieced together the story of a mysterious offshore bank account and the monthly transfers that funded it. He hadn't figured out every detail, but he would soon enough. He was closing in on the biggest moment of his career.

He could imagine the coming endgame. He would march into Ted Parker's posh office, handcuffs at the ready. His hair would be neatly cut for the occasion, his shiny gold badge dangling from his neck. In his finest blue suit, Joe would parade the lawyer out to a waiting car, a stream of police officers and reporters there to witness the spectacle. Onlookers would gasp. Cameras would flash. He would be the hero, Parker the vanquished.

As Joe planned his triumph, he imagined Parker would not be alone. Nobody ever worked alone, and Ted Parker was no exception. The secretaries would be led out with him. The associates would go too, news cameras recording their steps as they tried to hide their faces, ignoring the questions shouted at them. Maybe a jury would never convict them all, but that wasn't the point. Joe would make them household names just the same. Guilty or not, they would never overcome the specter of suspicion—never live down the shame.

And as he pictured Parker and his cronies marching before him, he knew exactly what he would say to them. "You're done," he would taunt. "You're all done."

# CHAPTER 12

Although they had worked together for a mere three weeks, Jack and Deb were becoming inseparable. Part of their deepening relationship was inevitable—as the two associates working most directly for Ted Parker, they spent significant amounts of time together each day. But for Jack, there was more to it than that. He had become captivated by the brashness of Deb's personality and the sharpness of her tongue, her level of drive and energy constantly reminding him how much more dynamic things were in New York City than they had been in Stamford.

In those few weeks together, he had also come to learn that she had, at best, a checkered dating history and was hardly in a position to give relationship advice. However, that clearly didn't stop her. Setting down her chopsticks on the tablecloth at Hunan Palace, she stared directly at him. "You need to shake things up a bit."

"Shake what up?"

"Your life. Your marriage. You keep telling me that your life is so boring. So do something exciting. Take your wife someplace warm and get some drinks with umbrellas in them."

In the brief time he had known Deb, she had shown an unusual interest in the intricacies of his personal life. Yet, strangely, she had never once referred to Amanda by name. "Take my wife someplace?" he parroted back. "We're not in college anymore. There's no spring break."

She let out an audible sigh and pursed her lips. "What, she doesn't get vacation at that job of hers?"

"Sure, she gets vacation. But do I? When's the last time you took a week off?"

She laughed then snatched her chopsticks off the tablecloth and used them to pluck a shrimp off her plate. "Yes, my dear, you get vacation. You can take a week off. The firm can survive without you. In fact, it did for, like, eighty years. I know that may be hard to accept, but it's true."

"That wasn't my question. When is the last time *you* took a week off?"

"Well, not everyone needs to be me. And I would take a vacation if I had someone to go with." She reached across the table and patted the back of his hand. Her touch startled him, and he slid his hand away.

"Okay, travel expert, what do I do?"

"Well, you've never made it through a New York City winter. By sometime in February or so, I guarantee you will have had your fill of snow and slush, overheated trains, and wet leather shoes. Plan a trip to the islands. Surprise your wife with the tickets for Christmas." Her broad grin made it apparent that she was relishing planning his little adventure, her dimples deepening with her increasing enthusiasm. "In fact, surprise her with the whole trip. Tell her you're going somewhere, but don't say where. Tell her to pack a bag and bring a passport. Be mysterious. Women love a little mystery."

"That's not really my style."

"Exactly!" She groaned as she slapped the table with her palm. "That's the point. Look at yourself, Mr. Gray Suit, White Shirt, and Red Tie. You need to shake it up a bit. Step out on a limb for once. You'll love how it feels—a natural high."

He had heard that all before. He had been called "risk averse" and "boring" more times than he could count, the terms tossed about blithely by people who had never buried their only sister nor watched their father struggle for breath in an ICU. They didn't understand how it could be a duty to be risk averse, a virtue to be boring. But Jack sure did. And so he had trod one safe road after another, allowing fear and obligation to shape his adult life, until finally he said those fateful words to his father, his law partner. "Dad, I have to leave."

R&H wasn't just a new *job*. It was a chance to remake himself.

"Okay, boss," he challenged her. "Where's my great mystery destination?"

She leaned back in her chair and rolled her chopsticks between her fingers. Her dark eyes glistened in the dim light. "Hmmm... I'm no expert about that. I've never been south of Florida." Seemingly finding a source of inspiration elsewhere, she continued, "But Ted's been everywhere: St. John, St. Barts, Virgin Gorda . . ." She cocked her head and looked up toward the ceiling, clearly deep in thought as she worked to select the perfect destination.

Suddenly she lurched forward in her seat, and her eyes snapped back to meet his. She again wrapped her hand over the back of his. "I've got it!" she exclaimed triumphantly. "It's perfect." After a slight pause, she delivered her verdict. "Grand Cayman. Gorgeous beaches. Sand, sun, your wife in a slinky bikini. You'll love it."

"I'm not sure..."

"Come on, you wimp." She yanked her hand back across the table. "What's not to be sure about?"

"Well, Amanda's been there. Spring break. Old boyfriend. You know what I mean."

"So what? Come on, it's supposed to have the world's best beaches."

"I'll think about it."

"That's what people say when they are not going to think about it. Don't be a loser."

"Did you just call me a loser?"

"I believe I did, loser. Mr. Nutmeg: the most boring spice in the rack."

"Oh yeah?" He leaned toward the table and stared right at her. "So, here's the deal. Pick another place. Any place. Your call, and I'm in."

"Seriously?"

"Seriously."

She sat back in her chair and swirled her chopsticks between her fingers. His heart began to race with anticipation as he waited for her to speak. Finally, an impish smile crossed her face, and she sat forward to meet him eye to eye. "Nevis. The Four Seasons. Totally, that's the place. Ted was there last winter and called it the best trip of his life. Come on. Do it." She got more animated as she urged him along. "It's the Four Seasons. Do it. What could possibly be better?"

"I'll do it," he said as his quickening pulse cascaded toward his temples. "Nevis it is. Done." He had never in his life made a more spontaneous decision.

"Just like that?" she asked, her mouth agape.

"Just like that. Your wish is my command."

"Super. You'll have a blast. See how I'm looking out for you?" she asked through a broad smile. Then her tone became notably more serious as her smile faded. "I told you, we have to stick together if we're going to make it at that crazy firm. We have to have each other's backs," she said as she returned her full attention to the shrimp on her plate.

"And I appreciate it."

"I know you do," she said without looking up from her food. "And I know you'll have a great time."

———— ◉ ————

LATER THAT NIGHT, WHILE Amanda was sleeping just down the hall, Jack sat at the computer in his home office. Typing as silently as he could, he found the website for the Four Seasons Resort in Nevis and booked an ocean-view room for the last week of February.

*Just like that.*

The spontaneity was completely out of character. And, just as Deb had promised, it was exhilarating.

# CHAPTER 13

Ted had always dreaded partnership meetings. They became even harder to endure when Daniel Reynolds, a great-grandson of the firm's cofounder, was elected R&H's managing partner. Reynolds had a penchant for taking fifteen minutes to deliver a report that warranted fifteen seconds—a valuable asset for a lawyer who billed by the hour but a significant liability for an administrator of a large law firm. With sixty of the firm's equity partners on site in New York and another thirty listening in from Boston and R&H's other offices, every minute Daniel Reynolds spoke cost his law firm nearly one thousand dollars in lost revenue.

By this measure, Reynolds had just spent more than ten thousand dollars reminding his partners that they would soon be voting on a list of associates nominated as candidates to the firm's partnership ranks. For those who were successful, partnership would be the culmination of eight to ten years of steadfast devotion to both the practice of law and the interests of R&H. Though a crowning achievement, partnership wasn't what it had once been. In many ways, the term itself was a relic from a generation past.

Technically, the partners at R&H weren't partners at all. In order to better shield the firm's lawyers from malpractice suits, the firm's general partnership had long since been reconstituted as a limited liability company, or LLC, and the partners officially renamed as *principals* of the firm. But no young lawyer dreams of becoming a *principal*, and clients expect to deal with lawyers who sound like owners rather than school administrators. And thus, while legally incorrect, the title of *partner* had endured.

The other secret truth about R&H's partners was even less well-publicized than the first. In actuality, there were two categories of partners at R&H—the *equity* partners, who owned the firm and shared its profits, and the *nonequity* or *income* partners, who had neither ownership nor management interests in the enterprise. While still a career milestone in the eyes of the firm and its clients, attaining the lesser rank of income partner left much to be desired. The title would get one a larger office and a modest raise. However, only the equity partners got access to the firm's detailed financial data. Only the equity partners voted on the promotion and compensation of the firm's lawyers. Perhaps most importantly, only the equity partners shared in the year-end distribution of the firm's profits.

Even in the most mundane details, the equity partners sought to differentiate themselves from their income-partner counterparts. For example, for decades, every lawyer at R&H was issued a brown leather litigation bag, a virtually indestructible briefcase large enough to hold a foot-thick stack of legal-sized paper. The bags had been passed down from lawyer to lawyer over the years, their scrapes and dings serving as badges of honor and remembrance, a visual reminder of all of the meetings, closings, and trials in which those bags had played a supporting role. Last winter, the firm decided to order a new supply of these cases to replace those that had become worn beyond repair. Dan Reynolds was droning on about the need for replacements when one of the equity partners chimed in with a seemingly ridiculous idea. Others soon added their assent. And Reynolds ultimately agreed to the plan.

And so, when the firm's equity partners traveled to and from today's lunch meeting, most carried their files in a black leather litigation bag, fitted with a bright brass lock and emblazoned with a gold firm logo. Few clients would ever even notice the difference in color between these new black bags and the firm's old brown ones, and fewer still would attribute any significance to the choice of leather. But everyone working at the firm understood this visual display of caste, for only equity partners had been issued the new black bags. Everyone else still used the old brown ones.

As Reynolds blathered on about the new carpeting recently purchased for the firm's Boston office, effectively doubling the cost of that project by spending so long explaining it, Ted looked down at the list of income partnership candidates. He was not the least bit surprised to see Deb Miller's name on the list. She had served by his side for nearly eight full years, joining him the summer after she graduated from NYU and staying with him ever since. During that time, nobody at R&H had worked harder than Deb had. Nobody wanted the title of *partner* more than she did. But nobody had burned more bridges and ostracized more coworkers than she had.

Ted felt a tap on his shoulder and turned to see Brian Lynch leaning toward him. He lowered his head to hear what the grizzled senior partner had to say.

"So, Ted," Lynch whispered, the faint scent of cigar evident on his breath, "what are we going to do about that barracuda you have working for you?"

"What are you talking about, Brian?" He wondered when the old man had begun paying attention to anything other than managing his stock portfolio and talking about his fishing trips.

"That Miller girl is yours, right? The secretaries tell me she's nothing but trouble."

"Look, Brian, if we listened to the secretaries—"

"Look, eh? I do *look*, Ted. I look around here every day. Like I have since you were back in grade school. You may think I've checked out of this place, but it still matters to me. And someone like her is not going to be my law partner. No way."

Ted nodded but said nothing further in reply. Instead, he eased his chair away from Lynch's, closed his eyes, and prayed for the meeting to end.

"I want you all to take this very seriously," intoned Dan Reynolds. "The future of this law firm depends on all of us."

"No way," Lynch mumbled in Ted's direction. "That one? No way."

# CHAPTER 14

The sound of footsteps at his doorway attracted Jack's attention. He looked up from his desk to see Deb leaning against his office doorframe. "You look like crap," she said.

"Thanks, that's really nice."

"You know what I mean."

"Of course I do. You mean that I look like crap, which is probably because I feel like crap."

"Come on, if you don't take care of yourself, that cold is going to turn into something a lot worse. Why are you still here?"

"I'm trying to finish up," he said through a series of coughs that burned the back of his throat. "I just need to finish some stuff for Ted, and I have to prepare for this speech tomorrow."

"Ted gave you a project?" She stared at him intently, her dark eyes locked on his.

"Yeah, but it's nothing of any consequence. It's basically scut work, but at least it's—"

"What's the speech?"

"It's a bar association thing tomorrow. Mary Vincent from tax asked me to cover for her. *Recent Developments in Estate and Probate Law*, or some similar snoozer."

"Mary Vincent?" The intensity had returned to her eyes.

"Yes, she—"

"Oh, right. Sorry. She told me about that. I was going to cover it but have another thing at the same time."

"Good. You seem upset. Something wrong?"

"Oh no, no. I mean, I'm just concerned about you. You're going to totally screw yourself if you don't get some rest. Summertime colds are impossible to get rid of. You're going to lose your voice."

"I know, but what can I do? I've got to get this done."

She threw her head back and cackled. "Come on, Jack. You think Ted would rather you do some silly research than be able to give your speech tomorrow? You obviously don't know him very well. Hand it over."

"The speech?"

"No, fool, the research. I know how to read the tax code just as well as you do. I'll handle it."

"Are you serious? You *hate* research."

She smiled at him as he struggled to suppress another cough. "Yes, but I'm a nice person. I'm nice to everyone." They both had a good laugh at that last part, his punctuated by another series of coughs. "Okay, sometimes I'm kind of a bitch," she conceded, "and we both know it. But you and I are teammates. We've talked about that, right? And I am glad to do this for you."

"But Ted asked me to—"

"And he'll understand. Seriously, it's not a problem. And for God's sake, rest your voice. You already sound like some sort of frogman."

He was convinced. "I really appreciate it," he croaked.

"My pleasure. Remember what I said about sticking together?" She punctuated the question with a broad smile. "This is sticking together. Besides, you'd do the same for me." She was right on that score. He would.

He turned his attention to his computer for a moment and then looked back at her. "I just emailed the draft to you." He then stood from his desk chair and grabbed a stack of files off his desk. He placed them in her waiting arms, feeling tremendous relief as he walked past her toward the door. He wanted nothing more than to get home and crawl into bed.

"You're the best. I'd hug you, but I don't want to give you the plague."

"Please don't. Just go take care of yourself. That's more important."

"You're a great friend. I really appreciate it."

"You've said that already. Just go home."

―――――◉―――――

ABOUT NINETY MINUTES later, right around the time that Jack's train should have arrived in Stamford, Deb stood in the hallway outside Ted's office. She had actually paced back and forth in front of his doorway a few times, her stomping footsteps and heavy sighs increasing in volume until he finally took notice.

"What the heck is going on out there?" Ted yelled.

"Oh sorry." She feigned embarrassment as she stuck her head inside his office doorway. "It's nothing."

"Sounds like a pack of elephants," he mumbled as he flipped through a stack of papers. "You sure it's nothing?"

She sighed for dramatic effect. "It's just... there's way too much to do."

"There's always too much to do." His eyes never lost focus on the document in front of him as he spoke. "Why would today be different?"

"You're right, it just..." Another dramatic pause. "It's nothing."

He finally looked up from the work on his desk. "Look, I hate pulling teeth. If you have something to tell me, then tell me. Or drop it and move on."

"Right. Sorry. I really don't want to complain, but it's just that this Olsen thing really has me pissed."

At the mention of his newest clients' names, Ted gave her his full attention. "Olsen? What are you doing for the Olsens?"

"Nothing, really. I'm just somehow trying to jam in that quick research project."

"I gave that to Jack. Where is he?" The backs of Ted's hands reddened visibly as he pressed his palms against his desk.

"Oh." She looked down at the carpet, trying her best to look befuddled. "I thought he talked to you."

"Nobody talked to me."

"Oh, I had no idea. All I know is he marched into my office, handed me this sloppy pile of paper, and begged me to finish it off for him. Apparently, Mary Vincent asked him to give some dumb speech tomorrow, so he wanted to be home early for dinner tonight."

"Early dinner? You're kidding me, right?" His right hand curled into a fist as his face reddened.

"Oh God, I'm sorry for even mentioning this. He just asked me to cover this. That's all I know."

"Okay, whatever," Ted said, his attention drifting back to the papers on his desk.

"I'll take care of it." She watched him for a moment as he flipped through a stack of documents. He seemed unaware that she was still standing there. "I'll take care of it," she repeated.

"Fine, Deborah," he said without looking up. "You run this place anyway." He had used her full name. Clearly time for this conversation to end.

"I'll get the Olsen thing done. It's not a big deal."

"Good. Are we done?"

"Yes, but please don't say anything to Jack about this. I want him to trust me."

"Oh, he can trust you, all right," Ted scoffed.

# CHAPTER 15

S taying at the Harvard Club was neither cheaper nor more convenient than staying at a nearby hotel. It did have one advantage over many other hotels in that its members and guests enjoyed access to a swimming pool, gym, and several squash courts located on its upper floors. As a result, Joe Andrews attracted little attention as he approached the club's doorway at dinnertime carrying a large black gym bag.

"Welcome to the Harvard Club." The doorman's black top hat was a somewhat haughty relic of ancient Harvard.

"Good evening," Joe Andrews said as he passed through the open door first.

"Hey, how are ya?" Special Agent Bob Masterson asked as he huffed and puffed a few steps behind.

Bob's poorly cut black hair and overgrown mustache glistened with sweat, and a pair of ratty, uneven sideburns made his globular face seem even wider than it was. A penchant for fast food and greasy diners had left the surveillance expert thirty pounds heavier than when he'd first joined the FBI. Just that easily, they were both inside. No guns nor badges needed.

"I thought Harvard was supposed to be tough to get into," Bob said.

"Maybe you should have applied."

After traversing the wood-floored lobby, the two men entered an ornately paneled elevator car. The two men stood silently as the old car lurched up four floors, arriving with a rumble at its intended stop. Joe stepped out and turned to his right, with Bob following behind.

When they arrived at room 402, Joe unlocked the door, and the two men stepped inside.

———————— ◉ ————————

SEVERAL HOURS LATER, Joe and Bob left the fourth floor and made their way downstairs and into a darkened corner of the club's main dining room. Having swapped out their dark suits for jeans and sweatshirts, they now looked every bit like the workmen they purported to be.

"Nice and quiet," Bob said as he put down the toolbox he had been carrying. "Harvard people all go to bed early?"

"Yup, that's how we keep up our good looks," Joe said with a smirk as he set down a ladder and unfolded it.

Bob looked up at the oil painting hanging directly in front of the two men.

"Well, this fellow is sure sharp looking. Good evening, Senator. I'm glad to meet you."

"You talking to the artwork now? I'm pretty sure he won't talk back."

"If he does, I'm outta here," Bob responded as he climbed up the ladder. When he reached the third step, he stuck his hand behind the framed portrait. "I got the power cord."

From the small toolbox, Joe grabbed a pair of wire cutters and a small black box, no larger than a pack of gum. Three small cords came out of the box, two ending with exposed copper wires and the third with a tiny microphone. He handed it all to Bob then watched as Bob removed a half inch of insulation from the electrical line behind the portrait, exposing two smaller wires inside. Working effortlessly, Bob wrapped one of the copper wires from the small box around each of the exposed wires and spiraled electrical tape around both splices. He tucked everything behind the frame, secured it all with one last strip of tape, and descended the ladder. The entire procedure had taken less than five minutes.

In the morning, when the dining room lights were lit, the club's electrical system would power both the lamp above the portrait and the small microphone now hidden behind it. In room 402, a receiver would hum to life and pick up the microphone's signal, capturing every word spoken at the dining table below.

"Have a good night, Senator," Bob said as he stepped off the ladder and onto the dining room floor. "Thanks for all your help."

# CHAPTER 16

Jack stumbled into the kitchen half-asleep to find Amanda leaning up against the sunlit kitchen counter, the morning newspaper spread in front of her. She wore black jogging pants and a long-sleeved pink T-shirt, the latter soaked with sweat and plastered against her back.

"Good morning," he mumbled as clearly as his pasty mouth would allow. He eased himself onto a stool, shielding his tired eyes from the sunlight reflecting off the countertop. "You already get in a run?"

"Sure did," she said as she poured him a cup of coffee and stirred in a copious amount of sugar. "More than four miles. To the cove and back. It's a little cold but beautiful." She slid the mug in front of him. "I guess you slept well. I can't remember the last time you got up after seven."

"Thanks for the caffeine," he said with a smile. He took a careful sip from the steaming mug and set it back on the counter. "I guess I needed the sleep. My commute is knocking the stuffing out of me."

"Well, at least you work for some famous people." She slid the *New York Times* in front of him, folded open to a page with a color photo of Ted and Deb standing in front of the New York skyline. "Apparently, they've come up with the perfect tax scheme."

He scanned through the article. "Oh yeah. The South Dakota thing. Pretty brilliant stuff. Ted figured out that if New Yorkers set up trusts in South Dakota, they wouldn't pay tax in either state. It's nuts. New York law treats the trust assets as taxable in South Dakota, and South Dakota thinks they are taxed in New York. So neither state actually taxes the trusts. Pretty cool, eh?"

"I guess."

"You *guess*? You don't think it's pretty darn smart?"

"Yes, it's pretty clever. But what's the point? Shouldn't people just pay their taxes?"

"Not any more than they have to."

"Yes, you're right. The rich are so mistreated. By the way, if you see my husband, could you send him back to the kitchen? And remind him that he's a Democrat."

"Very funny. Seriously, the more I deal with Ted's clients, the more I see that they spend their money a lot better than the government does."

"Right, and then there's all those bloated nonprofits funded by government grants. They don't do anything, especially the ones that hire *social workers*." Amanda, a social worker, groaned dramatically.

"You know what I mean."

"Don't you guys do any normal legal work, like the kind you used to do?"

"This *is* normal legal work. It's just really cool." He turned his attention away from her and back to the newspaper article. "Hey, did they mention me in here?"

"Sorry, just Ted and your pretty new friend. Good thing you only fall for blondes," she teased as she grabbed the coffeepot and topped off his mug. "Otherwise, I'd be nervous."

"I love this part," he chortled, raising the paper in front of his face and reading aloud. "'If the legislature didn't like it, they could have done something about it,' Mr. Parker said. 'But apparently, I work faster than they do.' I love it," Jack gushed. "Take that, *New York Times*."

"Yes, well said. And not even a touch arrogant."

Jack let the comment slide as he continued to read.

"Listen, I need to get out of these clothes," she said. "I'm going to take a shower."

"You need any company?" he asked, looking up from the paper. "I'll wash your back."

"'I can wash my own back, thanks. Besides, I'm all sweaty and gross."

"Is that a no?"

"That's a no."

"Please?"

"If you let me take a shower, I'll buy you breakfast."

"Deal."

He turned back to the newspaper and took a sip of coffee as he stared at the photo. Deb looked striking in a dark suit. Her arms were folded across her chest, a look that radiated a sense of confidence, of power. He could picture her standing in his office doorway, striking an identical pose. He saw her face as clearly as if she were in front of him. He could almost smell her perfume.

"See you later," Amanda said as she stepped down the hallway.

"Okay," he called after her without lifting his eyes from the page.

# CHAPTER 17

F or Deb, waking up in suburban Simsbury on a Sunday morning was like waking up in the middle of nowhere—which was exactly why she loved it. She slipped out from beneath the thin cotton comforter, grabbed her robe from a hook on the back of the bedroom door, and then tiptoed through the carpeted living room and onto the back deck. It was unusually crisp for late August, fifty degrees in the early sunlight—a welcome preview of the fall to come. In just a few more weeks, the first glimpses of orange and yellow would appear amid the lush green treetops at the end of the short back field.

Deb lit a cigarette and walked to the corner of the deck where an ashtray sat waiting atop the railing. The cigarette smoke mixed with her warm breath to create sheets of gray rolling upward into the morning air. She closed her eyes as a gentle breeze rustled toward her through the treetops. Puffing away at the cigarette, she felt her body relax, her mind totally at ease.

She pressed the stub of the cigarette into the ashtray and immediately lit another. Then the deck door creaked open behind her, and a man stepped onto the deck, ending both the stillness and her solitude.

"Man, it's cold out here," he said, pulling his bare arms against his T-shirt-clad chest. "Aren't you freezing?"

Although irked that the morning's silence had been broken, Deb couldn't help but smile at the twenty-seven-year-old man who stood before her. His wavy brown hair was ruffled on one side and completely flat on the other. She had given him that hairdo—working him into a sweaty frenzy last night until he collapsed into an uninterrupted sleep.

He handed her a cup of freshly brewed coffee. She warmed her face in the steam billowing out of the white mug then lowered her nose toward the rich brown liquid. She took in a deep breath of citrus and earth. "Kenyan?"

"Yes!" he replied, his deep blue eyes widening in amazement. "You're good."

She stepped toward him and tugged at the elastic waistband of his pajama pants, pulling him closer to her and planting a kiss on the end of his nose. "You were much more convincing when you said that last night."

He blushed and tugged back at the drawstring of her terry-cloth robe. "Maybe you were that much better last night."

She laughed, sending spastic clouds of coffee mist into the morning air. "Touché."

He bowed and turned back toward the house. "I'm going to take a quick shower. Want to grab some breakfast afterward?"

"Sounds divine."

"Give me five minutes." He walked back inside and pulled the deck door shut.

Alone again in the morning stillness, she turned back toward the open field and stared out at the trees. She took a drag on her cigarette and blew a gust of smoke toward the field, watching it disappear into nothingness. She smiled as she recalled the prior night—the romantic dinner that had ended in sweat-soaked bedsheets. Suddenly she was startled to find herself fighting back tears.

She was falling in love with him. That should have made her happy, but it did not. In fact, it horrified her. There was no way she was going to get married and settle down in sleepy little Simsbury. Nothing was more pathetic than carpools and runny noses. He wanted all of that. But it was not for her. Not part of her plan.

All she had wanted from him was information. An occasional loose comment or leaving his email open for her to peruse. She'd gotten all of that and more, learned everything she had hoped to find out. And it was all good news.

As she sent another puff of smoke cascading over the railing, she thought about how soon Ben's usefulness to her would come to an end. So then would their relationship. No more weekends shuttling back and forth between dynamic New York City and suburban Simsbury. No more art museums and Sunday breakfasts. Thinking of it made her miss him already.

*Poor Benjamin*, she thought as she took one final drag from the cigarette and headed back inside. He was so adorable, so trusting. And he was such a sucker for her charms.

In this last way more than any other, Ben Parker was exactly like his father.

# CHAPTER 18

As Jack ran eastward along 44th Street toward Grand Central Station in a vain effort to catch the 6:42 express to Stamford, what had been a light drizzle became a steady rain. He was not prepared for this weather, and wet wool clung to his arms as his suit jacket paid a hefty price for his lack of forethought. His shoes sloshed through puddle after puddle as he dashed from the temporary shelter of one awning to the next, trying to minimize the soaking.

An ambulance roared past as he dashed out from under the overhang of the Iroquois Hotel and bolted toward the Harvard Club. Distracted by the lights and siren, he saw the young woman stepping out of the club's doorway just before they collided, giving him barely enough time to slow himself and minimize the force of their impact.

"I'm so sorry," he stammered as he disentangled himself from the tall brunette. "I didn't see you."

"I'm fine. Don't worry." She smiled at Jack as she tossed her wavy hair back over her shoulders and straightened her bright-blue raincoat. "I'm fine," she repeated.

She might well have been fine, but he was not. *A passing ambulance. A brunette in a blue raincoat.* His stomach sank as his thoughts drifted to the past. Suddenly it was eleven years earlier. *That day, yet again.*

Back then he was a senior at Harvard. One hundred and eighty miles away from home. As far as he would get before the gravity of family responsibilities pulled him back toward Stamford.

The bells in the steeple of Memorial Church sounded at noon that day, just as he passed through the massive brick archway that separated the main campus, Harvard Yard, from the city streets of Cambridge. He had two hours to make it back to his dorm for lunch and then return to the Yard for a two-o'clock class on the history of the Civil War—plenty of time.

Leaving the Yard, he crossed Massachusetts Avenue, dodging a few taxis and a tour bus along the way. The tour buses that circled his college always amazed him. He never understood how a university could be a major tourist destination, but Harvard clearly was. He turned back toward the tour bus and waved. A battery of camera flashes went off. Twelve women from Idaho now had a picture of a completely unrecognizable college student, noteworthy only because he happened to attend America's oldest college. The tour buses provided Jack with his daily moment of fame. It worked every time.

Like all the parks in Boston and Cambridge, or *commons*, as true New Englanders call them, Cambridge Common was a jungle of intersecting paths. There were nearly a dozen ways for him to get through that park from Harvard Yard to his room in Cabot House, and his mind never knew which path he would follow until his feet made the decision. Each trip through the park, like each day itself, brought a new path, a new journey, and new consequences.

Today he chose to enter the park at its southeast corner and circle the walkway along the common's eastern edge. This path along Massachusetts Avenue was the long way around the park but with the advantage that it was typically sunnier and warmer than the short route. Since Professor Carter had let his English class sneak out a few minutes early, Jack could afford the extra time.

As he headed north, he basked in the warm sunlight of a glorious fall day. A rich amber-and-yellow canopy of elm and maple soared above his head as he sucked in a deep breath of cool, clear air. The park was largely still. His fourth gray winter at Harvard would be here soon enough. But for the moment, he was lost in the splendor of fall.

He soon reached the point where the green expanse of the common morphed into the brick and asphalt of Cambridge. Running directly in front of him was Waterhouse Street, the midpoint on his walk home. He reached the edge of the crosswalk.

And then, across the street, he saw her.

She seemed to be about his age—tall, athletic, with wavy brown hair cascading past the shoulders of a bright-blue raincoat. The coat was unbuttoned, revealing a short dress and long, toned legs. She was beautiful. But there was something even more enchanting about her. Just looking at her, he could sense that she was happy, vibrant, joyful. She seemed to be laughing to herself as she stood framed in a patch of sunlight. His heart began to pound, each breath he took shallower than the one before it. His palms grew damp, his mouth dry. He had never been more drawn to someone at first sight.

He was about to step forward when a piercing sound sent him back onto the curb. His heart lurched forward in his chest as his head instinctively snapped toward the noise. An ambulance, lights and siren blaring, emerged into view as it raced down Garden Street. The blur of white and red darted and swerved as it hurtled past the common's northwest corner and turned with a squeal onto Mason Street. Three police cars followed, while countless others could be heard in the distance, their wailing sirens echoing from every direction. Their urgency was unmistakable.

After he watched the lights and sirens make their retreat, Jack faced back toward the crosswalk. He felt a strange trembling in his legs as he forced a deep breath and stepped off the curb, finally ready to cross the street and engage the mysterious brunette.

But she was gone.

In her place was a black-and-white taxi. And it was slowly pulling away.

His mouth agape, Jack watched the taxi turn around the west end of the common and grow smaller and smaller as it accelerated away. He made no movement. He uttered no sound. A rogue cloud brought a chilling shadow as the car disappeared from view.

It had been eleven years since that moment, but he had not forgotten it. Despite the passage of time and distance, he could never quite shake what should have become a trivial memory. So many times when he questioned the shape his life had taken, he was somehow drawn back to that instant in time. To the lights and noise and pounding heart. To the moment of hesitation that had left him wondering what could have been. It had become the epitome of all the bad luck and cautious choices that had continued to shape his life—the many, many times since that day when he metaphorically stood on the curb instead of darting across the street.

"Hey, are you okay?" he heard someone asking. "Seriously, are you okay?" The young brunette's tone was now bordering on frantic. Her arm was wrapped around his shoulder. "Are you all right?"

He snapped back to reality. "Huh? Oh yes, I'm fine. Fine." He pulled away from her and stood on his own power, struggling in vain to straighten his drenched suit jacket.

"Good. I'm glad," the woman said. "You had me kind of freaked out."

He stared into her dark eyes. "Me too," he said.

He excused himself and continued his journey toward Grand Central. After a few paces, he stopped and stared back at the woman. He watched as she silently stepped farther and farther away from him, the outline of her body growing less distinct with every step.

And then, she was gone.

# SEPTEMBER
# CHAPTER 19

Jack hadn't yet decided whether he loved Ted or despised him. The truth was probably a blend of both. On the positive side, he was still in awe of Ted's public persona. In the few client meetings he had attended during his first few weeks at R&H, he had watched in silent admiration as Ted magically turned skeptical prospects into lifelong clients, showcasing his unusual yet effortless combination of intelligence and charisma. Jack had heard stories of Ted's legendary ability to charm a host of audiences, from streetwise reporters to seasoned politicians, resulting in both news stories and tax legislation being written exactly the way he intended. In interactions with his clients, Ted had lived up to every one of those stories.

But Jack had seen another side of his boss as well. When neither the clients nor the public was looking, he could be humorless and intimidating. He rarely engaged in casual banter—no discussions of politics or sports when he was around. Every second Jack had spent in Ted's presence had been as tense as the very first.

Sitting in one of the burgundy guest chairs across from Ted's desk, Jack listened intently as his boss rattled off information about his latest potential clients, Walter and Margaret Harrington. Mrs. Harrington was the only daughter of one of the former owners of the Baltimore Orioles. When her father died, he left her a piece of the team, which she'd wisely sold at the first opportunity and reinvested in the stock market. Over the ensuing years, the S&P 500 had far more winning seasons than the Orioles.

Mr. Harrington had made his money in investment banking. A longtime employee of Morgan Stanley, he was a managing director responsible for sports and entertainment transactions. When one of the owners of the Orioles died unexpectedly, Harrington was one of the bankers dispatched to Baltimore to help the owner's daughter explore options for selling her inheritance. He ended up making a number of proposals to the heiress, including that she become his wife.

Ted slid a thick stack of documents across his desk. "All right, kid, are you ready to impress me?"

"Absolutely."

"Good. These are the Harringtons' existing wills and trusts. I want you to read them. Dissect every word, and—here's the important part—find every mistake."

Jack nodded enthusiastically. "Sure."

"These were done by Tom Klein's firm," Ted said, patting the thick stack. Jack recognized the name of one of New York's finest lawyers. "So let's show up that high-priced windbag, shall we?"

"You bet."

"Great. Take a day or two to read through these, and write a memo pointing out every potential weakness in them. I'll use it at my next meeting with the Harringtons to convince them they should switch firms."

"Got it. I'll start right away."

"That's great." Ted pushed the stack closer toward him. "Look, I need you to really go after this one. These are clients we want, and I need to give them a reason to dump Klein. So trash what he did for them. Show them that we're the smartest guys in town."

Jack ran his tongue along the inside of his parched mouth. "I understand. I'm on it."

"I know I can count on you."

Jack stood and stepped toward the office door, the documents tucked under his arm.

"Oh, one more thing," Ted called as Jack reached the doorway. He stopped and turned back to face his boss. "Don't mention this to Deb."

"So don't show her a draft?" Jack asked quizzically.

"Not a word to her. You work directly with me on this one."

# CHAPTER 20

Abigail was waiting just inside her apartment door when she heard the doorbell ring. She generally didn't open the door to strangers. But this particular stranger came with fairly impressive credentials. She looked through the peephole to see that her visitor was holding up his gold shield. She opened the door and welcomed him inside.

"Mr. Andrews—excuse me—*Agent* Andrews, won't you please come in?"

Joe Andrews placed his credentials back in the pocket of his suit jacket and stepped inside. "Please, call me Joe."

"Very well, Joe, can I offer you some tea?"

"No, thank you. I'm fine."

Abigail escorted him into the living room, where he settled into a waiting armchair. "I would like to ask you just a few questions, if that's all right."

"Of course, that's fine," she replied, pressing her palms together to try to calm her trembling hands. "But I'm afraid this is all a waste of your time. As I told you on the phone, Mr. Parker's firm handles all of my tax matters. They are the ones you really need to speak to."

She had made that point clear to him during their initial phone conversation, yet Andrews had persisted. And even though she and Ted had spent a long phone call trying to figure things out, Abigail had no idea what exactly had led the FBI to her doorstep. Ted assured her that her tax returns contained nothing even resembling fraud. So defying conventional legal advice, she had yielded to Agent Andrews's admittedly unconventional request to meet with her alone, at her home, without the benefit of counsel.

"I know that Ted Parker is your lawyer, and I know he handles your taxes," Andrews said. "However, as I told you on the phone, I thought this matter would be best discussed without him."

"Well, why are you here?" As soon as she finished the question, she knew that it had sounded too brusque. She forced a smile. "How can I assist you?"

He set his briefcase across the knees of his solid navy suit then pulled out a stack of paper. "May I show you something?" he asked.

"Of course. Please do." The trembling in Abigail's palms radiated up her arms as she anticipated his next words. She had just taken two Xanax but already needed more.

"This is a computer printout from an account at a bank in the Cayman Islands." He handed her the piece of paper and stared intently at her. "Now, this particular outfit, Atlantic Coast Bank, is notorious for dealing in some shady financial matters. As you can see, it looks like... Are you okay, Mrs. Walker?"

"Yes, yes. Of course." She pressed her lips together as she struggled mightily to mask their quivering. "It's just..." She swallowed a mouthful of froth. "I'm not sure what this is about."

"Well, I'll try to make it as simple as I can. Our government signed something called a tax information exchange agreement with the Cayman Islands. The deal is pretty simple: they promise to let us know if they think any of their bank accounts are being used for US tax fraud, and we promise not to land our navy on their beaches."

He chuckled, but she didn't appreciate the humor. To the contrary, she clenched her teeth as her pulse throbbed in her temples. *Stupid idiot,* she thought. *I'll have your badge.*

As he babbled on about "information exchanges," she lowered her head into her hands and rubbed her forehead. She struggled to remember what Ted had told her to do if she sensed this kind of trouble. He had told her that she could ask Andrews to leave at any time, that she could assert her Fifth-Amendment rights and refuse to answer questions, that at any point she could simply refer the matter to her attorneys. But while he had empowered her with these tools, he had also counseled her not to use them lightly. This request for a private meeting was unusual and suggested that she herself wasn't the target of a criminal probe. The last thing she needed to do was to invite more scrutiny by appearing uncooperative.

"I'm just..." She paused and offered a forced smile. "I'm sorry, Joe, it's just..." Her lips shuddered as she spoke. She dropped her head back into her hands. Despite all her preparation, she had not seen this coming. She'd never envisioned that he would be asking about the transfers to the Caymans or that he would already know so much about them. Now that it was too late, she realized that he had fully anticipated her surprise and was there to prey upon it. She never should have let him come. *You fool,* she thought.

"Ma'am, are you okay?"

Trying to suppress her racing heart, she lifted her head and struggled to speak as calmly as she could. "I am. Yes. You see, Agent Andrews," she began again, this time reverting to formal titles rather than first names, "I'm just not sure what you're accusing me of."

"I'm not accusing you of anything, ma'am. As I told you earlier, you're not the target of an investigation, at least not now."

"Well, then, who is?"

He leaned forward and stared directly at her. His gaze was uncomfortably intense, as if he were trying to look straight through her eyes and scan her brain.

"Mrs. Walker, you don't know?"

"Don't know *what*? I would appreciate your telling me what you have come to tell me. I do not like playing games."

"Mrs. Walker, this is Ted Parker's account. Ted Parker," he repeated. "You've been sending this money to your lawyer's account."

"Nonsense!" A loud buzzing began to echo in her ears. "My goodness! You must be insane, young man."

He pointed to the top of the ledger, where he had highlighted Ted's name with a bold yellow slash. "I assure you, ma'am, I am not. This is *his* account."

She shook her head. "Agent Andrews. I do not like tricks. I've known Ted Parker for thirty years. I do not appreciate whatever game you are playing."

"Mrs. Walker, this is no game," the agent said calmly. "The point is that—"

"I know what you *think* that printout says, or at least what you *say* it says." The buzzing in her ears had now become a rhythmic pulsing. She needed to get this idiot out of her house. "You have made a terrible mistake. Terrible. You cannot come into my home and speak this nonsense. And be assured that your supervisors will hear about this." Her voice boomed louder with every crisp syllable. She was doing everything that Ted had warned her not to do.

"You are welcome to contact my supervisory agent, Brian Sanford," Joe offered robotically. "He will assure you there's no mistake."

"You listen to me, young man." She sprayed spit as she spoke. "Hear what I'm telling you. You are making a terrible error. Terrible. It pains me to see you wasting your time. But it is simply intolerable to have you waste mine. I will hear nothing more of this." She forced herself out of her chair, stumbling for a moment before righting herself.

"But, ma'am, all I'm asking for is—"

"I couldn't care less what you're asking for. So drop this foolishness. Drop it now! I am not a well woman. This is not how I want to spend my final days."

The agent stood from his chair. "Mrs. Walker, it—"

She raised her hand and pressed the palm toward him.

"*Enough!* This meeting is finished. Ted Parker is my attorney. Please call him if you wish to discuss anything."

"Call *him*? Given the allegations, how can I—"

"Good day, Agent Andrews," she said as she offered a handshake. "I appreciate your service. I really do." Attempting to invoke a higher authority, she continued. "Senator Walker would have appreciated your service as well. But let's end this silliness, shall we? Your computers are making a fool of you. I do not want to see a black mark on your fine career."

After shaking her hand, the agent followed her to the apartment door. "It was a pleasure meeting you, ma'am. Thank you for your time." He handed her a business card, which she accepted without comment. "Please call me if you wish to speak further."

"I will."

After closing the door behind him, she crossed the living room and entered her small pantry. She filled a Waterford glass with two ice cubes and a hefty pour of vodka then returned to the comforts of the Queen Anne chair.

She rolled the glass around in her hand, mesmerized by the rays of light reflecting off the brilliant crystal and shooting out in every direction. Then she threw back the glass of vodka and downed its contents in a single gulp. As the alcohol seared the back of her throat, she picked up the phone on the small end table and dialed.

"Hello, Claire, is he in?"

"I'm sorry, Mrs. Walker, he's out of town today. He should be back late tonight."

"Oh yes, Boston. He did tell me that. I'll try his cell. Thank you, dear."

Her hands were trembling as she put down the phone, yet her voice had not quivered in the slightest. Notwithstanding her encounter with Andrews, she was still able to appear composed. Being a senator's wife had taught her that skill.

But the false front of calmness began to crumble as she dialed Ted's cell-phone number. The dam of emotion then fully broke as she heard his voice. "What the hell are you up to?"

"Abby, what's wrong? What happened with Andrews?"

"Don't be coy with me, you *bastard*. After all I have done for you, this is how you repay me? Haven't you caused me enough heartbreak for one lifetime?"

"Abby, I really don't know what—"

"I'll tell you *what*. Agent Andrews just showed me the records for your offshore account."

"Oh Jesus... the account?"

"Not *the* account. *Your* account. Bastard. How dare you?"

"Abby, please just listen."

"Listen to what? I saw the paperwork. It was printed right there. This charming federal agent made me look like a damn fool."

"I can explain. You know I would never—"

"You would never? Hah. There's *nothing* you would *never* do. I'm quite certain of that. A liar and a cheat. Nothing ever changes."

"Abby, stop it," he snapped. "Put down the booze or the pills or whatever the hell you are using to dull your senses today and just think for a minute."

Her jaw dropped open. It had been years since he had spoken to her like that.

"Get control of yourself, Abigail. Pull it together right now. We've been through too much for you to turn on me like this. I would never hurt you, and you know it."

She remained silent for a moment. This conversation was becoming pointless.

"Enough, Ted," she finally said. "Just get yourself back to New York and come straight here. And cancel my lunch with Deb. I can't deal with her drama today."

"Look, I really can explain," he said calmly. "Maybe I should have told you earlier, but I thought it was better—"

"I said *enough*. So stop your blather. If you have an explanation, I will hear it when you get here. If you don't, I suggest you slit your own throat to save me the trouble."

He tried to say something further, but she was done listening. She slammed the phone down. She then picked it up and slammed it down again before hurling it across the room.

The sound of the phone shattering against the plaster wall echoed through the apartment. It masked only briefly her wails of grief.

# CHAPTER 21

Deb knocked on the mahogany doorframe as she stuck her head inside Jack's office. "What are you doing for lunch?"

"Are you asking me on a date?"

"You wish. I need you to have lunch with me and Abigail Walker. Ted's in Boston, so you're buying."

"Fine. I feel so used."

"Oh, I intend to use you." Her voice dripped with mock seduction. "And I promise you'll like it. A lot."

Although he had known her for only a short time, the continued intensity of their interaction had been unmatched in his life. And although he could feel the slightest blush spread across his cheeks after her last comment, he wasn't about to end the flirtation. "You can use me anytime you want."

She laughed but offered no other immediate response. He momentarily feared that he had gone too far—that he had crossed some line in their still-budding friendship that would end up with a phone call from HR. But soon he was reassured that he had not.

"I love you, Collins," she said as a broad smile crossed her face. "You can dish it out with the best of them." Her smile growing more mischievous, she continued. "Maybe one night after work, I'll take you up on that offer. As for lunch, we already have reservations. I'll swing by just before noon."

"Okay. I'll be here."

As she turned and walked back into the hallway, he scanned down the length of her tight black skirt, tracing the outline of her hips then watching her calf muscles strain in her high heels. His pulse quickened as he mentally replayed her words. *Maybe one night after work...*

JACK KNEW DEB WELL enough to realize that a few minutes before noon actually meant a few minutes after. Accordingly, he continued to work until about five past twelve then stepped out of his office just as she came striding down the hall. She smiled at him but didn't measurably slow her pace as she continued past him toward the lobby. "Come on. Lunchtime."

He pursued her down the hall and through the reception area, where a group of other lawyers had begun to gather for lunch.

"Can you guys join us downstairs?" asked Steve Oswald, a counsel in the tax department. Steve acted as the self-appointed marketing department for the building's cafeteria, where he ate at the same table at the same time every day. Unlike most of other lawyers at R&H, who worked and socialized in insular groups, Steve had gone out of his way to try to make Jack feel welcome, including inviting him to lunch every time they saw each other. On the few occasions when he had been able to accept, Jack had found the food decent and the conversation interesting, especially when the topic inevitably drifted to the recent history of R&H. As those at the table recounted story after story, the prevailing themes had become crystal clear: Ted was the most brilliant lawyer in the history of the firm, and Deb the most ruthless.

"Sorry," Deb said without even looking at Steve. "It's Friday. Mrs. Walker's day."

"Too bad," Steve mumbled as one of the elevators chimed to life, the red down arrow flashing as the door opened to receive them.

Offering a little spectacle for the other lawyers, Deb tucked her arm through Jack's and led him into the waiting elevator. "Come on, handsome, time for our lunch."

"Oswald is such a prick," she said as the elevator door rattled shut. "Don't even bother with him."

"Um, okay." Jack was momentarily stunned by the randomness of the comment. "What's his deal?"

"Nothing. He's just some fancy-pants from Scarsdale. Thinks he knows everything but is really just a windbag."

Staring awkwardly at his distorted reflection in the elevator's brass doors, Jack said nothing in reply. Clearly there was some history between the "windbag" and the "cold-hearted bitch," as Deb and Steve so lovingly referred to each other behind each other's back. Steve actually seemed to hate Deb more than she hated him, going so far as to warn Jack that Deb's legendary mood swings were some form of personality disorder. But Jack wasn't convinced. Yes, her personality could flip without warning, darting from proper and professional one minute to cunning and sarcastic the next. But, on balance, he found her chaotic personality alluring. She was smart, tough, and the number-one associate of one of the firm's most powerful partners. Certainly a fair dose of jealousy clouded the others' views of her.

The elevator headed toward the lobby, the two of them standing side by side in silence. As the floors ticked down on the elevator display, Jack cast a sideways glance at her. Her tanned cheeks were accentuated with just the right amount of blush. Her dark-red lipstick glistened in the elevator light. A faint scent of strawberry wafted off her wavy hair, filling the elevator car with the smell of summer.

He inhaled slowly through his nose and savored the sweet aroma. He couldn't care less what the others thought about her. He liked her. *A lot.*

# CHAPTER 22

As Jack and Deb entered the Harvard Club dining room, Raymond, the tuxedo-clad maître d', rushed over to them. "Mr. Collins, Ms. Miller, I am so sorry. Claire called to tell me that Mrs. Walker isn't feeling well. Perhaps she just missed you?"

"Or just too lazy to do her job right," Deb mumbled in Jack's general direction before turning back to Raymond. "Well, it *is* Friday, and traditions are traditions."

"Very well, ma'am, please follow me."

Raymond led the two of them to the table in the far corner. He sat Deb in the chair usually reserved for Abigail, the one beneath Harold Walker's portrait. Jack sat next to her, and Raymond cleared the remaining place settings. A waiter appeared moments later with two glasses of Chardonnay they did not need to order.

After twenty minutes of lighthearted conversation, Deb made a quick trip to the bathroom. She returned with Raymond, and two more glasses of Chardonnay, in tow. As soon as the maître d' had dropped off the wine and turned away from the table, Deb looked intently at Jack. "Why does Oswald hate me?"

"Huh?" He'd heard the question but hoped it might change the second time around.

"Stop it. You know it as well as I do. That whole little lunch bunch at R&H can't stand me."

"I don't know that. Nobody has ever said anything about you."

"Bullshit."

"What?" *Where the hell is this coming from?*

"Come on, you are full of crap." She reached across the table and grabbed the cuff of his suit jacket. He could see her jaw pulsing. "I know you had lunch with Oswald and that crew last week. I'm sure they talked all kinds of trash about me."

"Huh?" He felt his collar tighten around his neck. "They may have mentioned you, but nothing serious. Maybe some petty stuff, but I figured they're probably just jealous." He shrugged.

"Jealous of what? I'm thirty-three and single. My apartment is the size of this table. All I have to show for my life is my work. You have your wife. That bald loser Oswald has his perfect little family. And he's jealous of me?"

*Yeah, that tone of voice will win you a lot of friends,* Jack thought. He had seen her talk that way about people before. Heck, he'd seen her talk that way *to* people before. There was a very fine line separating spunky confidence from cutting contempt, and she loved darting over that line. That was why some people did hate her, including Steve Oswald, "the bald loser," as she lovingly called him.

"Yes, he's jealous of you... and your box seats at Yankee Stadium." He flashed a broad smile at her. *Come on, Deb, please calm down.* She met his smile with a cold stare.

"Those are my uncle's." She paused, and her expression softened into a smile. "They are pretty cool seats, though."

"I wouldn't know. Nobody's ever invited me to sit in them."

She took a healthy gulp of wine. "It's not my fault that Ted relies on me like he does. I've worked hard for that. And I deserve it. I am paying the price in other ways. Rest assured, I am."

"I'm sure that—"

"But all of you who have other things in your life hate me."

"Hold on. How did *I* get on that list? What's up with you today?"

"You know you're just like them. You have a *life*. All I have is my stupid job. I didn't want it to be that way, but that's what it is, for now."

"Well, I certainly don't hate you. Far from it. I mean, I think you're awesome."

She stared past him as he spoke. "And why do people say things about me and Ted?"

Now *that* was a topic he didn't want to touch. Rumors persisted throughout the hallways of R&H that Ted and Deb enjoyed a somewhat more intimate relationship than most colleagues. Jack at first had dismissed her actions toward Ted as being part innocent flirtation and part manipulation. But as time went on and he heard more rumors of their past interactions, he had become less certain about his assessment. In any event, he wanted no part of that debate.

She went on. "It's so hurtful." Her eyes grew moist. She looked away as she continued. "I know what they call me. I know they say I do my best work in Ted's apartment." She stopped talking and dabbed her napkin at her eyes.

The pause gave him a chance to speak. "Just ignore it. Some people are jealous, or sexist, or just plain mad that you're moving ahead of them. Don't let it rattle you."

He tried to pat her hand in reassurance, but she slid it away from him and off the table. Then she laughed, almost maniacally. "Great pep talk. Did you practice that? That's the best cliché you could come up with? People hate me because I'm a strong woman?"

"Yeah, 'cause it's true. Sure, Ted likes me. At least he likes me *enough*. Sure, he brought me to R&H to join him. He gives me a cool project here and there. But we all know who gets first call on the best projects. We all know who's number one. I don't hold that against you. But you have to see how some people might."

She sat back in her chair, tapping her red fingernails against her wineglass and staring across the dining room. Just as the silence became awkward, and without looking back at him, she resumed the conversation.

"My father." It was a complete non sequitur. "For some reason, I started thinking about him on the walk over. I guess I'm still trying to impress him."

Another tear formed in the corner of her eye, but she quickly wiped it away. "I need you to like me." Another non sequitur. She lunged forward and grabbed his hand in hers. "Not just *endure* me. Not just *work with* me. I need you to *be* with me. Through thick and thin. I've never really had that."

"You do have that. I mean, I've known you for six weeks, and it feels like forever."

"You have no idea how much that means to me."

He enjoyed feeling the warmth of her fingers on his own, her smooth skin pressed against his. But that enjoyment was tempered by guilt. He slid his fingers out of her palm and returned them to the stem of his wineglass. She sat silently in her chair, her eyes gazing past him. She slowly began to smile, clearly entertained by whatever she was thinking about. Her emotional storm had retreated as quickly as it had gathered.

"I'm sorry," she said, matter-of-factly. "That was crazy. It's just that my mother called me before and stirred up some old memories." She patted the back of his hand. "You're a great friend."

"You're a great friend too. Teammates, right?"

"Absolutely. But enough drama on this team for one day. Let's order lunch."

---

WHEN LUNCH WAS DONE, Deb and Jack made their way slowly back toward 1593 Broadway. She consciously slowed her pace as they ambled down a sunlit sidewalk. She was not at all anxious to return to the pile of paperwork she had left on her desk. It could wait.

As she walked in silence, she thought back to the lunchtime conversation. *You're a great friend,* Jack had repeated time and again. What an idiot he was. Adorable. Loyal. But a terrible judge of character. Steve Oswald was so much savvier than he was. Which was why Oswald had needed to go.

But Jack could stay, at least for now.

"I didn't expect to be alone with you," she said, breaking a long silence. "But I'm glad it worked out that way."

"Me too. Maybe we should make this a new tradition. I can only eat Chinese so often."

"Sounds great. Sorry again for the sloppy part."

"You don't need to keep apologizing. Really." For the next block, she kept the conversation breezy, making no further mention of the emotional intensity of less than an hour before.

As they turned north, she stopped short.

"Hang on for a second." She turned away from him, lit a cigarette, and tossed the match to the curb. She subtly straightened her skirt, pressing it against her leg as she slid her left hand slowly down her hip. *Poor Jack,* she thought. He was obviously dying to sleep with her. More than once, she had watched him subtly trace the outline of her clothing with his eyes. She had seen him blush whenever she positioned herself to give him a glimpse of her bra. He was probably so confused right now—struggling mightily to balance his surging hormones with his desire to be her protector, her pathetically loyal teammate.

But as much as he was like all the other men who had come and gone in her past, he was different in one key way. He needed to be the hero more than anyone else ever had. He wouldn't just sleep with her and get it over with. That would be the self-serving easy way out. Instead, he had this bizarre need to always say and do the right thing—to solve her every problem. That was his most endearing trait. It was also his greatest weakness. She just needed to keep being the vulnerable and sad friend, and he'd do her bidding.

As she placed her cigarettes in a jacket pocket, her hand brushed against a slip of paper. She pulled it out and saw the phone message Claire had handed her at noon as she stepped out of her office—the pink slip of paper that told her that Abigail had cancelled lunch. She crumpled it into a ball and stuffed it back into her pocket.

*Thank you, Abigail. Lunch was so much better without you.*

# CHAPTER 23

Ted's heart raced as he fumbled with the lock to Abigail's apartment. She had not answered her phone in over two hours. His imagination had long since gotten the worst of him.

He raced into the apartment and headed straight to the Queen Anne chair. In the dim light slipping through a crack between the drawn curtains, he saw the outline of her figure slumped sideways in the chair, her chin tucked into her chest. He cradled the sides of her face in his hands and breathed an audible sigh of relief as she raised her head.

"Well, there's the bastard himself," she slurred. "Sure took you long enough to get here."

"It was three hours." He could feel a warm trickle rolling down the back of his spine, his shirt and rumpled suit both soaked with sweat from his frantic journey from Boston. "My trip was fine. Thank you for asking."

As he turned on a lamp, she moaned and placed her hand across her eyes.

"For God's sake, turn that off."

Ignoring the request, he strode over to the window and flung open the curtains. "How many pills did you take?"

She laughed and licked her lips. "Seven or eight. It's been a lousy day."

He grabbed a small armchair and slid it beside the Queen Anne. "All right, so tell me about Andrews."

"What's to say?" she asked, rubbing her temples. "He knows all about your account. Ready to make a fool of me and arrest you. Our government at work."

"Abby, it's not *my* account."

"Of course it's not. Just a typographical error by the bankers. Little mistake, I'm sure."

"Seriously, Abby. I know my name is on it, but it's not mine."

"Oh yes, that makes perfect sense." She attempted to stand up but slumped backward into the chair. "Just like all my other bank accounts. It's my money, but your name is on all of those too."

"Look, that's not—"

"I trusted you. I trusted you with everything."

"Think about it," he said as she closed her eyes. "A blackmailer sets up an offshore account. It's a numbered account, probably set up over the Internet. Did you expect him to use his own name and address? Did you expect him to be that stupid? Would you expect *me* to be that stupid?"

"I don't know what I expected. Nothing's turned out the way I expected, so why would this be different?"

"Just think about it."

Neither of them spoke for a full minute, the stillness in the apartment punctuated only by Ted's still-labored breathing and the distant ticking of a grandfather clock.

"It does makes sense," she said, breaking the silence. "Nobody would expect the brilliant Ted Parker to be so sloppy. Which is exactly what you might have planned."

"Oh, spare me. Look, this is precisely why I didn't tell you in the first place. If you're not going to trust me, then I'm gone. You can find another lawyer. I mean it."

She said nothing.

"I mean it," he repeated, even more sternly this time.

"And why should I care?" she asked, her voice drifting off.

"Because." He paused. "Just because."

"Because, because, because," she parroted back at him, her eyes now clamped shut and her voice becoming weaker and weaker with every repetition.

"Because I love you," he blurted, the words jumping past his lips before he could stop them.

He looked over at her sleeping figure and wondered if she had heard him. Her snoring suggested that she had not.

"I love you," he whispered as he stroked her graying hair. "I always have."

# CHAPTER 24

Joe Andrews looked up from his computer screen to find Bob Masterson standing beside him, a Styrofoam cup of coffee in one hand and a messy pile of paperwork in the other. As authorized by Judge Vivian Martinez of the US District Court for the Southern District of New York, the stack of papers included the transcript of every lunchtime conversation involving Ted Parker or one of his associates in the past week, as captured by the listening device located in the Harvard Club dining room.

Bob placed the cup to his lips with one hand and handed Joe the papers with the other. After downing a swig of coffee with an audible gulp, Bob provided his professional assessment. "We got nothing." After a brief pause, he continued. "Lots of chitchat, talk about family, stupid stuff. A bunch of babble. That's all."

*You're the one who's babbling,* Joe thought. He flipped through the pages, struggling to read the text in front of him while his oblivious colleague continued speaking. "It's been this way the whole time. I'm thinking we're spinning our wheels here."

"Hang on," Joe replied, extending one finger in Bob's direction—a further attempt to silence the incessant chatter. Smiling involuntarily, he looked up. "Who's the new voice from Friday?"

"Some guy named Jack Collins," Bob replied between slurps of coffee. "A new associate at the firm. We already checked his background, and nothing came up. Don't think he matters here."

*Not so fast.* "Can you pull up the file?"

"Of course." Bob lumbered to the other side of the room, where he began pounding on the keys of a laptop. He returned a few moments later and handed the computer to Joe.

"I won't know anything until I hear this."

The sound of conversation soon filled the small room. Joe listened intently as the faceless voices engaged in seemingly idle conversation.

Bob again took a slurp from his paper cup. "See, boss, we got nothing. Absolutely nothing."

Joe ignored Bob as he focused on the voices on the recording, his smile broadening as he listened to every passing exchange. *What unbelievable luck. What were the odds?*

Turning toward his counterpart for just a moment, he paused the playback.

"Actually, we got something much better than we ever hoped for."

# CHAPTER 25

Jack glanced up from his desk to see Claire stepping through his office doorway, her eyes barely visible above the thick stack of files she held in front of her. She dropped the files with a thud on the corner of his desk. "A little present from Ted," she said with a smile. "He's dictating a memo about them."

He snatched the first file off the top of the stack. His heart surged in his chest as he saw the name on the label. "Oh God, this guy owns half of Greenwich," he said.

"So I hear," she replied nonchalantly. "Plus the Chrysler Building."

"I can't believe Ted is letting me work on this. This is so cool."

"Apparently the client asked for you, so try not to do your usual lousy job."

"What are you talking about? Michael Putnam asked for *me*?"

Claire eased one of the guest chairs away from Jack's desk. "Yeah, I think his stepdaughter may have mentioned you."

"Putnam's stepdaughter?" He struggled to think back if he had ever met anyone even remotely connected to the Putnam family.

"I'm sure you'll figure it out," she said as she slid her chair closer to the desk. Although she was looking downward at the floor, he could see that she was struggling to conceal an impish smile.

His pulse pounded again. "No way, *seriously*?"

"Seriously."

"Your mom is Leslie Putnam?"

"That's her."

"Holy shit," he exclaimed then recoiled in shock. "Sorry for that." He took a deep breath.

"It's shocking, just shocking," she said through an affectedly clenched jaw. "The Putnams do not tolerate vulgarity."

"I'm sure," he said, laughing. "No cursing allowed in the real estate world." After a pause, he continued. "So why the hell are you a secretary? Oh man, that came out wrong. I just mean how did you end up working for Ted?"

"Don't worry, I get that all the time. The NYU English major turned legal secretary. Must be some great story. And I'm not sure I have much of an answer. Ted and my dad went way back, and Ted was so good to us after my dad died. He even gave my mom a part-time job once I was old enough for school, and that's how she met Mike. They get married, and suddenly it's my graduation day. Ted gives me a temporary spot so I can figure out what I want to do when I grow up. I guess I'm still figuring."

"Nothing wrong with that. It's an honest living."

"I guess. The work's not bad. I meet a ton of interesting people. And hanging out here pays more than making caramel lattes. Plus I can keep a good eye on the family lawyers."

"Now hold on," he said sternly. "What's wrong with making caramel lattes?"

"Nothing, if you make them right. Not like that crap at Starbucks. You want a decent latte, then trudge up to Dylan's on Seventh and 53rd. I've never had a bad day their caramel latte can't cure."

"I'll try it sometime."

"So while we're trading life secrets, why are *you* here?" Claire asked, sliding her chair still closer to the desk. "You had a pretty good thing going in Connecticut. Why not just stay there? Why R&H?"

Jack tapped his finger on the file label. "To work for people like Michael Putnam."

"He is a pretty cool guy. I'll make sure you meet him. But really, is that it?"

"It kinda is. Is that a bad thing?"

"No, it's not."

"It's just that I didn't exactly take a lot of chances in life. I went to the same law school my father and grandfather did. I went to work in the family firm in my hometown. I live down the street from Mom and Dad. I married the first girl I ever seriously dated."

"There's nothing wrong with any of that."

"Maybe not. But you start to wonder that there's a whole world out there you've been afraid to step into. A few months ago, I'd finally had enough. I decided it was time for a fresh start, a big challenge. So here I am."

"And how's it working out?"

"Pretty well, best I can tell. Apparently even the Putnams have heard of me."

"They have. They speak of you almost every night." She flashed him a smile before pressing her lips together. "But all kidding aside, nobody here knows a thing about me. Besides Ted, of course. So can we keep it that way?"

"Of course."

"I mean it. I had to tell you because my name is everywhere inside those files. But I don't want anyone else knowing my business, especially *her.*"

"I'm sorry," he said, turning his head askew as he stared at her. "Have I seen you before?"

"Very funny."

"Oh, you're Ted's secretary, right? Thanks for dropping off the files, Ted's secretary," he said through a wide grin. "Enjoy the rest of your day."

"I will, Mr. Associate," she said as she stood. "I'll bring you the Putnam memo when it's ready."

# CHAPTER 26

Ted leaned back in his oversized leather chair, his hands folded in his lap and his mind drifting back through the events of the past few years. For all his success as a lawyer, he had been a relatively poor manager of his own staff. Perhaps that was not unexpected. A trusts and estates lawyer needed the intellectual focus to memorize the smallest details of his clients' lives and navigate the densest provisions of the Internal Revenue Code. Being a good manager required an entirely different set of skills, including a willingness to waste precious time dealing with the garbage of staff personalities and office politics.

He had once thought that Deb was his own perfect counterpoint. Unlike him, she seemed genuinely energized by the human drama that came with a trusts and estates practice and could be gracious and amiable when listening to the same old client stories. But, as even the senior partners had apparently noticed, she did have the charm of a pit bull when her coworkers didn't live up to her unreasonable expectations. The clients adored her—the staff feared her. For years, that had been a useful combination.

But things had changed. In the past year or two, Deb's already thorny personality had grown increasingly acerbic. Her sense of entitlement had become evident. Sloppy mistakes had begun to appear in her work. And the take-no-prisoners attitude, which he had once found refreshing in the young Deb Miller, became increasingly grating as she inched her way toward middle age. Instead of mellowing with the passage of time, she had become an increasingly polarizing figure within R&H.

For years, he had chosen to dance with this devil. She was far too intelligent and productive for him to ignore. She could run intellectual circles around the Clay Warrens and Steve Oswalds of the world. She had thus become the mainstay of his practice. He had no better choice.

But that had just changed.

He had just finished reading the best legal memo he'd ever seen. And Deb had not written it. Indeed, she didn't even know it existed—just as he'd instructed.

Ted leaned forward and looked at the memo on his desk, focusing on Jack's name on the first page. He'd expected Jack to be smart. However, he'd assumed he would be undertrained and underprepared, a minor leaguer overwhelmed by the expectations of a firm like R&H. Ted had interviewed Jack as a favor and hired him on a whim. But based on what he had seen these first several weeks, he just might have ended up with something much greater than he'd ever thought possible.

Jack did lack Deb's tenacity. In fact, he was downright lazy in comparison to her. He was soft and suburban, preferring early dinners to Deb's all-nighters. But he had a maturity and poise that she could spend years trying to develop without ever succeeding, even with the help of her psychiatrist and her medicine cabinet. Plus, as Jack's analysis of the Harringtons' estate plan showed, he could already go toe-to-toe with some of the best lawyers in New York. With one memo, Jack had given Ted something he had never had: a real alternative to Deb.

Ted wasn't into charity work. He wasn't into training young lawyers to benefit the future of the profession or the good of the public. That was all feel-good crap. While his critics reviled him for it, he held steadfast to his own simple philosophy about the legal business: the free market was the antidote to all of society's ills, and the pursuit of money was the purest, and most easily manageable, motive. He discounted those who wanted to *help people* or *do interesting work*. Sure, he got a chance to do that. But when he sat at his desk at ten o'clock on a Thursday night, it was not the desire to help others that got him through the piles of paper. It was the search for profit, nothing else.

Everyone at R&H knew both that he could spend money with the best of them and that he viewed his compensation as a measure of his self-worth. What they didn't know was how sick Abigail had become, nor how relevant her health would be to the future of this law firm. Just as she would not live forever, he wasn't going to stay at R&H forever. In fact, he was just months away from opening the doors to a new practice, with a new name, a new location, and a new junior partner. He had slowly developed this plan over several years. It was the key to his financial future—a way to finally reap the financial rewards of all of his efforts. Once he ran his own firm, he would no longer have to share the fruits of his labors with the likes of Daniel Reynolds and Brian Lynch. He would easily double his own income and free himself from the death spiral of spending and debt that had driven him to the verge of bankruptcy. It was his great escape.

In the past few days, Ted had begun to question one long-standing detail of this master plan. There would still be a new law firm. There would still be a new junior partner. But what if that new partner was named Jack Collins, not Deb Miller? As he thought about the idea, he grew to like it more and more. It felt impulsive. But it also felt right.

He had grown so tired of Deb's drama. He had long since lost patience with the emotional rollercoaster that was her life. And as he sat alone in reflective silence, he thought ahead to what his own life would look like if he simply left her behind.

Abigail would soon leave behind a fortune. A dozen trusts would hold her vast net worth for generations into the future. Thousands of hours of legal work would follow. Millions of dollars would flow into the hands of whoever controlled her financial legacy. *He* would be that person.

He had worked hard to earn this future. He had done things he wished he could forget. He had made choices that filled him with remorse, virtually selling his own soul to solidify his position as the Walkers' family lawyer. Now it was time to reap the spoils.

# CHAPTER 27

Jack and Amanda Collins had just finished a perfectly mediocre dinner. The problem was not the food at Burning Tree Country Club. On the contrary, the wild Copper River salmon had been cooked perfectly, and the apple pie tasted homemade. Nor was the problem with the Collins's hosts, Marie and Larry Levitt—Amanda's boss and her husband. The problem was with Jack, who spent too much of the dinner in stony silence, disengaged and detached, lost in his own thoughts. Although the Levitts hadn't seemed to notice Jack's behavior, his wife certainly had.

So as they drove north on the Merritt Parkway, Amanda turned to her husband and asked the question she'd been itching to ask for over an hour. "Is everything okay with you?"

The car veered slightly to the right as he turned his head toward her. "Yeah, why? What did I do?"

"Not much. That's the point. You seemed to be somewhere else at dinner tonight. What's on your mind?"

"Nothing really. I was trying to just let you do your thing."

"*My thing?* How is eating dinner *my thing*?"

"You know what I mean. This lawyer did that, this judge does that. I don't even know half the people you were talking about."

"Well, I don't know half the people you talk about lately. That doesn't mean I don't try."

"I did try. It's just hard. My life is becoming completely different. Different people. Different conversations. It was just hard to change gears tonight."

She stared at her husband's profile, watching as the passing head-lights reflected off his face. His eyes were focused on the road ahead of him, but his thoughts, yet again, were somewhere else entirely.

"Don't let them take you away," she said.

"Huh?"

"R&H. The big-shot lawyers. The fancy clients. Don't let them change you. The guy I fell in love with never forgot his high school friends even when he went off to the Ivy League. That guy never needed to rub elbows with the rich and famous."

"Not true. Scott Mitchell is rich and famous," he teased, referring to his former roommate and current congressman from Tennessee's Fifth District.

"I'm serious. Just remember who you are and what you are about."

He reached over and rested his hand on her leg. "I do remember," he said.

"Not enough. Not nearly enough."

He let out a heavy sigh. "I hear you. I'm sorry."

"For tonight or for swiping that bar stool from M. J.?" They both laughed at the reference back to the evening when they'd first met. Mary Jane Elliott, one of Amanda's Holy Cross roommates—and her subsequent maid of honor—still maintained that Jack had all but pushed her off a barstool so he could sit next to Amanda.

"Maybe for both. Maybe I ruined two nights of your life."

She softened. "No, just one. Just tonight. As to that barstool thing, I wouldn't have wanted anyone else on that barstool."

"I'm glad I have you," he said. "I need to say that more."

"I'm glad you have me too," she deadpanned, generating a laugh from her husband—his second of the entire evening.

# CHAPTER 28

The Wadsworth Athenaeum in Hartford was the nation's oldest public art museum and boasted one of the world's finest collections of paintings from the Hudson River School. Deb stood in the middle of one of the museum's galleries, transfixed by amid-nineteenth-century work by Asher Durand, *View Toward the Hudson Valley*. The museum was fairly crowded on this rainy Saturday afternoon, but she stood alone in front of the Durand and surveyed the unspoiled landscape of early America.

She felt a hand on her waist and turned.

"Amazing, isn't it?" Ben asked.

"It is. Absolutely beautiful," Deb replied, lowering her head onto his shoulder.

"Just like you," he said, kissing her hair.

She lifted her head off his shoulder and took his hand in hers. "Did you see the Coles on the other side of the room?" she asked, tugging him gently. "Those are my absolute favorites."

The two continued to hold hands as they walked to the far side of the room and looked up at the wall that housed nearly a dozen paintings by Thomas Cole. "Amazing," Ben said. "I never get sick of this place. Growing up, it was all about the Met. That's the one place my dad always made the time to take me. But I've come to love it here even more."

As they strolled from one corner of the room to the other, she paused in front of a smaller work, entitled *Life, Death, and Immortality*. "Perfect for an estate planner, don't you think?" she asked.

"Absolutely," he said. "You should hang it in your office. Let's check the gift shop on the way out."

The two soon separated again and moved into different galleries. After fifteen minutes or so, she found him in front of a John Trumbull painting of the Battle of Princeton.

"Look at George Washington," Deb said as she approached him from behind and patted him on the buttocks. Lowering her voice to a whisper inaudible to the silver-haired woman standing just a few paces away, she pressed her chest into his back and continued with her assessment of the famous general. "He's looking kinda hot in those tight little pants."

"He was riding a horse," Ben groaned. "They're riding pants, you freak."

"Still a little tight, if you ask me."

"Okay, if we're talking about Washington's ass, I assume you've had enough of this place. So what are you thinking next?"

"I'm thinking we should go see your office."

"My office? It's just a crappy desk covered with paper. Why the hell would you want to go there?"

"I'm thinking we could move the papers off to the side."

His eyes widened, and a smile crept across his face. "You're a wicked one, Deb Miller."

"I am. And I hope your office door has a lock."

# CHAPTER 29

"Five iron," Ted said calmly.

Although there wasn't a hint of a question mark at the end of Ted's request, his caddy, Mike Rose, hesitated ever so slightly. "One ninety-five to the flag, Mr. Parker. Bunker in front. I'm thinking the four, Mr. Parker."

"It's downwind, though. It'll play one eighty-five."

Mike pulled the five iron from Ted's bag and presented it in silence to the former club president.

As Ted adjusted his grip and looked back and forth from his ball to the waiting flagstick, he overheard one of his opponents, investment banker Pete Hoffman, mutter, "Not enough club."

*Go screw yourself, Pete,* Ted thought as he swung the club forward, launching the ball and a small slice of turf toward the green. The minute he struck the ball, he knew it would be close. "Go, go," he heard Mike urge, as if the ball were actually listening. Reaching the peak of its flight path, the white sphere began its slow return earthward while Ted mentally computed its speed and distance. "Get moving. Get there," Ted pressed.

The ball seemed to respond. As it plummeted toward the greenery below, it cleared the rear edge of the sand trap by less than a yard, took a favorable bounce off the thick fescue, and rolled onto theeighteenth green, stopping just inches short of the flagstick. The tap-in putt would win the hole and the match.

Ted and his playing partner exchanged broad smiles, while Pete and his partner groaned in audible agony. "One foot shorter, Parker..." Pete barked.

"One foot longer, and it would have bounced straight into the cup," Ted countered as he flipped the five iron into Mike's hands and began his triumphant march toward the putting green.

Ted heard someone approaching from behind him and turned back just as Pete reached him. The banker put his arm around his old friend's shoulders. "Awesome shot, I'll give you that. Gutsy call. I didn't think you had enough club."

"I didn't either," he confessed.

"Hey, Ted," Pete said. Just from the way his friend had said his name, Ted knew what he was about to say. "I really need an answer on that oil thing."

The "oil thing" to which Pete referred was a limited partnership he had put together with some of his underlings at Goldman Sachs. The basic idea was to raise the funds needed to drill for oil in previously untapped reserves in the southwestern US, hopefully earning enough money in the process to pay Goldman a management fee and provide a generous return to the investors. The deal was highly speculative, at least from the investors' standpoint. In fact, the hefty management fee was the only sure thing in the entire transaction.

"I'm still noodling it over. Not sure I can take a full share, though." As much as he liked Pete and trusted his judgment, there was no way he would ever be willing to commit five hundred thousand dollars to Goldman's questionable search for oil in New Mexico. "I might be able to swing a half share," he offered, lying effortlessly. "I'll call you about it this week."

As he stepped away from Pete and approached his ball, he forgot about the great shot that he had just played and thought instead of his rapidly eroding personal finances, silently wondering how he had allowed himself to slide so deeply into debt. He knew that the answer lay in part in the company he kept. For the early part of his career, he had accepted that he would never keep pace with the wealth accumulated by the Pete Hoffmans of the world. Guys like Pete earned money by combining companies and packaging investments. There were un-limited companies that could be combined, unlimited investments that could be created and sold. But Ted earned his money by devoting his time to client work. And the undeniable truth was that there were only so many hours in the day.

At some point during his career, Ted and his lawyer brethren had begun a silent, ill-advised revolt. The investment bankers were no smarter than they were, the lawyers reasoned to each other. They worked no harder. They had no greater education. They shouldn't live so much higher on the hog. And so, lawyers in all the nation's biggest cities had begun to claim their rightful place in the economic pecking order. They raised their billing rates, slashed administrative costs, and piled increasing burdens on associates and paralegals. They devoted less time to training young lawyers, nibbled away at employees' medical in-surance, and, perhaps most nefariously, pushed into unwilling retire-ment some of their firm's oldest but least productive partners—the now *dead wood* that had built many of these storied law firms.

For the lawyers at R&H, that plan worked, but not nearly fast enough. In the past decade, Ted's annual income had grown from eight hundred thousand dollars to more than two million. But Pete Hoff-man's annual bonus alone would likely exceed ten million. Try as he might, Ted could not keep pace with his golfing buddy. Trying to do so had led him to join too many clubs, pick up too many dinner tabs, and buy his wife too much jewelry. His desire to live as conspicuously well as those with whom he surrounded himself had only driven him into debt.

"Hey, let's have the ladies meet us at La Panetière for dinner, shall we?" Pete suggested. It was an excellent choice. The food at the elegant French restaurant was among the finest in Westchester County. "You're about to have a thousand of my dollars in your pocket," he added.

"Great idea," Ted replied, trying not to think about the fact that the wager he was about to collect wouldn't even pay for one of the bottles of Château Margaux they would consume that night.

# CHAPTER 30

Jack stood up from his desk and pulled his cell phone out of his pocket. As he eyed the buzzing phone, he felt a twinge of panic in his gut. Only his parents and Amanda ever called his cell during the workday and usually only when something was wrong. His second reaction was one of confusion as *Restricted* flashed on the display. *What does that mean?* He placed the phone against his ear. "Hello?"

"Hey, bud," came the reply in Joe Andrews's distinct Boston accent.

"Joe? How are you?"

"Doing well. I'm actually in New York."

"That's great. Want to get together?"

"Yeah, that's why I called. Mind if I come by your place tonight?"

"Not at all. You want to do a late dinner?"

"I'm thinking after dinner. It's business."

Jack's throat felt tight. "Business? What's going on?"

"Let me explain in person. It may take a bit of time."

"Am I in trouble?"

"Not personally. I just need your help on something."

"Not *personally*? That's not exactly reassuring."

"Don't worry. I'll explain it all tonight."

"Okay."

"Great. I'll get there as soon as I can."

As the voice on the other end of the line fell silent, Jack slipped his phone back into his pocket. He exhaled deeply and rubbed his sweaty palms against the legs of his pants. His heart still beating at a frantic pace, he sat back in his desk chair and forced a few more deep breaths.

He'd known Joe since the day Jack walked into his freshman dorm room in Weld Hall and saw the Bostonian sitting on the top bunk. As roommates for all four years of college, they were all but inseparable. After graduation, they drifted somewhat apart. Weekly phone calls soon became monthly ones and then largely stopped, their long silences punctuated by occasional birthday or anniversary greetings when they actually remembered such events. Before today, it had been at least six months since they'd last spoken. And while Joe hadn't said anything particularly foreboding, it was clear that today's contact was no social call. It was a sign of trouble.

Jack's deliberately slow breathing had some modest effect. His heart rate gradually slowed. The pain retreated from his stomach. But his palms continued to sweat, and his mind continued to race. He tried in vain to redirect his focus to the stack of papers sitting on his desk, but he couldn't clear his head of the conversation he'd just had.

He grabbed his suit jacket off the back of his office door and headed toward the elevators and the fresh air waiting forty-four stories below him. Besides taking a walk around the block and obsessing about his fate, he had no idea how he would pass the next several hours.

# CHAPTER 31

Startled from his slumber, Jack forced open his eyes and looked at the clock on the living room wall. It was nearly midnight. Using the sleeve of his sweatshirt to clear the drool from his chin, he stood up from the sofa and headed toward the kitchen, turning off the television as he passed by.

He heard the faint knock again.

He crossed the kitchen linoleum and opened the door to reveal a familiar face.

"I like the overcoat. My taxes pay for that?"

"No, but they paid for the Glock." Joe pulled open the left side of his overcoat to reveal the holstered handgun.

"Okay, you win. I yield to your superior weapons. Come on in."

Joe stepped onto the kitchen linoleum, wrapped his arms around Jack's shoulders and hugged him. "It's good to see you, bud."

"Good to see you too. You look sharp."

"You look like you were sleeping on the sofa," Joe replied then tapped him on the face where a cushion had etched a deep groove.

"Can I get you something?"

"Nope. I need to head back out in a minute. Hey, is anyone else here? Amanda?"

"In our bedroom. Asleep."

"Good. It's better that way," Joe said, quickly adding, "You know what I mean."

Jack nodded. "Of course. Come on in." He led his visitor into the living room and slumped back onto the sofa.

Joe neither sat down nor removed his overcoat. "How's it going, bud?" he asked.

"I thought it was going well until about three o'clock this afternoon," Jack said as he stood back up.

"Yeah, sorry about all this. And sorry for the delay. I got caught up leaving the city. Thanks for having me over."

"Sure thing. So, what's going on?"

"I need you to understand something first," Joe said after an awkward pause.

Jack rolled his eyes. *Please get to the point.* "You're stalling."

"I'm not stalling. I am being careful. You understand I'm not technically supposed to be here, right?"

"What do you mean?"

"That's not how we roll. We don't just call people on the phone to chat. We don't just walk into people's living rooms and tell them what we're working on."

"I get that. But I also get that it's almost midnight, and you're standing in my living room two hundred miles from home with your freaking overcoat on. I assume there's a reason for this little social call?"

"There is a reason. Abigail Walker."

"What did she do?" Realizing that Joe probably knew the answer to his own question, Jack added, "I don't think we do her tax returns."

"It's not her tax returns. It's something else." Joe again paused awkwardly. "What do you know about Atlantic Coast Bank?"

"Never heard of it."

"Okay, then, here's what I can tell you. Atlantic Coast Bank is a small outfit in the Caymans. Nice New England name. Nice New England client base. Doctors. Lawyers. Drug kingpins. Rhode Island politicians. You get the picture?"

Jack had only limited experience with the intricacies of Cayman Island banking firms, but he knew Grand Cayman was a haven for dollars moving offshore and beyond the reach of US banking laws and regulations.

Joe continued, "Every month, your dear Mrs. Walker wires money from Constitution Trust to Atlantic Coast Bank."

"So?" Jack knew there were a hundred legitimate reasons why someone like Abigail would have a bank account in the Cayman Islands. He also knew that she was probably pretty unlikely to be a major player in the world of financial crimes. "Sorry, but I'm still not getting it. Did she forget to check the box?" he asked, thinking about the box on an income-tax return one is supposed to check if they own an offshore bank account. None of the thousands of people illicitly hiding their money offshore actually check that particular box, and thus its existence serves only to add tax fraud to their list of federal offenses.

Joe's stern facial expression answered the question. Clearly, they weren't dealing with a missing checkmark on a tax return. "I'm afraid that's all I know."

"You mean that's all you're going to share."

"That's all I know," he repeated mechanically.

"Okay, so what can I do?"

"Just keep your eyes and ears open. Anything involving Atlantic Coast Bank and Abigail Walker. Anything about the Caymans. Any money sloshing around where it shouldn't be. Okay, bud? Got it?"

With that, Joe stepped forward and offered a handshake.

"I can't do it," Jack said.

"Can't do what?"

"You know I can't do it. I can't just discuss my clients with you because you show up and ask me to. Remember that thing called attorney-client privilege? Did they forget to teach that at Columbia?"

Joe sighed. "You're one funny guy. Only you forgot something. Ever hear of the crime and fraud exception? You know, the part about lawyers being obligated to disclose ongoing crimes? Or did they forget to teach that at Yale?"

Jack was getting more and more confused. "What the hell are you talking about? How does one Cayman bank account make Abigail Walker into Al Capone?"

"It doesn't. And I didn't say it did. You've just got to trust me on this thing. All I'm saying is for you to keep your eyes and ears open. That's all." Joe began to edge back toward the kitchen door.

"Okay, but we have to play by the rules."

Joe stopped again and laughed incredulously. "Seriously? Play by the rules? Do you have any idea of the mess you've stepped into? Any idea what you're talking about? This is not legal ethics class. This is the real world." For the third time in as many minutes, he resumed his movement toward the exit. This time, his steps were noticeably less subtle than they had been before.

"I still have no idea what you're talking about," Jack called to the retreating figure.

"It's better that way."

"Says who?"

Joe stopped in his tracks and glared back at him. "Says me. Says the United States government, okay? Trust me, all I'm saying is keep your eyes and ears open. That's all you need to do."

Jack had heard the "trust me" line one time too many. "Fine. But I'm not squealing on a client. I didn't wait all these years to get to where I am to toss it all away as a favor to you."

"A favor to *me*?" Joe looked down at the floor and shook his head. "Just don't overthink this."

"I'm not."

"Yes, you are," he said, his voice rising as he crossed into the kitchen with Jack in pursuit. "You think I'm supposed to be here? You think I got approval to knock on your door in the middle of the night and tell you one of your clients is involved in an investigation? You think that's the way it works? Or you think maybe, just maybe, I'm sticking my neck out a little bit here too? Come on, bud, get a brain."

"I'm sorry. I'm not trying to be difficult. But your cryptic half sentences are pissing me off a little bit." He took a deep breath. "I have no idea what I'm supposed to do right now."

"I've told you like three times. Keep your eyes and ears open. Abigail Walker. Money moving where it shouldn't be. Transfers from Constitution Trust to Atlantic Coast Bank. Surely you see things at that firm of yours. You know what kind of stuff I'm looking for."

"So what if some old lady is hiding money in the Caymans? Don't you have terrorists or something to keep you busy? Why the hell do you even care about Abigail Walker?"

"Boy, Collins, you really are as dumb as you look." Joe sounded serious, but then he smiled. "Just keep your ears open, but be cool about it. Keep your head down."

"My head down? What's that supposed to mean? I'm supposed to be afraid of Abigail Walker? Not sure her right hook is what it used to be."

He laughed heartily. Joe did not.

"I don't think you need to fear Abigail Walker," Joe replied calmly.

"Then what are you so worried about?"

Joe completed his path across the kitchen, opened the storm door, and stepped out onto the concrete stoop. Turning back toward the house, he finally gave Jack the answer he had been begging for.

"Ted Parker. The money is going into *his* account."

Jack could feel the color drain from his face. "Huh? Ted? What the hell is he up to?"

"That, my friend, is what I need you to help figure out."

# CHAPTER 32

Ted had spent much of the prior evening thinking about the conversation he was about to have. He had considered inviting Deb out to lunch instead of summoning her to his office. However, he couldn't bear the thought of making small talk before getting to the point of this meeting and feared that small talk afterward might not be possible. He was about to disappoint her. He had seen her disappointed before. It was not a pretty sight.

The concession he had made to try to lighten the formality of this occasion was to sit with her at the round table in the corner of his office, thus removing the awkward power dynamic of him perching in his imposing leather chair while she sat in one of the smaller, less comfortable guest chairs on the opposite side of his antique desk. Maybe being together at the table would project a sense of collegiality, of camaraderie.

As soon as they had settled into their chairs, he got right down to business. "Look, Deb, I want to talk about the partnership vote."

He could see the tension creep across her face as he spoke, the skin growing taut across her cheekbones, her lips pressed tightly together. His tone had not the slightest air of celebration to it. She probably already sensed what he was about to say.

"First, I want to compliment you. You're a very talented lawyer, and you've been an integral part of my success here. I do expect you to be a partner of the firm."

She nodded but said nothing.

"However, it's not going to happen this year."

He paused and let out a deep breath, relieved to have so efficiently delivered his message. His spine tensed as he prepared to receive a

tongue-lashing in reply. Much to his surprise, she said nothing. No ob-
jection, no attack. Instead, she sat mute, leaving an awkward void.

"I don't want you to get down about this," he said. "You know we
have lots of ninth- and tenth-year associates around here. You're still
very much in the hunt." He paused again for a reply but was met only
with silence. *What the hell is she thinking?* He continued to throw ex-
planations in her direction, hoping one would generate some kind of
response. "It was just a tough year economically for the firm, and we're
a small department. A number of folks around here don't know you all
that well, and I just didn't have the votes to get it done this year. Perhaps
that's my fault," he rambled on. "Perhaps I should have started lobbying
earlier in the year. I'll remember that for next year."

After another long pause, she finally spoke. Her words were calm
and restrained. "I really appreciate your support. I'll admit to being disappointed. You know how hard I've worked. You know how important
this firm is to my life."

"I do, and others do as well. But politics is politics. The other de-
partments got their people through this year. I fought tooth and nail
but came up just short. The time will be right. Then you'll get the recog-
nition you deserve."

He smiled at her, and she smiled warmly in return. He had been
prepared for her to storm out of the room once he delivered the bad
news, but she had not. Instead, for the next several minutes, they chatted amicably about their future together

"Maybe next year," she said with little enthusiasm.

"Hopefully. You deserve it."

"Is that all?" Her demeanor was so calm, her tone so measured, that
it made him nervous.

"Yes, and thanks for being such a good sport about this. I know
how disappointed you must be."

"I am. I won't lie to you." She paused and looked down at her
hands. "But just tell me one thing."

"Sure."

"If it were up to you, just you, would you have made me a partner?" She barely looked up at him as she spoke.

"Ha!" he chortled. "What a silly question! Of course I would. If they had listened to me, you'd be running the whole damn firm."

———◦———

AFTER SHE ULTIMATELY excused herself from Ted's office, Deb walked quickly down the hallway. Passing office doors and secretarial desks, she headed toward the end of the corridor, where the firm had recently built a new eight-person conference room. This new space was furnished with dark woods and rich fabrics and felt more like a client's living room than a lawyer's work space. For this reason, Ted often used this room for will-execution ceremonies and family meetings with his most important clients.

Deb's favorite feature of this space was the fact that it had a private restroom, far more elegant, and affording far more privacy, than the larger communal restrooms located near the center of the floor. She entered the vacant conference room and stepped into its small restroom, locking the door behind her.

By the time she reached the sink, tears had begun streaming down her face, leaving jagged black trails of mascara in their wake. She splashed cool water on her eyes and cheeks and patted herself dry with a paper towel. Breathing as slowly and deeply as she could, she valiantly tried to calm herself down. But the tears continued to pour. She found no comfort in the cold water splashing on her face, just as she had found no solace in Ted's pathetic attempts at reassurance.

She quivered with fury as she looked at herself in the mirror and wiped mascara off her face. She imagined the partners of R&H meeting in their plush conference room. A group of elitist snobs with half her talent and a third of her energy. A bunch of fat-cat profit hoarders, most long since past their economic prime. And they dared not invite her into their little club? After all of the hours she'd billed? After all the money she had made for this firm? Oh sure, she might still be a partner at R&H *someday*, Ted had reassured her. Well, screw that. *Next year* was not what she wanted, and it was not what she deserved.

Her body kept shaking as she thought of all the time and effort she had expended at R&H. The work had been intellectually rewarding. The pay had been good. But she had spent the last eight years in pursuit of a different goal—an affirmation that she was in fact special, that her skills were exceptional, that she was integral to Ted's practice and this entire firm. *How dare they deny me that validation? How dare they!*

She turned away from the sink and faced the toilet across the small room. As if approaching an altar, she slowly knelt before it. Wave after wave of tension swept through her body as bile burned her throat. Holding back her hair with her right hand and bracing herself against the toilet rim with her left, she began to vomit.

# CHAPTER 33

Jack looked down at his nearly empty plate and pierced the last piece of broccoli with his fork. He had come to love the $11.95 lunch special at Hunan Palace. He had come to love it even more whenever he was there with the woman sitting across from him.

Deb looked at his empty plate and then smiled at him. "Didn't you say you were getting sick of this place?"

"I guess not." He returned her smile with a somewhat sheepish grin, slightly embarrassed that he had taken less than five minutes to scarf down a heaping plate of chicken and broccoli. "Plus, I want to be sure I get my twelve dollars' worth."

His smile widened, and she responded with a broadening smile of her own. "Collins, you are adorable."

His budding friendship with Deb was liberating, so very different than anything he had experienced before. They had become the best of teammates, just as Deb promised they would. And now he needed his teammate's help.

"Hey, remember when we were talking about the Cayman Islands?" he asked, a slight quiver in his voice undermining his attempt to appear nonchalant.

She looked up from her plate, and her eyes locked on his. "Excuse me?"

"I was just curious if you knew much about the Caymans. You said there were really nice beaches, right? I was thinking that maybe..."

"Well, I've never actually *been* there," she said before a knowing smile crossed her face. "Oh come on, you chicken. Don't tell me you're rethinking those vacation plans. I thought you had decided on Nevis?"

"No, no, that's not..." He paused. She had given him a chance to change the subject. And maybe he should. At first, he had sensed something off in her tone, something disconcerting about the expression on her face. But now she seemed perfectly serene, even giddy. *Just another one of her mood swings.* He leaned toward her and pressed his hands into the tablecloth.

"I need to tell you something," he began softly. "I'm not sure I should be telling you this. Actually, I'm not sure there actually is anything to tell. But I've been racking my brain on this and getting nowhere. You might be able to help me."

"Sure, what's up?"

"This may be completely crazy." He paused and took a deep breath then closed his eyes and spat out the next phrase. "I think Ted is up to something with Abigail Walker. Something wrong."

Her head snapped back, and her eyes darted around. "What are you talking about?"

He leaned back in his chair. *This was probably a bad idea.* Deb likely knew nothing about Ted's financial dealings, and raising the issue with her was probably just stupid, especially when she was in such a weird mood. "It's nothing," he said in the most reassuring tone he could muster. "It's just some crazy idea I had. I don't even know why."

"Not so fast, Collins," she said, her eyes fixed on his and her jaw muscles visibly tense. "You didn't just make that up. What did Ted tell you?"

He stared down at the tablecloth. "It's really nothing. That was just silly." After a pause, he went on. "Ted didn't say anything. I thought I saw something on his desk, but I probably was just confused. You've worked with him a lot longer than I have. If you've never seen anything that makes you think that, then I probably am just crazy."

He looked up and saw that her facial expression had not softened.

"Let's forget the whole thing, okay? Let's just drop it," he said.

She was now leaning forward halfway across the table, her nostrils flaring. "No! I can't just 'drop the whole thing.' I really need to know what you saw. If there's something wrong at R&H, I need to know about it."

"I'm really sorry for mentioning it. It was a crazy idea. Let's just drop it."

*Oh shit.* She looked like a lion about to pounce, her eyes still fixed on his as she leaned silently across the table. The silence filled him with dread, his legs beginning to quiver with increasing panic.

"Can we just forget I ever said anything?" he pleaded. He took two twenties from his wallet and placed them on the tablecloth. "Come on. Starbucks? My treat."

Just as he stood from the table, she began to speak.

"You can't just say things like that if you don't have proof," she said sternly. "I know you're too smart for that. So tell me, what did you see?" Her eyes were blinking furiously. She was as agitated as he had ever seen her.

He sank back into his chair. "Okay, okay, let's forget it. It was just a weird hunch I got from something someone said, and I'm not even sure anymore where it came from. Please, let's just drop the whole thing."

She seemed like she was about to say something but then simply smiled. "Of course we can drop it. I'm sorry I got so worked up. You caught me off guard, and for some reason my first instinct is always to be protective of Ted. Makes sense, right?"

*Thank God.* Jack's shoulders relaxed as he accepted the explanation. "Of course I understand that. It was stupid of me to even mention this."

"No, it wasn't. I told you way back when to always keep me in the loop, and I meant it. We should be able to talk about anything, anytime. So here's what I think," she said through another broad smile. "I need to use the bathroom, and then I will let you buy me some coffee."

"Okay, that sounds great."

"I'm sorry again for sounding upset," she said as she stood from the table. "I have a confession to make. I'm a little jealous of your travel plans. Talk of tropical islands just made me a little nuts."

"Jealous?"

"Yeah, I was being kind of a brat, I guess."

"It's okay, really."

She stepped beside his chair and rested her hand softly on his shoulder. "Good. Because I've been thinking of you and your wife strolling on the beach this winter, and the truth is I'm jealous as hell. You know nobody ever takes me to the Caribbean," she added as she slid her hand off his shoulder. "Which is too bad, because I look pretty darn good in a bikini."

She turned and headed toward the bathroom.

Jack watched her as she retreated. As he did so, he imagined her in a skimpy bikini, sunlight reflecting off her wavy hair as she walked away from him down a deserted sandy beach.

# CHAPTER 34

Abigail stood at the living room window of her twelfth-floor apartment. She held a steaming cup of Earl Grey tea in her hand and gazed out at the sun-dappled treetops rising from the pavement below. She inhaled a deep whiff of orange and took a sip that nearly burned her tongue. It was a beautiful morning in New York City. But her thoughts were filled with dread.

Exactly eleven years ago today was the last time she'd seen her husband alive. Eleven long years. That day, like this one, had started with sunshine and light. It had ended in darkness at noon.

He was supposed to have been back in Washington for the day. He was supposed to have been hundreds of miles from Cambridge. But at the last minute, he had changed his plans. He had chosen to come home, to come to *her*.

She closed her eyes and imagined what it must have been like for him that morning, what he must have seen and felt in his final moments.

She hadn't heard him open the front door and let himself inside. She was oblivious as he closed the door behind him and set his bag on the tile floor. She never saw him remove his overcoat for the very last time and hang it neatly in the front closet.

She would never know for sure if he had gone into the kitchen and seen the two dirty coffee mugs on the kitchen table, the two plates covered with the remnants of eggs and toast. Even if he had missed that clue, he hadn't missed the scene waiting for him as he climbed the oak staircase to the colonial's second floor. He'd certainly seen her skirt and stockings tossed on the hallway floor, a trail of scattered clothing leading right into their bedroom.

She could still hear the creak of the old hinges as he swung open the bedroom door and revealed her lying in bed, moaning in the throes of passion. Her pounding heartbeat nearly stopped as she looked up to see him standing in the doorway.

His hands clenched into fists. "*You slut*," he hissed at her as she pulled the sheet over her naked body and began to cry. "After all I've done for you, *this* is how you repay me?"

"Hal, I'm sorry. I'm so sorry." She kept repeating the phrase as her trembling hands desperately searched for her silk bathrobe on the floor beside the bed.

"And *you*," he continued, turning to the man cowering across the bedroom. "I will *ruin* you." His voice rose as he continued his tirade. "So help me, you are finished. *Finished.*"

Tears streaming from his eyes, his face red with fury, Harold Walker turned from them and stomped away. Crossing back through the bedroom door, he reached the hallway, then the top landing of the stairs.

"Wait, wait. Hal. Hold on," she called after him as she bolted from bed and threw on her robe. "Please, wait."

From the top of the stairs, he turned back to face the bedroom. "You *snakes*. You *ingrates*." He sprayed spit as he spoke. "I'll ruin you both."

"Wait, Hal," she begged again. She was now in hot pursuit, desperately trying to tie the belt of the wrinkled silk robe as she crossed the hallway. "Please, please, I can explain."

He turned away from her. His rigid posture said it all. There would be no pleading. There would be no explanation. She had done something that could not be undone.

As he descended a step, she grabbed his suit jacket and spun him back to face her. "Get off me, goddamn it," he said as he stared at her through misty eyes. "I hate you."

The words stung. "Oh, Hal," she said, tugging on the soft wool of his suit. "Please, oh please, just listen."

"No, you bitch," he barked as he swatted her hand away and turned back toward the staircase. "There is nothing you could possibly say."

As he took another step down, she grabbed his arm from behind. "You can't do this!" she screamed. "You can't just go." She clenched a wad of fabric tighter and tighter, afraid that if he slipped from her grasp, he would never come back.

He turned back to face her, his reddened eyes meeting hers. "I can do what I damn well please," he said as he pried her hand off him. "And I'm done with you." He turned away again.

"Oh no, you're not," she growled. *Not like this.* She grabbed the back of his collar, yanking him toward her with all of her might as he attempted to continue down the stairs. "You can't leave me." Tears streamed down her face. "I won't allow it."

"Get the hell off me," he snapped. "I'm going to fall."

"I don't care."

She tugged even harder on his collar as he tried to step forward. In the battle between opposing forces, gravity soon dictated a winner. The senator's shoulders spun back toward her as his legs continued forward. He twisted awkwardly as his feet slipped out from under him. He grabbed for the banister only to have the tips of his fingers bounce off it as his hand slid by. His look of rage turned to one of panic. His eyes widened, and his lips parted in fear.

His head hit one of the oak risers with a sickening thud as his body tumbled and rolled toward the foyer below. Abigail's scream as she watched him was decibels louder than any of her earlier cries. Her panicked call to 9-1-1 was immediate, yet far too late.

An ambulance arrived and whisked the senator down Garden Street toward Mount Auburn Hospital. While that journey took mere minutes, it was a trip that Senator Harold Walker did not survive. As the sounds of sirens and squealing tires echoed across the Cambridge Common and into Harvard Yard, Abigail watched helplessly as her husband whispered what would be his last words.

"I'll never forgive you."

# CHAPTER 35

J ack knew that in some guidebook to proper office decorum, it probably said a married man shouldn't take a single female coworker to dinner to celebrate her birthday. And yet here he was, sitting across from Deb in one of New York's most romantic French restaurants. During dinner, they had traded tales of their youth, with him telling stories of growing up in urban Stamford, while she countered with stories from Wellesley. Despite their different geography, they'd had largely similar childhood experiences. Both were popular in school. Both were academically successful. Both had lawyers for fathers.

On that last point, however, their two paths diverged. While Jack saw a career in law as a means of emulating and continuing his father's life work, Deb clearly had a far more tortured relationship with her father's legacy. Staring into the bottom of her third glass of wine, she began to tell yet another story.

"My father and I were very close when I was young. After he and my mother split up, we drifted apart. But we still had our traditions. Football was his passion. At least once a month during the season, I'd go to Cambridge to visit him. It would be our time. Our alone time."

She took another sip of wine and continued. "He had such a great apartment. One of those old brick buildings just north of the common. From his study, you could see right over the park, the domes of Harvard peeking over the treetops in the distance. I loved looking out that window." She paused and swirled her wine around in her glass, sending ruby-colored reflections dancing across the tablecloth.

"I know those buildings. I walked past there all the time when I lived in Cabot. I would—"

"I loved that window," she continued, still staring down at the tablecloth and playing with her wineglass as she spoke, "but I've never seen it since. We made our peace, sort of, but it was never the same. We didn't speak at all for years. I could never forgive him. It was my birthday. That was my day. My day. Not his."

She opened and closed her fingers, the skin blanching as her fists closed tighter and tighter each time.

"Wait, you've lost me," he said. "What day?"

"'Meet me at the Faculty Club for lunch,' he'd said as he left the apartment that morning. 'I have a big surprise.' He'd given me the exact time. He had been so perfectly clear, and I was so excited." She looked up to make eye contact for just an instant before her eyes darted back to the tablecloth. "I was like a pathetic little schoolgirl. Lunch with Daddy. And believe it or not, I was *early*."

"Early, seriously?"

"Yes, Collins, for once in my life, I was ahead of schedule. That's how excited I was. That's how pathetic I was. So I sat at the restaurant in this fancy little dress, waiting for him. He was five minutes late. And then ten. The waiter kept coming back to the table. 'Are you okay, Miss?' 'Do you need anything, Miss?' And I sat there like an idiot. Like the stupid little girl waiting for the father who lied and cheated and never had a moment for anything that really mattered. And you know, for all those years, we had mostly ignored it. The great genius. The nation's authority on criminal law. Mr. Talk Show, Mr. Journal Article, Mr. Front Page of the *Boston Globe*."

"Where was he?" Jack asked when she finally paused for breath. But she carried on, yet again oblivious to his questions.

"Pathetically waiting at that table, I realized that there was nothing special about me. Nothing important about my life."

"Where was he?" Jack asked again.

"Finally, I called his secretary. She told me he'd just run off. Some sort of emergency. He never even called me to cancel lunch. Do you hear me?" Her pace and tone had become far more deliberate as she paused after every word. "He *never* even called. My birthday, and I'm sitting at this table, alone, waiting. Pathetic.

"That made it all so clear to me. It had always been about him, just him. His books. His classes. His women. His needs. I swear I went to law school to spite him. To show him that I could master what he could master. And that's probably why I hate the law but also why I can never leave it. It reminds me of him, but I can't let it beat me. I can't let him beat me. God, eleven years later, and I'm still trying to get over it—trying to make partner just to prove something to my dead father."

She continued, but Jack had stopped listening. *Eleven years?* He was staring off across the restaurant, trying his best to ignore the distraction of her ramblings and force his Burgundy-impaired brain to think back through the years. *It was the right month for sure. But was this the right day?*

He snapped back to attention, staring right at her as she continued the story. "I never went back there to see him. I saw him again after that, sure, but never there." She was shaking her head from side to side, staring down at the tablecloth. Her hands again clenched into fists, rhythmically banging on the table. "I was so angry at him."

As she spoke, he looked at her carefully. His eyes traced every line on her face, measuring every angle. Her high cheekbones. Her strong chin. Every feature. One by one. *Could it have been her?* He waited for a pause in her monologue and put out his hand to touch hers. The contact stopped her in her tracks. Her eyes rose to meet his.

"Your birthday?"

"Yeah, that totally sucks, right?"

"*Eleven* years ago? Are you sure?"

"Yeah, eleven years ago today. Happy birthday to me."

He could feel his heart beating, its sound whooshing in his ears. His body trembled with a sudden surge of adrenaline as sweat began to pour down his temples. He could hardly see, or hear, or breathe.

"What the hell is wrong with you?" she asked. "Why are you staring at me like that?"

"I'm fine."

"Fine? You look like you've just seen a ghost."

He had. The pounding in his head was nearly excruciating as his own memory of that same day came rushing back. *Could it really be?*

Almost unaware that he was speaking out loud, he offered a comment. "You looked so happy."

"Damn right I did. Wait, what?"

He was lost in his thoughts as he muttered on. "The blue coat. The ambulance."

"Hello? Jack? What the hell are you talking about?"

For a moment, he was twenty-one again. He was back in that vast Cambridge park, staring across the street at an opportunity that a moment later was gone. He saw the trees overhead and the leaves on the path and the light at the crosswalk. He heard the sirens and shivered as he felt the passing shadow.

"What's going on with you?"

He whispered his question, already knowing the answer. "What time did you leave for lunch?"

"What the hell? Why does that matter?"

"Just tell me, was it noon?" he asked, knowing that in fact it was. He knew it as certainly as if he had been there. For he had.

She looked at him quizzically. "No, you weirdo, it wasn't *noon*," she said with a smirk. "I didn't even get into the cab until a few minutes past."

He pictured the black-and-white taxi pulling away from the curb.

"I know. I was there."

"Huh? You were *where*?"

As he drifted into the dream world of his past, a stream of thoughts ran through his head. And only one of them made it past his vocal cords. "I remember that day."

"Jack Collins." His name snapped him back to attention. She was staring straight at him. "You're acting crazy. What the hell is going on?"

He inhaled deeply and slowly let out his breath. Stifling a firestorm of emotions, he attempted to regain enough composure to seem at least somewhat rational. "Let me explain."

And so he did.

# CHAPTER 36

After a fifteen-minute walk, Jack and Deb somehow made it to Grand Central Station. The bottles of wine had left both of them giddy and uncoordinated. The crosstown stroll had been filled with stumbles and giggles, and at least one near-miss encounter with a truck driver who clearly had the right of way.

They arrived at the platform of Track 23, where the 10:06 express would soon depart for Stamford. She stopped in her tracks. "Okay, bucko, this is the end of the escort."

He turned to face her. Without thinking, he reached down to grab her hand and hold it in his. "Happy birthday," he said. "I had a really great night."

She offered a meek smile.

"What's with the long face?" After a moment of silence, he prodded again. "Come on, what's wrong?"

He watched with elation as her look of sadness softened into a seductive smile.

"I'm just bummed that you didn't make the traffic light that day," she said, squeezing his hand. "Who knows what could have happened."

She loosened her grip as if about to slip her fingers from his but then retook his hand and clenched it more firmly than before. "Actually, there's one other thing I'm really bummed about."

She leaned in closer, as if prepared to reveal her life's ultimate secret. He felt a few stray curls of her hair brush against his ear as she closed in on him, her telltale scent of lemon and flowers radiating from her neck. "Yes," she whispered, "one big bummer."

Before he knew what was happening, he felt her lips upon his. They were warm and soft, and just as he closed his eyes and kissed her back, the warmth was gone.

He opened his eyes to see that he was still leaning forward while she was once again standing perfectly upright. He was speechless, aroused beyond words. As he struggled to regain his composure, a mischievous smile crossed her face. "You're not really going to get on that train right now, are you?"

"I've got to get home. I really need to—"

He was interrupted by her lips against his. This time she didn't stop when he kissed her back. His head pounded from the wine as his heart pounded with excitement. He wrapped his arm around her waist, balling a handful of her skirt into his hand and pulling her closer, driving his lips and tongue against hers.

"I really need to get home," he repeated as they paused for air. "This is wrong."

"Yes, terribly wrong," she said, running her hand all the way up the inseam of his pants. "Oh yeah, I can tell you're hating this."

"You know I have to go—"

She interrupted him by planting one last kiss on his lips.

"Yes, I know you have to go. I get it." She ran her hand down the sleeve of his suit jacket before pulling it away. "Have a good trip home," she added curtly before turning away from him and walking back toward the station.

"Hey, are you mad at me?" he called after her.

She turned back to face him and flashed a broad smile. "Never," she said. "Not possible."

# CHAPTER 37

As the train rolled toward Stamford, Jack sat back in a tattered blue seat and watched the darkened scenery whirl by. He'd taken the safe route so many times in his life. In the process, he'd missed so many opportunities, shied away from so many possibilities. To the outside world, he seemed happy and successful. Fancy degrees, a good job, a beautiful wife. Yeah, he had all of those. But he also had a growing collection of gnawing doubts, a scrap heap of regrets.

The last two months had begun to change all that. At last, he was working at a place he could be proud of, serving one famous client after another. He was making more money than ever. He was more important than ever. Plus, there was Deb.

He closed his eyes and remembered the feeling of her warm lips on his, the flowery scent of perfume as he clutched her tight. He hadn't wanted that moment to stop. Perhaps it shouldn't have. And what to make of the fact that they had nearly met once before? He had never been able to completely shake her memory, and now she was suddenly back in his life. That was some crazy coincidence. Was it always meant to be?

*Maybe it was.* Maybe he should have grabbed her hand tonight and let her lead him away from Grand Central, a path that would have ended in her apartment, in her bed. Maybe he should have yielded.

*But then what?* A gnawing pain in his gut brought him back to reality. So he'd almost met her once before. So what? It was just a fluke, a random twist of fate. And it was years ago. He was not twenty-one anymore. His life had moved on. A wife was waiting for him at the end of this train ride. A *wife*. He couldn't just magically restart his adult life. It would be painful, messy.

And even if he could simply start over, did he really want to? The Deb he had come to know over the past two months was alluring as hell but far more complex than some smiling schoolgirl he remembered from a decade earlier. Could he really make a life with her? Was that even possible to think about? And what about Ted and Abigail and the Caymans? Was there a path through this minefield? Would he ever make his way out?

He stared out the train window at the passing headlights on I-95, his head pounding, stomach churning. His thoughts jumped randomly from memory to memory—from Deb standing across a crosswalk to Amanda in her wedding dress to Joe Andrews knocking on his kitchen door. To call his life complicated would be an epic understatement.

He rubbed his aching temples and closed his eyes. After eleven years, he was back at the edge of a crosswalk, staring across the street into a future he couldn't predict. The time had come to make some serious choices about both his marriage and his career. He had gotten a second chance to revisit old choices, a second chance to define his own destiny.

There would be no third chances. This time he had to get it right.

———— ◉ ————

AS THE TAXI SPED DOWN Fifth Avenue, Deb thought back to that day eleven years earlier. She had loved her father dearly. But she had also hated him. Or at least parts of him. And the part she hated the most was the part that ruined her twenty-third birthday, like so many days before—the part that always had something more important to do, the part that always needed to be someplace else. As much as her father had loved her, and she knew he had dearly loved her, on one level she had always been an afterthought.

Given that background, it was ironic that she would end up employed by Ted Parker, her father's former student in both law and in human relations. Ted embodied so much of what she had disliked in her own father. His mere presence in her life provided a constant reminder of all the attention the great professor had heaped upon others and withheld from her. Of course, that was exactly why she ended up working in Ted's office. Her psychiatrist had explained it all long ago. She was trying to prove her strength by facing her worst demons. It was her version of Stockholm Syndrome, or some similar bullshit. It had taken her years of therapy and a cabinet full of medicine to conclusively determine what she had always known: that her relationship with her father had messed her up.

Yet among a lifetime of affronts, that infamous birthday remained the worst. She could no longer keep track of all the times she had replayed that scene in her mind. How pathetic she must have looked sitting in the Faculty Club that day—the fully grown daughter still praying for her father's affection, sitting alone at a table, sipping a glass of water, waiting for the man who would never appear. Something more important had come up. *It always did.*

So when she found out who had pulled her father away from her that day, she could think of nothing but revenge. This time she would be important. This time *her* needs, *her* demands, would be all that mattered.

Her plan had been brilliant from the start. So far, it had been executed to perfection. But there had always been one nagging concern—one last problem she still needed to solve.

Tonight the solution had come to her.

As the arch of Washington Square Park came into view through the taxi windshield, she knew she was almost home. She also knew how Jack was going to solve her biggest problem.

She exited the cab and crossed the sidewalk to her apartment, thinking of the nine million dollars at Atlantic Coast Bank that she had systematically extracted from Abigail Walker during the past four years. It really had been a brilliant plan. An offshore account. No tax forms or IRS reporting to trip her up. And opening the account in Ted's name—that was her smartest idea of all. If anyone ever followed the paper trail from Hartford to Grand Cayman, it would lead right back to Ted's office. Even if he could somehow prove his innocence, it would be so very messy for poor Ted. The great Ted Parker, mired in scandal. She laughed at the thought of it.

At some point, she would use Ted's forged signature to move her millions from the Cayman Islands through a series of other accounts in other countries, each jurisdiction more secretive than the last, the paper trail growing colder and colder as the money moved from nation to nation. Finally, it would find its way home to her. Then she would have a little compensation for all they had put her through. She could finally tell R&H to screw off. She could free herself from all of them, finally able to live the life she had always deserved.

It was a brilliant plan. But even brilliant plans were rarely perfect. She often worried that she had left some unintended clue in her wake. In her frequent sleepless nights, she wondered if her fling with Ben was as transparent as it felt, or if someone with enough time and resources could find her old travel records, or if anyone knew about her uncle in the Caymans. She had been too patient and too careful to fall prey to such an error. She always felt a need to add one more twist in the money trail that began with Abigail and ended with her. Tonight the way to do that had come to her—she had just kissed him.

God, she was such a whore. She would have taken Jack home if he had let her. And what a stupid move that would have been. She didn't need any more ties binding the two of them together. And she certainly didn't need another lover.

But dear Jack didn't need to know any of that, at least not quite yet. She'd drive him off soon enough. But first, she needed him to buy her just one more dinner. One last meal together, his own last supper. Then she could swing the ax and cut him loose.

She had felt only the slightest remorse for what she had done to Abigail these past four years. She felt much more guilty about what she was about to do to Jack.

# OCTOBER

# CHAPTER 38

Jack knew he should never drink red wine. He had known that since college. There was something about red wine. He was allergic to the tannins, somebody had once suggested. But whatever the reason, there was no denying that red wine made him angry and grumpy. *Demonic* was the word Amanda used to describe it. Yet nothing went with a steak like red wine.

"Do you think we are in a rut?" he asked as he sliced a piece off his filet mignon.

"A *rut*?"

"Yeah, you know. Like the same old thing over and over again." He noticed her eyeing his half-empty wineglass. "It's not the wine talking."

"You sure? Because I think that wine is giving you amnesia. Remember that new job? Big building in New York? Ring a bell?"

"Yeah, I remember, but that's not the issue."

"So then what is the issue?"

Silence.

"Oh, so it's *me*? Are you sorry you married me?"

"Of course not. I'm really glad I married you. It's just that..."

"It's just *what*, Jack?" Her face was turning crimson. Apparently, she'd had some red wine too.

"It's just all of it. R&H has been great, but I'm still living out here, just down the road from my parents. It feels like I haven't really gone anywhere."

"Yeah, I get it," she snapped, her voice rising. "Kind of hard to restart your life in the big city with Mom, Dad, and your wife holding you back? Is that the problem?"

*Okay, keep it down.* Jack looked around the dining room to be sure her intensifying voice wasn't drawing any attention. Fortunately, Kirkland's Steakhouse was half empty on this Wednesday night. Those who were there were too absorbed in the effects of their own red wine to be concerned about the problems caused by his.

"Let's just drop it."

"Just *drop it*?" She sighed audibly then grabbed his hands in hers, setting them both on the white damask tablecloth. After taking a visible, slow breath, she began again in a more inviting tone. "Please. Tell me what you're feeling."

"I'm guess I'm just feeling unsure."

"About what?"

"About everything, *okay*?"

"No, not okay." She nearly barked the words but then lowered her voice again. "Sweetheart, listen to me." She tucked her hair behind her ears, leaned in toward him, and flashed a smile. "You're living a great life. You have a great family. Well, a little overbearing," she added with another grin, "but still great. You've had some rough luck, but you've also been blessed. And now, finally, you're on a new course. So see where that takes you before you talk about being in a *rut*. If things work out, maybe we'll move to New York. Maybe we'll move to Paris. But let's take one step at a time."

He stared down at the tablecloth. He knew that he was being unreasonable, too hard on both himself and his wife. But that was a part of his personality. Even though she might want him to, he couldn't simply stop. "I kissed her."

The randomness of the comment apparently surprised her as much as it had him. She stared at him with a quizzical look, her obvious confusion offering him one last chance to avert the firestorm he was about to unleash. He didn't take it. "Deb. I kissed Deb."

Her eyes burned with fury before softening into misty anguish. "Excuse me?"

"I kissed her. Nothing else happened," he added quickly, "just a kiss, but—"

"Oh, I'm so glad that 'nothing else happened,'" she mocked. "Listen to me," she said through clenched teeth. "You want some new life so bad, then go for it. Really, go for it. Become the New York City big shot. You can kiss everyone in the entire city if you like. Why not fuck them all while you're at it? But leave me out of it."

"Leave you out of what?"

"Don't play stupid with me. You know what I mean. You want to cheat, then go for it, but I'll be gone. You'll come home to find your crap on the front lawn and the locks changed. Do you get it?"

"Yeah, I get it. Just calm down."

"Don't tell me what to do," she snapped. She pushed her chair back from the table and stormed out of the restaurant.

He looked down at the tablecloth to avoid the accusatory stare of a gray-haired woman sitting two tables away. *Mind your own damn business,* he thought.

He took another hearty swig of red wine and closed his eyes. He could taste the bitter tannins as he swallowed.

# CHAPTER 39

The black Town Car exited the highway and turned onto the access road leading to LaGuardia Airport. Sitting in the back seat, Deb knew that she was running out of time.

She slid forward and leaned toward the driver. "Terry, I've got a problem."

Terry O'Reilly looked into the rearview mirror and reached up to adjust it slightly. "What's wrong?"

Although Terry drove her to the airport several times a year, she had never made anything other than idle small talk with him. "Maybe I shouldn't even drag you into this," she said. "It's just that we've got a big problem at the firm, and I don't know what to do about it."

He laughed awkwardly. "I'm not exactly sure how I can help you on that one, Deborah. Police work I know something about, but lawyering is supposed to be your job."

"Well, this may be kind of like police work."

He was now looking back at her in the rearview mirror, his eyes meeting hers. "Deborah Miller, I've known you for years, and you've never been one to share your troubles. What's going on?"

She intentionally paused for a moment. "I don't know. It's this new guy, Jack Collins. I think he's up to something." She glanced out the window and tried to compute how much longer she had until they arrived at her terminal.

Terry seemed more interested in navigating his way through the taxi-clogged airport than he was in becoming embroiled in R&H's politics. "I really think you should be talking to Mr. Parker," he said, looking straight ahead. "I drive for you folks when I can. That's pretty much it, as far as I'm concerned."

She knew that he was understating his own importance. While his only formal connection to R&H was his service as a very part-time driver, he had far greater influence by virtue of his primary avocation. For over a dozen years, he had overseen all aspects of Abigail's private security. Sometimes personally escorting her in public, sometimes merely making telephone contact with local law enforcement, he devoted much of his life to protecting her from a host of security threats, both real and imagined.

As the Town Car passed the first terminal and continued toward its destination, Deb's panic grew. She had begun this conversation too late. Abandoning subtlety in the name of efficiency, she made her case as plainly as she could. "I think Jack is stealing from Mrs. Walker," she said.

Terry's eyes were suddenly visible in the mirror.

"I think he's blackmailing her," she added.

"Jesus," he muttered, slamming on the brakes. After the car screeched to a halt, he waved apologetically at the taxi driver unloading a suitcase from the open trunk of the car in front of him. She could smell burning rubber.

Terry jammed the transmission in park, took off his seat belt, and twisted around in his seat to face her eye to eye. "Excuse the hard landing, Deborah. Now what exactly is going on?"

"I know you go way back with Mrs. Walker. I know she trusts you more than anyone else, even Ted." She added a subtle emphasis to those last two words.

"Okay, so let's have it. What exactly is this fellow doing?"

Tears began to flow from Deb's eyes. She batted dramatically at the wetness with the back of her hand as he repeated the question, a little more empathetically this time.

"Deborah, what did this guy do?"

She sniffled and wiped her eyes again. Looking out the front of the car, she felt her stomach tense as a police officer headed in their direction, his yellow vest rapidly approaching. "I don't have any evidence. But Jack and I have become close, and he's started to confide in me. He's said things about Abigail that make me nervous. I know he's up to *something*."

He laughed. "Deborah, I'm really not sure what's going on, but if there's a problem with someone at your firm, you really need to talk to Mr. Parker."

The yellow-vested officer was now waving at Terry to move his car.

"Ted is the last person I can talk to," she said as her pulse started to race. She continued on in a breathless monologue. "I'm stuck. Totally stuck. I can't trust Ted any more than I can trust Jack, and I can't talk to Mrs. Walker without losing my job or my head. You see, I went out with Jack the other night. He got sloppy drunk and started talking about how he's been working on some scheme. He seemed to know way more about Abigail than he should. Kept talking about how she was a terrible person. I know something is going on."

She paused for air to give him a chance to respond. He didn't take it. His eyes, which had previously been locked like lasers on hers, now drifted out into space. She knew exactly what was going through his mind and repeated it back to him.

"Ted has done a lot of good things for the Walkers. But he hasn't been there for them in the ways that you have. He's certainly never taken a bullet for them." She saw him instinctively flex his left arm, where a would-be assassin's bullet had torn through two muscles and shattered a bone as Harold Walker had stepped out of the lobby of the Copley Plaza hotel some twenty years earlier.

The police officer tapped on the car window. Terry didn't react until the tapping became a pounding. "Move it along," bellowed the officer. "Or I'll tow you and the friggin' car both out of here."

Terry snapped to attention, dutifully replaced his seat belt, and pulled back out into the traffic on the terminal road. His eyes were fixed on the road as he accelerated away from the curb. Nearing Deb's terminal, he continued to look straight forward as he responded to her.

"I can't go into detail, but if Mrs. Walker was being blackmailed, I would know about it. And if you have a problem with Ted or someone else at R&H, then you guys need to deal with it yourselves. Mrs. Walker isn't going to want any part of that. And she doesn't talk personal business with me anyway. It's not my place."

"*Please*," Deb begged. "Jack's up to no good. He was boasting about how he's got something on Mrs. Walker. If ever she needed you, this is the time. I can't help her," she said, crying. "I can't do this. You're the only one who can help her."

The Town Car reached the unloading area of Terminal B. As Terry grabbed her luggage from the trunk, Deb slid across the rear seat and stepped onto the airport curb, tears flowing from her eyes.

"Just warn Mrs. Walker," she pleaded through sniffles, her chest heaving. "Please, help her. This is not stupid law-firm politics. This is something really bad."

He finally nodded his assent. "I'll speak to Mrs. Walker this afternoon."

She swatted a tissue against her eyes. "Thank you so much." She took one step toward him and was about to hug him when she thought better of it. Instead, she simply smiled. "You're a hero, Terry. You always have been."

"Have a good flight, Deborah. And don't worry about things. I hate to see you so upset."

She turned and walked off toward the airport terminal, her black suitcase in tow. "Terry, you're the best," she called back to him as he nodded goodbye.

She headed through a revolving door then wiped her eyes and nose one last time before erupting into laughter.

# CHAPTER 40

Jack stopped in front of Claire's desk and extended a large blue coffee cup in her direction. "Happy birthday," he said, placing a small wrapped box atop a pile of mail.

"Is that from Dylan's? You know it's the best coffee shop in town, right?"

"You may have mentioned that once," he replied with a smile. "Sometimes I remember things."

She took a sip of the caramel latte. "Oh wow, you do remember things. Best birthday gift *ever*."

"Hardly. It's probably cold from the walk from 53rd. Besides, I hear Ted gets you some amazing swag."

"That he does." She reached into her desk drawer and pulled out a platinum credit card. "He has excellent taste—hands me his Amex and tells me to buy myself something nice. A little impersonal, perhaps, but I can't be offended. I buy all of Suzy's gifts too," she added, smiling.

"There's something in the box as well. I have to admit Amanda picked that out. Guess I'm no better than Ted."

Claire tore open the box and pulled out the silk scarf. "Wow, it's beautiful. You didn't have to do any of this. Technically I don't even work for you."

"Yeah, that's the point. Diane seems totally annoyed anytime I ask her to do anything. But you've been such a great help to me. I owe you big time."

"I'm glad to do it." She tied the brown-and-gold scarf around her neck. "Thank you again. And thank Amanda for me. She's got great taste, in scarves as well as husbands. You're lucky to have her."

"Yeah, I know," Jack said sheepishly. "Hey, since I'm here, can you do me a favor? Can you email me the PowerPoint for that speech I did for Mary Vincent a couple months back? It's the standard recent update thing. I'm supposed to do that again next week."

"Sure thing," she said as she began typing. "Just one little tip," she added awkwardly without looking up from her computer.

"Of course, what is it?"

"Play it just a little cooler this time. Like, don't make a big deal about going home early to practice."

"Huh?"

"Sorry, not trying to butt in," she said, looking up from her monitor. "It's just that I heard Ted grumbling to Mary about the last time."

"The last time? I'm not following you."

"I just heard a piece of their conversation. You were giving a speech for Mary one time, and so you left early the day before. I wouldn't worry too much. They were both laughing about it, so it's no biggie."

"I still don't know what you're talking... oh, wait, I do. That's when I had laryngitis. Deb basically threw me out of here."

"Oh geez. What a..."

"What a *what*? It's not her fault Ted got confused."

"You think?"

"Yeah, I'm sure of it. She was covering for me. If Ted got it wrong, it wasn't her doing."

"Don't be so sure. Ted doesn't notice anything that she doesn't point out to him first. You've probably seen that she likes to stir the pot."

"Yeah, I know. She is little chaotic. But on balance, she's been a good friend."

"That's what everyone thinks at first," Claire replied, rubbing her new scarf between her fingers. "Then they learn."

# CHAPTER 41

Terry sat nervously in Abigail's living room, a glass of ice water clutched in a trembling hand. "Abigail, I don't like doing this. You know how much I love this family."

"Of course I do. And you have the scars to prove it."

*Oh, not that again.* Although he knew she was trying to be complimentary, he resented how often she and others constantly marginalized his years of devotion to the Walker family by referencing that single day. Ignoring those thoughts, he smiled warmly at his boss, took a sip of water, and began speaking again. "You know that I don't want to interfere in your personal business, ma'am."

"Did you just call me 'ma'am,' Terry? *Ma'am?* Are you suddenly back on the force?"

He tugged at his shirt collar and stared nervously at his shoelaces. He indeed felt as if he were reverting to another time and place, back to the days when the former cop was part of the senator's security detail and Abigail was a senator's wife.

Finding his rhythm, he continued in a muted tone. "I had a very troubling conversation with Deb Miller this morning. I'm not sure what to make of it, but I was driving her to the airport, and out of nowhere she starts crying and telling me that this new fellow Jack Collins is nothing but trouble and that you need to be worried about him. But we've checked him up and down, and there's nothing there."

"Well, then, isn't that the end of it then? We hear crazy rumors all the time, don't we?"

"We do, but this somehow feels different. She seemed really upset. That's why I thought I'd bring it to you. Is there anything I don't know about? Has he given you any sort of trouble?" Taking a breath, Terry looked up from his shoelaces.

"Jack Collins?" Abigail's befuddled tone matched her facial expression. "Nothing of the sort. I've seen him just a few times, and he's been a perfectly polite young man."

He was now sure that his first instinct about this whole mess had been the correct one. This meeting had been an error. "Well, I honestly don't know what to make of all of this. Deb was clearly upset about something. She even said that she thought that Ted somehow knew what Jack was up to and either didn't care or was even somehow involved."

Abigail laughed heartily. "Preposterous." She added another laugh that reverberated throughout the apartment. "Absolutely preposterous."

Terry again looked down at his shoelaces, feeling his face redden as she continued chuckling. "I've known Ted Parker even longer than I have known you, and neither of you would do anything to hurt me. So I appreciate your concern, but there is nothing you need to worry about here. All right?"

He looked up at her. "Yes, ma'am."

They both laughed.

"Sorry, old habit," he said. "And sorry for troubling you with this." Such was a strange statement coming from the man who had routinely briefed her on kidnapping fears and death threats. "This one was a false alarm," he said as he stood up.

He and Abigail exchanged pleasantries as they walked from the living room to the door. As he said goodbye to her, he looked directly into her eyes. Her pupils seemed too wide, her blinking too frequent. Forgetting for an instant all notions of place and propriety, the former policeman reverted to his training. "Abigail, is there something you're not telling me? Really," he added rather sternly, "this is the time to say something."

She held up her palm. "Please, Terry. Enough of this."

"Sure, Abigail... sorry." Thanking her again for her time, he opened the door and stepped out into the hall.

Leaving the apartment, he looked back one last time. What had been a hunch on his part a moment ago was now a certainty. Her smile was too broad, clearly forced. The darting movements of her eyes and the evident tension in her cheeks betrayed her efforts to seem at ease. He had seen that same facial expression countless times before. It was the look of someone who was hiding something.

———◉———

AS TERRY WALKED DOWN the hall to the elevator, Abigail shut the door behind him and turned the deadbolt. She leaned against the door for a moment, listening to the sound of leather on marble echoing through the hallway as Terry moved away. It took every ounce of her mental strength to stand there idly as the sound grew increasingly faint before fading into nothingness.

Although she wouldn't allow herself to do so, she desperately wanted nothing more than to call him back into her apartment and tell him the secrets she had been keeping for all of these years.

# CHAPTER 42

On this Sunday morning, the Hartford headquarters of Constitution Trust was largely deserted. Deb and Ben hadn't encountered another soul as they entered the building and headed to the third floor.

"What do you have to do to get a window around here?" Deb asked, spinning from side to side in Ben's desk chair as she surveyed the contents of his small workspace. This was her second visit to Constitution Trust, and his office seemed even crappier than she remembered it.

"Kiss more ass than I have, I guess," he replied.

"Well, windows are overrated. Plus, we wouldn't want to shock the good folks of Hartford." She stood and pressed her body against his. After planting a passionate kiss on his lips, she pawed at the front pocket of his jeans. "I need your card," she said before kissing him again. "Ladies' room."

He dug into his pants and handed her his ID badge. "You want a chaperone?"

"No, I remember where it is. Stay right here. I have a surprise for you."

"A surprise?"

"Yes, but no peeking. I'm serious—stay right here." She shut the door behind her. "I'm serious. No peeking," she yelled back at the closed door.

After waiting a minute, she hurried down the dimly lit hallway toward the exit from the custody department and the restrooms just beyond the department's locked doors. She passed two empty offices then stopped at the beige secretarial station located just in front of the third.

Looking back to confirm that Ben's office door remained shut, she sat in the secretary's chair and opened the lower right desk drawer.

She had never met Maria Alfonzo, the administrative secretary of the custody department, but she had heard much about her from Ben last month as he took her on a mind-numbing forty-five-minute tour of Constitution Trust. Maria was about fifty, divorced, a mother of three, and a legendary baker of birthday cakes and treats for all of the custody officers. Deb didn't give a crap about any of that. All she cared about was the fact that Maria's lower right desk drawer contained a pile of stamps and seals, including the notary seals of all of the bank's custody officers.

The clutter in Maria Alfonzo's desk said much about the increasing complexity of the modern financial world. As forgers had become more sophisticated and photocopiers more high tech over the past few decades, it grew increasingly difficult to tell if a signature was genuine. For this reason, almost any banking transaction of significance required all signatures on documents to be notarized. To assist customers in meeting these requirements, Constitution Trust long ago began to require all of its custody officers to become notaries.

However, technology and human ingenuity had continued their relentless march. In the past few years, just about anyone could become a duly authorized notary public by filling out a form and taking a test many third graders could pass, and anyone with five dollars to spend could find a notary willing to sign just about anything under just about any circumstances. As a result, notarized documents began to become relatively useless in the world of sophisticated financial transactions. The larger the transaction, the more likely a notarized document wasn't good enough. For that reason, many of the notary stamps in Alfonzo's desk rarely saw the light of day.

A signature guarantee, however, was something wholly different. When the special green ink of that stamp was applied to a document, the authenticity of the signature was backed by the full resources of the certifying financial institution. If Constitution Trust's signature guarantee adorned a signed document, the genuineness of the signature was backed by the bank itself, rather than some unknown notary in a check-cashing store. And that was precisely why the documentation for any account opened by mail at the Royal Bank of Nevis, West Indies, had to be backed by a signature guarantee.

Although he didn't know it, Ted Parker would be opening a brand-new bank account in Nevis on Monday morning. Deb opened her purse and removed an envelope containing the copies of Ted's passport and driver's license that she had lifted from Claire's desk a week earlier, along with a letter of instructions bearing his forged signature. Pulling at random out of the drawer, she looked at the metal stamp that contained the signature guarantee for Christine Chan, a second vice president of Constitution Trust—and a "super-smart Princeton grad," if Deb remembered Ben's description properly. Smart or not, Christine's signature guarantee would now adorn the copies of Ted's letter of instructions and accompanying documents, thereby validating all the places where Deb had neatly forged his signature.

Once the paperwork was safely back in her purse, Deb headed back toward Ben's office. On her way, she stopped in the windowless office next to his to make a slight modification to her wardrobe.

"I was getting worried," he said when she opened the door and walked back into his office.

"You can't rush a lady." She wrapped her arms around his waist and kissed him.

After a few more passionate kisses, he eased his face back away from hers. "And when do I get my surprise?"

"Ah, yes." After taking a step back from him, she reached into the front pocket of her jeans and pulled out the royal-blue thong that she had removed just a moment earlier. Pressing the underwear into his hand, she planted another kiss on his lips before whispering in his ear, "Surprise."

# CHAPTER 43

J oe Andrews tucked his hands in the pockets of his black raincoat as
he strode down Madison Avenue. The gray sky sent down a steady
mist, casting a mournful pall over the October morning. For him, the
weather added another depressing element to an already depressing day.

He had just spent the past half hour in the FBI's New York office,
facing a barrage of criticism unprecedented in his career. While largely
ignoring all the other matters on his desk in DC, he had become nearly
obsessed with his pursuit of Ted Parker for weeks, the last few of which
he'd spent hunkered down in the Harvard Club at the government rate
of three hundred dollars per night. Other than rapidly accumulating
expenses, he had little to show for his efforts. His superiors had taken
note.

"I never liked this fishing expedition," Special Agent Brian Sanford
barked across his paper-strewn desk. "This was your brilliant idea, and
all I'm seeing are hotel bills and useless transcripts." Sanford, under
whose auspices Andrews was operating in New York, frowned as he detailed all of the expenses the government had incurred in pursuit of
Joe's great hunch. "If this Parker guy is guilty of anything other than
egomania, I'm not seeing it."

"Parker is dirty, and I can prove it."

"Then why haven't you?"

"You know some of these cases take time, and this is one of those.
There are a lot of moving parts to pull together."

"You know how tight our resources are, right?"

"I do. I don't like being away from home any more than the Bureau
likes paying for it, but I'm sure of this. I know I'm right."

"Confidence will only get you so far."

"I understand."

"I'm getting pressure from above," Sanford said. Joe cringed as the conversation abruptly reached the generic *pressure from above* line he and his fellow agents had heard countless times before. "I could use twice the number of agents I have," Sanford continued. "I need to make tough choices."

"Okay, got it. I'll move on it as quickly as I can." Joe took a step toward the door, expecting that would be the end of it.

"Three weeks."

Joe stopped in his tracks. "Three weeks until *what*?"

"Until I pull the plug on this whole damn operation."

# CHAPTER 44

"Where are you going?" Deb yelled out her office door as she spotted Jack bounding past.

"Oh hey. I thought you were already gone," he said meekly as he stuck his head into her office.

"Bullshit. You've been avoiding me for more than a week. Good thing I didn't let you into my pants. I'd feel so cheap."

He laughed nervously. "I'm sorry. It's just really complicated."

"Do you want to talk about it?"

"I don't know. I wouldn't even know where to begin."

"How about we begin with dinner Thursday night? I know a great place on the Upper East Side."

"I don't think that's such a good—"

"Come on, it's just dinner. Please don't let things get awkward between us."

"Okay, fine. Thursday it is. But now I'm heading out. Do you need anything before I go?"

She glanced over at the clock on her monitor. It was nearly eight.

"Can you do me a huge favor?" she asked nonchalantly. "I need a plain envelope. No letterhead. Just a white one." Seeing the blank look on his face, she added a further detail. "I need to mail my rent check, if it's okay with you."

"Sure, where are they?"

"I think Claire has a box behind her desk."

"Got it. Be right back." He headed out into the hallway and could soon be heard rifling through cabinets. He returned to Deb's office a minute later, a box tucked under his right arm. "Found them."

"Awesome, you're the best."

He placed the box on her desk and smiled. "I try." After a pause, he added, "Anything else? I really need to catch the next train."

She looked at the box of envelopes and then back at him. "Hey, klepto, don't you think Claire will notice the missing box? I really only need *one* envelope."

"Problem with your hands tonight?" He opened the box and grabbed one envelope, dramatically flinging it across her desk and landing it on her brown leather blotter. "Anything else from the overpriced delivery boy?"

"I'm such a pain in the ass, aren't I? I don't know why you put up with me. I think it's because you're trying to get your hands on these," she said cupping her hands beneath her breasts. "Maybe you will on Thursday."

His cheeks and ears turned bright red. "You're nuts."

"And you love it. I'll see you tomorrow."

"Sounds great."

"Super. Now, since my hands aren't working tonight, would you kindly take that industrial-sized box of envelopes out of here."

Jack dutifully grabbed the box of envelopes, bid her good night, and stepped into the darkened hallway.

After allowing several minutes to pass, she shut her office door and returned to her desk. She then opened her briefcase and pulled out a pair of latex gloves.

It was time for Abigail to get one last letter, an ultimatum. Although coming from the same source, this letter would be so very different from the last. It would demand more money. It would involve a new bank account in a new country. And it would arrive in an envelope covered with Jack Collins's fingerprints.

# CHAPTER 45

McGuigan's Bar was not a place you went to impress a first date. The lighting was dark, the food was greasy, and the crowd was largely upper middle-aged and lower middle-class. For Terry O'Reilly, the place represented a throwback to the way things used to be—a life of fried food and boorish buddies. That was before the bullet that shattered his arm, before Harold Walker came into his hospital room and promised to help him make a new life, before he traded his patrol car for a Town Car, his dress blues for navy suits. Flagging down the bartender, Terry ordered yet another round of vintage scotch for himself and the companion seated next to him.

When the glasses arrived, David Dalton threw back his scotch in a single gulp and slammed his glass down on the bar. He swiveled his barstool slightly in Terry's direction. "Okay, now I'm ready. What's going on?"

Terry had known Dalton for nearly thirty years. The two men had been cadets together at the police academy, then partners within the Boston PD. Working side by side for nearly four years, they had come to share each other's every secret, to anticipate each other's every thought. They had seen each other an instant away from death. And they had killed for each other.

Neither man had even been charged with murder, but they both had come awfully close. Terry was the first to take another's life under questionable circumstances. During their first year together, Officers Dalton and O'Reilly responded to a robbery at a neighborhood liquor store. While pursuing a suspect into a dark alleyway, Dalton got careless and ended up on the wrong end of a stolen Smith & Wesson .38. An instant before that error nearly cost him his career and his life, Terry fired his service revolver and staggered the suspect. Although the robber had dropped his gun in response to the first shot, the rookie officer's adrenaline got the better of him. He discharged five more shots into the unarmed man, spraying his blood across a twenty-foot section of Dorchester.

Three years later, when Terry was shot by a would-be assassin, Dalton repaid the old debt. While his partner recovered at Massachusetts General Hospital, Dalton tracked down the crack-addicted anarchist who had fired the crippling shot and beat him to death in his own apartment. He filed a report claiming that the violence had become inevitable after the suspect lunged at him with a kitchen knife, a story every cop in the precinct knew to be either exaggeration or fabrication, but which both the internal affairs division and the state prosecutor judiciously declined to challenge.

In the years that followed, the two men pursued divergent paths. While Terry had transitioned into civilian life, Dalton had taken a very different road. He sank deeper into the world of violence and criminality. Working on the Boston city vice squad for nearly two decades, he earned a file full of commendations for his service but left a trail of bloodied criminals in his wake. The fissures on his face and slightly reddened nose revealed the cumulative effect of too many cigarettes and too much alcohol. A scar on his right cheekbone commemorated the night a pimp had lunged at him with a broken beer bottle for refusing to pay for services rendered. And yet his jet-black hair remained blacker than ever, the dye-assisted product of his vanity rather than the result of good genetics. Sitting together at this bar, the two made an odd pair. Nobody could have guessed that twenty years ago, they were often mistaken for brothers.

Turning to face his old friend, Terry began to speak. "I need a favor. More precisely, Abigail Walker needs a favor."

"Ah," Dalton said in response to the mention of America's most famous widow. His small black eyes widened as he rubbed the stubble on his face. "*Now* you got me interested."

Terry handed him a manila file containing a photo of Jack Collins along with his background, personal information, and approximate daily schedule. "This guy is an associate at the law firm that handles her legal work. I got a tip that he's up to something. Find out what you can."

"You got anything more than that?"

"Not really. Not yet. Just kick the tires on him, and then we'll talk."

"Okay, I got it."

"Thanks. I appreciate it."

"No problem. And we'll handle the money the same way as last time?"

"Yes, David. You'll be paid later. And paid very well."

# CHAPTER 46

As Deb walked east on 71st Street, the signs of autumn were everywhere. A smattering of yellow and brown leaves swirled across the sidewalk in front of her. The air was decidedly cooler than it had been just two weeks prior. And each night's dusk now approached measurably earlier than it had the evening before. It was not even quarter past seven, but it already felt like it was late at night.

She eyed the passersby as she approached the street corner. An old man walking a scrawny little dog. A woman toting groceries. A thirty-something pretending to jog, trying to justify her purchase of designer leggings. A skinny teenager in a navy blazer, toting a matching backpack. She looked at his hands. *Him. He's the one.*

"Excuse me," she said as she took a step toward him. "Do you know where the Corinthian is? I can't figure out the building numbers around here."

"Did you say the Corinthian?" he asked as he popped his earbuds out of his ears. "It's just a few doors up."

"God, I'm the worst assistant in New York. I must have walked past it twice." She pulled a white envelope out of her handbag and held it firmly between two gloved fingers. "Can you do me a huge favor?"

"What do you need?"

"Can you just drop this off with the doorman when you walk by? I promised my boss I'd do it, but now I'm running way late."

"I guess so. Sure."

"That's awesome." She reached into her handbag and pulled out a crumpled twenty. "Can I give you something for your trouble?"

"Nah. I have to go by there anyway," he said, waving her off with the palm of a gloved hand.

"You're awesome. Thanks so much." She smiled as she flipped back some of her bright-blond hair and straightened her equally bright-pink scarf. Both had been acquired solely for this occasion, and both would be discarded in the trash within the next five minutes.

"It's nothing," he said before walking away northward.

She crossed the street and watched as he ducked into the lobby of the Corinthian and quickly re-emerged. Without looking back toward her, he resumed his path uptown.

Within two blocks, the naturally brunette Deb Miller entered the Café Stanhope and checked her black overcoat and royal-blue scarf. Picking a stray blond hair off the overcoat just before the coatroom attendant whisked it from view, she stepped off to the side to wait for her dinner companion.

# CHAPTER 47

As if on cue, Jack walked through the restaurant door. "Waiting long?"

"Not at all."

Within minutes, the two were seated and working on a bottle of wine.

"So, should we talk about it?" she asked.

"I guess we should. But I don't know where to begin."

"You Harvard boys sure know how to kiss," she said as she leaned in toward him and allowed her blouse to gape open. "Let's begin with that."

She could see the redness spreading from his cheeks to his ears.

"I feel like such an idiot. I haven't handled things very well."

She reached across the table and grabbed one of his hands with hers. She dramatically wiped her eyes with the back of her other hand and feigned a labored breath.

"Are you okay?" he asked.

"I am." She sniffled again and dabbed at her eyes with her napkin. "Yeah, I'm fine," she said, ending the impromptu theatrics and turning back to her rehearsed script. "You and I have a special bond. I *really* like working with you. And it's so nuts that we almost met years ago." She paused for a second to be sure she had his full attention. "*But* you need to quit."

"Huh?" he yelped like a boxer who had just been hit in the gut. "Quit *what*?"

"*R&H*, fool. I think you're on the wrong path, that you've found the wrong place. Ted's a lousy boss. You don't need to spend your career with him. The firm's a rat's nest. Why the hell do you want any of this?"

"Because I—"

"Hang on a minute." She raised a finger and continued talking over him. "Here's what I think. You had a great thing in Connecticut. Go back there. Live a safe little suburban life. Just accept that's your fate. And it's a great one. Certainly better than being the single seductress who tries to maul her hot coworkers," she concluded as she slid one finger seductively across the back of his hand.

"I don't get it. Where is this coming from?" He pulled his hands away from her.

"It's not coming from anywhere. As I said, I love working with you. I love *being* with you. If there were no consequences in life, I'd beg you to take me on that little island jaunt with you. But I can't."

"Can't?"

"Oh yeah. Great idea. Right in line with your daredevil personality."

"Well, haven't you told me that's my problem? Mr. Safe, Mr. Boring. I can't stop thinking that I should have jumped across that street and met you that day. Maybe I should have come to New York right away—made my own life instead of listening to what everyone else wanted."

"Oh, spare me. You once saw me across a street. So, big deal. That's not part of some great message from the universe. And what exactly do you think would have happened if we had actually met on that day? If they hadn't screwed up both of our lives? You think that would have magically changed your life?" Her pulse quickened as she pondered the answer. "So maybe we would have talked, or dated, or even had some awesome sex followed by a nasty breakup and never spoken to each other again. Big deal."

"You're probably right. But at least I would have tried. That's the point. I would have just crossed the damn street and given it a shot. And whether being back here with you is a coincidence or not, I finally feel like I'm on the right path. No way I'm just walking away. *No way.*"

"There's a difference between taking a chance and being stupid," she said.

"Believe me, I know that."

"Fine," she said, picking up her menu. "Ignore my advice. But don't say I didn't warn you."

———— ◉ ————

SIXTY UNEVENTFUL MINUTES later, Jack called for the check and paid it, slipping his credit card back into his wallet when he was done.

Once they were outside the restaurant, Deb spotted a passing taxi, which lurched to a stop before them. "Do you want it?" she asked.

"No, no. I should probably walk anyway. I need some fresh air."

She slipped into the taxi's back seat and shut the door. "See you tomorrow," she called through the open window as the cab pulled away. As the taxi headed south, she sat back in her seat and thought back to some of the more awkward moments from dinner. Her personal favorite had been when she showed him a fabricated file memo Ted had supposedly written to document Jack's *mediocre performance*. The charade had been as painful as it was necessary. She was pretty sure she had scared him off. It was time for him to go.

Hopefully, tonight had been the final act of their Shakespearean romance, the curtain drawn when he picked up the restaurant check just as she expected him to. For if anyone ever checked his financial records, and she expected that day might come, they would see exactly what she wanted them to see—that Jack had been just two blocks from Abigail's apartment on the evening someone delivered a blackmail letter to her.

*Sorry, Jack*, she thought. *I had no other choice.*

# CHAPTER 48

Abigail lifted her head off the pillow and squinted at the clock. Oh God, quarter to seven. Way too early to start a day.

She dropped her head back into the soft feathers and forced her eyes shut. She rolled from side to side, turning herself onto one aching hip and then the other. But try as she might, she couldn't get comfortable. Her mouth was bone dry. Her head was pounding.

She looked at the clock again. Still not even seven.

"Rosa," she called into the hallway beyond her bedroom. "Are you here yet?" She knew full well that her housekeeper wasn't supposed to arrive until eight. "Rosa, damn it, why aren't you here?"

She stumbled out of bed and grabbed her bathrobe off the back of her open bedroom door, tying the belt around her waist as she walked. *Who needs Rosa anyway?* she thought as she headed toward the apartment door. *I can fetch my own damn newspaper.*

She opened the apartment door and snatched the *New York Times* off her doormat. As she pulled the newspaper toward her, it revealed an unmarked white envelope beneath it. She grabbed that as well and turned back into the apartment.

She walked into the dining room and tossed the newspaper on the sideboard. *This first,* she thought, sliding a finger under the envelope's flap. She tore it open and pulled out a folded sheet of paper. As she read through the page, her temples began to pulse. *Oh God. It can't be.* Her stomach heaved up toward her chest. The typewritten words read eerily like the words of a letter received some four years earlier. The demand was set out with equal clarity. There was a new bank account this time, located at a bank of which she had never heard on an island she knew quite well. She had honeymooned on Nevis. Now her tormenter wanted ten million dollars sent there.

*This is the last demand*, said the letter. *This will be the end. The final price to pay for the lives you ruined. The price to pay for your peace.* It ended as had the previous letter from the same sender. *He will never forgive you.*

Senator Harold Walker had been dead for over eleven years. But he was still haunting his widow.

Within moments after reading the letter, she was on the phone with Ted, catching him on his cell phone as he entered a taxicab in front of a Boston hotel. "I'll be back in New York in time for lunch," he promised. It was not soon enough for her. "It will all be okay," he assured her. She was not the least bit comforted. "I can't be there any sooner," he reasoned before disconnecting the call. "I really can't."

She bolted into the pantry and flung open a cabinet. There was only one solution for her racing heart—only one way to counteract the burning feeling creeping up her throat. She found the bottle of Xanax and tapped several blue pills into the palm of her hand. *That should be enough*, she thought as she flung her head back and tossed the pills into her mouth.

# CHAPTER 49

Ted rose from his chair in the Harvard Club dining room as soon as he spotted Abigail walking toward him. As always, she was the model of elegance, today wearing a fashionable yellow wool suit accented with a red-and-blue scarf. She moved slowly toward the table, exchanging a few words with anyone who made eye contact along the way.

When she reached Ted, they embraced for a moment, kissed each other on the cheek, and sat in their usual seats. She appeared much calmer than he expected, presumably due to a healthy helping of Xanax. After they had settled in, he was the first to speak. "You look lovely, as always."

"I have no choice. Two photographers on the sidewalk want a picture of me looking like I'm dying. I won't give them the satisfaction."

Two glasses of Chardonnay appeared on the table, the waiter who delivered them disappearing as quickly as he had appeared. In an instant, Abigail had her glass in hand.

As he watched her hand trembling on the stem of her wineglass, Ted wondered how many tranquilizers were coursing through her veins and whether adding alcohol to the mix was a good idea. Nevertheless, there was no way he was going to pick that fight. Yielding to his powerlessness, he raised his glass and tilted it in her direction. "To your health. And your happiness."

"Lovely, but empty, words. You can't deliver on either front."

She took a number of large swallows before placing her empty glass back on the table.

"Now, that's better. Time for business."

She lifted her purse off the dining-room floor and pulled out a sheet of paper. After handing it to him, she leaned back in her chair and drummed her fingernails on the tablecloth. "You want me to be happy, my dear?" Her tone was suddenly full of frustration, the alchemy of drugs and alcohol clearly wreaking havoc on her mood. "Then tell me what to do about *that*."

Ted scanned the letter, his face getting warmer each time he read the single page of text. "Bastard," he muttered. He then looked directly at her and spoke in a slightly louder tone. "I don't like this, Abby. I thought we had this under control."

"*You* don't like it? It's not *your* money we're talking about."

He frowned. "Look, we've been down this road before. You and I are in this thing together. If this were just about money, it would be a lot simpler."

A waiter arrived with a fresh glass of Chardonnay. Abigail snatched the glass off his tray then swallowed nearly half in an indelicate gulp.

"This has gone on too long. I'm tired of it. I'm tired of everything," she said.

Ted slowly read through the letter again before offering his reply. "So, then let's stop."

She gave him a quizzical look as she replaced her wineglass on the table. "What do you mean, 'Let's stop'?"

"I mean exactly what I said. Just ignore this letter. Pretend it never happened. Let's keep doing what we're doing and simply ride this thing out. Enough is enough."

He watched as the tension spread across her face, large creases extending outward from her eyes. "Just 'ride this thing out'?" she echoed. "Isn't that awfully risky?"

"Of course it's risky." His increasingly strident tone was now that of a man fully committed to his chosen course of conduct. "But do you think giving in is going to make us any safer? You're dealing with a blackmailer, Abby. An extortionist—a terrorist. People like this have no souls. You can't negotiate with terrorists. We give in to this now, and next month it will be a new demand and then another. It just keeps going."

She looked down at the tablecloth. "I don't want to anger this person."

"Neither do I. But I'm sick of this. We've already given in to one demand. We've made a deal with this devil, and a fair one at that. If we give in to this next threat, there's no telling where it will stop." His decisiveness was clear as he refolded the letter and placed it in the inside pocket of his suit jacket.

"I think I should talk to Terry."

"Oh, I don't think that's a good idea."

"Why not? He is my director of security. He has been by my side nearly as long as you have. How can he do that job if we continue to keep him in the dark?"

"I see your point," he said in his most reassuring tone. "But we made that choice a long time ago. Terry is a good man. But deep down, he's a Boston cop in a fancy suit. He always wants to see justice done. He always looks for vengeance. All you want is peace." He continued to press his case. "He's just not the right guy for this job. If you bring him in on this, everything will change. Everything."

Ted didn't want to overstate his point, but he feared Terry's rash judgment and quick temper. Despite his years in elite private security, the former cop had never fully transitioned away from the world of paid informants and street justice. Ted had previously seen him overreact to even the most minor of threats, using a crackpot's rambling letter or incoherent phone call as an opportunity to cast himself in a long-lost starring role. He was the wrong guy for the job.

Abigail wrung her hands. "I don't know. I just don't know."

"Ultimately, it's your call. I'll honor your wishes. But my vote is clear. Keep doing what we're doing. Keep paying what we're paying. But not a penny more." With that, the lawyer rested his case.

She sat back and stared across the dining room in silent reflection. He never asked her what she was thinking about, for he was certain he knew. After a full minute of tortured silence, her focus returned to him. "Okay, you win. Let's do it your way," she said before returning to her pensive silence.

A few moments later, the waiter's reappearance interrupted the awkward stillness. "Mrs. Walker, Mr. Parker, have you decided what you would like to eat?"

Although he didn't have much of an appetite, Ted suitably feigned enthusiasm for the daily special, an Idaho rainbow trout with a beurre blanc sauce. "We'll have two," he said.

"An excellent choice," said the waiter. "Chef Austin has been talking about this all morning."

As the server disappeared from view, Ted and Abigail simultaneously raised their wineglasses and took long sips.

"It will be okay, Abby," he assured his famous client. "It really will."

# CHAPTER 50

Joe Andrews had dealt with a lot of people in his years with the FBI. But without a doubt, he found Ted Parker the most perplexing of all of them. Reading through the transcript of Ted's lunch with Abigail, Joe was completely confused.

"What the hell is going on here?"

"I know, I know," Bob Masterson replied from across the room. "I don't get it either."

This should have been a triumphant moment for Joe. In their lunchtime conversation, Ted and Abigail had provided the clearest evidence yet about the transfers to the Caymans and the reasons behind them. Joe now knew that Abigail was being blackmailed, that millions of her dollars had flowed into Ted's offshore account. The obvious conclusion was that the lawyer was extorting money from his most famous client. And yet, he had just read a transcript of a conversation in which Ted unequivocally urged her not to meet the blackmailer's demands. It simply didn't make sense.

In that moment, for perhaps the first time in his career, Joe felt tremendous self-doubt. His seven years in law enforcement had been blessed with never-ending good fortune, a series of well-chosen assignments and lucky breaks that had propelled him through the ranks. Coming to New York had brought all that to a grinding halt. He was starting to feel like Hemingway's Santiago, led by pride to pursue a fish beyond his ability. Was he slowly being pulled out to sea?

As he finished reading the transcript for the second time, he felt a burning sensation deep in his gut. He had seen with his own eyes the paperwork used to open the account at Atlantic Coast Bank, the photocopies of Ted's driver's license and passport undeniably connecting him to that account. He now had Ted's voice on tape acknowledging the blackmail plot used to fund the account. But the jury that would hear that evidence would also hear Ted urging his client not to meet the blackmailer's latest demand. The result was far from an airtight case. And time was ticking away.

Joe had underestimated his target.

Depressed and perplexed, he kept rereading the transcript, each time hoping some further clue would emerge. In frustration, he jumped from theory to theory in a vain effort to make sense of what he was reading. Maybe Ted was setting Abigail up for something else. Maybe he was just playing with her emotions. Maybe, just maybe, he knew they were listening to him. He was sure there was an explanation for Ted's incongruous behavior. He just couldn't figure it out. At least not yet.

<hr />

ACROSS THE ROOM, BOB Masterson had his own theory. He was reading the same words that so confused Joe, yet he had no problem understanding what they meant. He was not as emotionally vested in this matter, not as obsessed with nailing Ted Parker. And blessed with the superior clarity provided by emotional distance, Bob accepted the reality that Joe could not even begin to consider: they were tracking the wrong guy.

# CHAPTER 51

Jack slid the thick pile of tax returns off Abigail's dining room table and into his waiting briefcase then extended his hand toward his client. "Thank you for your time, Mrs. Walker. It was a real pleasure to see you again."

"I'm the one who should thank you," she replied, smiling warmly as she returned his firm handshake. "You were kind to come here. I'm so pleased we got all of that finished."

Jack made his way to the door. "It was my pleasure, Mrs. Walker," he repeated in the most professional tone he could muster. "Anytime you need me, I'd be glad to help."

"Thank you again. I'm so grateful to all of you."

He swelled with pride as he turned the heavy brass doorknob. This had been his first meeting alone with Abigail, and it had gone incredibly well. He had guided her ably through a year's worth of trust tax returns, answering her every question as she reviewed and then signed each document. It had not even been three months, but his transition to big-city lawyer was nearly complete. Here he was in the opulent Corinthian Building, alone with one of the country's most famous women, carrying a briefcase full of documents that contained her most sensitive financial information. He was so far away from his old life that he could barely remember it. Deb had been wrong. This *was* his calling.

He pulled open the door an inch but then closed it back. "By the way," he added as he turned back toward Abigail, "I just planned a trip to one of your favorite spots—the Four Seasons in Nevis. It looks amazing." He smiled giddily. "Too bad you have to rob a bank to afford the place."

His stomach dropped as the smile disappeared from her face. She stared at him with an unsettling glare.

"I'm not sure I know what you mean, Mr. Collins," she offered coldly.

His heart began to race. "I'm sorry," he said meekly. "I just thought that..." He stopped there. Sometimes a simple apology and a rapid exit were better than a drawn-out explanation.

She nodded but said nothing.

*Wow, she's pissed off*, he thought. "I'm very sorry if I said something wrong," he repeated as a wave of nausea overtook him. "I didn't mean to."

She stared at him, offering no response to his repeated apologies. *Oh crap*. A sour taste filled the back of his throat. Ted was going to be furious with him. The standing orders with respect to Abigail were pretty simple: keep her happy. Do anything she needs. Say "please, Mrs. Walker" and say "thank you, Mrs. Walker." No freelancing. No straying from the script. He had screwed up royally.

Backing out through the doorway and into the hall, he stammered yet another apology. "Again, Mrs. Walker, please forgive me if I said something wrong," he said meekly as he continued to inch away. "Have a nice evening, Mrs. Walker."

"Goodbye, Mr. Collins," she replied coolly as she closed the apartment door.

Jack flinched at the sound of the deadbolt sliding into place. Head hanging low, he trudged toward the elevator. *Wow, what an epic screwup*. Hopefully she had accepted his apology. Hopefully that would be the end of it.

# CHAPTER 52

Ted saw Abigail's name flash on his telephone display and picked up the call on the first ring. "Good afternoon."

"We have a problem. A very big problem."

"My God, what's wrong?"

"How does your Mr. Collins know about our little issue?" Abigail demanded.

"Huh? What are you talking about?"

"On the way out my door, he mentioned Nevis to me. And he gave me this knowing little smile, the smug bastard."

Ted could feel his jaw tense. He didn't like not knowing what was going on within his own law practice. He had no idea why Jack had been at Abigail's apartment in the first place. He knew even less about how, and when, and why, his youngest protégé had stumbled into information he had no business having. And so, despite his escalating fury, Ted offered what might have been one of the largest understatements of his long career. "I have absolutely no idea."

"What is that supposed to mean? This is intolerable."

"It means that I honestly don't know. Look, I'll talk to him and get—"

"Forget it, Ted. *I* will take care of this."

"What does that mean?"

Displaying a fierceness of tone that he had never before heard from her, she repeated her directive. "I told you to just forget it. I will take care of this myself."

"Let's talk about this."

"No, Ted," she snapped. "I will take care of this. You may not want to believe it, but I'm in charge here. *I* am. Not you." With that, the line went dead.

# CHAPTER 53

Deb tried her best to stifle a laugh. She allowed her phone to ring twice more while she exhaled slowly and composed herself.

"How'd it go?" she asked, cheerfully. "Everything all set?"

"Thanks for leading me into disaster."

*Poor baby.* He had seemed so excited just two hours ago when she asked him to do her the favor of having Abigail sign a pile of tax returns. And now he sounded heartbroken. "What are you talking about?" she asked. "Was there a problem with the returns?"

"No, everything was fine with that. We exchanged the usual hellos, she signed everything, and I was nearly on my way. But then I mentioned Nevis, and she went crazy on me."

"What do you mean, 'crazy'?" Deb tried her best to convey a tone of confusion. "In eight years, I've never seen that woman anything less than completely composed."

"Well, then I got a special treat. Because there was something wild in her eyes when I talked about taking a vacation. I clearly pissed her off. Hey, hang on a sec." Deb heard a car door slam, followed by Jack directing the driver to return him to 1593 Broadway. A moment later, he was back on the line.

"You led me into a mess. You *told* me to mention Nevis to her. You said she would 'love talking about the place,'" he mocked. "Well, apparently not." He was clearly flailing, a stream of questions rolling off his tongue. "What was her problem? Who gets pissed off by a Caribbean island? What the hell did you get me into?"

Holding the phone away from her ear, she allowed him to continue to boil over for a few more moments before she spoke. "I'm sorry. I didn't mean to give you bad advice. I know that she does love Nevis.

She's been to the Four Seasons a dozen times. I know that for a fact. But the senator loved that island too. Maybe you just brought up a bad memory? Maybe it was just a bad day. Who the hell knows?"

"I think you *do* know. Maybe she had laryngitis there once?"

"Huh? You're making no sense."

"Maybe I am, and maybe I'm not."

"Well, you're not. Abigail can be a bit thorny, in case you hadn't noticed. I'm sure she's just having a bad day, and I'm really sorry. I truly was trying to help you."

"Whatever."

"Come on, don't be such a baby. How can I make it up to you?" She let her words hang out there for a moment. "How about dinner again soon? My treat. Please?" Then, in her best begging tone, she added, "Don't make me beg."

"Yeah, whatever," he replied lifelessly. "Everyone keeping telling me to stay the hell away from you. I'm thinking they are all right."

———⊳●⊲———

JACK STEPPED INTO THE lobby of 1593 Broadway and headed straight to Steve Oswald's office.

"Well, I just got set up," Jack said as he sat down across from Steve. "Deb told me exactly how to handle Mrs. Walker, and somehow the whole thing blows up in my face."

"Not an accident."

"No, not an accident. You were right all along. She's trying to run me out."

"So, want me to talk to Mary Vincent? See if she'll take you on?"

"Not yet. I'm not willing to admit defeat. Oh shit, no offense."

"I know what you mean."

"So what's her next move?" Jack asked.

Steve leaned back in his chair. "Let's think. What cards has she played so far? Did she try to seduce you?"

"Check."

"Undermine you with the clients and with Ted?"

"Check. Check."

"Then you're at the point where Clay and I threw in the towel. You're entering uncharted territory. If you stick in there, I don't know what her next move will be."

"Well, then, I guess we're going to find out," Jack said. His decision made, he stood from his chair.

"Wow, good for you, Collins. I would have expected you to give up by now."

"Yeah, me too. But not this time."

# CHAPTER 54

David Dalton made quick work of the old lock securing the Collinses' back door and was soon inside the kitchen. After taking a quick loop through the living room and master bedroom, he headed into the second, smaller bedroom a few steps down the hall.

In contrast to the otherwise neat home, this room was crowded and cramped. An old desktop sat perched on a dinged-up desk. Brown cardboard boxes filled with books and mementos littered the floor, nearly covering a threadbare red Bokhara rug. For the next hour, he searched through many of the boxes. He read old bank statements and flipped through photographs. Finally, he copied the contents of the computer's hard drive onto a portable drive he now carried in his pocket. His work here was nearly done. He was about ready to retrace his steps down the narrow hallway and out through the kitchen door.

But then he heard that door rattle open.

As the door shut with a thud, Dalton pulled a black ski mask over his face and retreated to the far side of the room. The click of high heels on the kitchen floor turned into muffled footsteps as the unexpected visitor approached. He could tell from the footsteps that it was a woman who had just entered the house, and the fact that she had taken off her shoes gave him one likely suspect: Amanda Collins was home.

*What the hell is she doing here?* When he had called her office an hour earlier to check on her, her secretary had made clear that she would be in meetings until five thirty. *Stupid bitch.* It was not even four o'clock, and she was in the house and heading right for him. He moved silently toward the bedroom's only window, a small double-hung that was painted shut. *Crap.* He was trapped.

He slipped his Glock 19 from its holster and stepped out of sight behind the bedroom's open door. He wasn't going to shoot her. But he'd whack her on the side of the head if need be. It would all come down to which way she walked. If she went straight into the master bedroom, she'd be fine. If she turned into this room instead, she was going to get a huge headache.

He took slow and measured breaths as he strained to hear the sound of her approach. Floorboards in the hallway creaked louder and louder until she was nearly at the doorway. Then, as he steeled himself and raised the gun, the moment of truth came and went. Passing the doorway, the footsteps continued down the hallway, growing increasingly faint until Amanda reached the master bedroom.

Silently, Dalton slipped out from behind the bedroom door just far enough to be able to see. Still largely hidden behind the doorframe, he watched the female figure moving in the bedroom just down the hall. As she unbuttoned her pink silk blouse, he watched with growing arousal. She turned away from him as she tossed the blouse onto her bed then turned back as she removed her bra. *Now this could be fun*, he thought as he admired her exposed breasts. His breathing grew faster. *Yeah, just like the old days.*

As Amanda turned away from him and stepped out of her skirt, Dalton could no longer restrain himself. He stepped out from behind the doorway, tugged on his mask and headed toward the bedroom.

# CHAPTER 55

Deb and Ted sat at the small circular table in the corner of his office, three large stacks of paper piled up on the table's surface. The paperwork belonged to Mrs. and Mrs. Reginald Ashford, the chairman of the New York City Opera and his wife of thirty years.

"There are nine trusts in total," he explained as she took feverish notes. "Two discretionary trusts for each child—one GST exempt and one nonexempt. Plus a pot trust for the grandchildren."

He continued to explain the nature of the Ashfords' current documents and then relayed her specific assignments. She set them out neatly on her yellow legal pad. "I understand," she said. "I'll get it done."

"Super."

She stood from the table and gathered the stacks of paper as he retreated to his desk. Placing the documents neatly in a cardboard file box, she turned to face him. He was already leafing through another pile of papers.

"Hey, how long has Jack been here?"

"I don't know," he replied without looking up. "Maybe two months?"

"Has it been that long? It seems like he's still so clueless."

"He'll get the hang of it. You two still getting along okay?"

"Yes, Ted." She laughed reassuringly as he shuffled through a stack of papers. "We've been playing nicely in the sandbox. He's my buddy. Tells me all about his great vacation plans."

"*Vacation?* I guess we're not keeping him busy enough."

"Oh, he's not going until February, but I think we're going to hear about it constantly until then."

Ted mumbled "mm-hmm" and turned to pick up his phone.

"Yeah, he's going to Nevis," she continued. "He said something about how he didn't care how much it cost."

"Nevis, eh? Nice place." He placed the phone receiver to his ear and began to dial. "I love Nevis. The boy has good taste."

# CHAPTER 56

Amanda leaned forward and rummaged through her top dresser drawer. Her hands soon found her jogging bra, and she snatched it from the drawer. A faint sound echoed behind her. As she pulled on the bra, she heard the sound again then snapped in its direction. *Shit*, she thought as her pulse quickened.

She pounced toward her nightstand just in time to stop the vibrating phone from slipping off the edge. "Hey, Kerry," she said as she pressed the phone to her ear. "Yeah, I was expecting two hours."

"Nothing better than a meeting cut short," came the reply through the phone. "Makes up for all the late nights."

"I'll say. I'm going for a run. Do you want to join me?"

"Yeah, great idea. Let me get changed."

"I'll swing by your place on the way to the Cove."

Amanda heard another noise, this time coming from the kitchen. "Jack?" she called as she covered the phone with her hand. "Hello?"

She stepped cautiously into the hallway, her pulse quickening with every step. She heard a faint thud. *The door?* "Jack?" she called again.

"Everything okay?" Kerry asked.

"I think so. Hold on."

She lowered the phone from her face and turned the corner into the kitchen.

# CHAPTER 57

Abigail wrapped her arms around Terry O'Reilly as soon as he stepped through the apartment doorway. "Thank God you're here."

"Abigail? Are you okay?"

"Oh yes," she whispered, still clinging onto his suit jacket. "I'm sorry to be in such a state," she slurred as she lifted her weight from him and stood erect. "I imagine I'm quite a sight." She rubbed her hands across her eyes and dried them on her sleeves, leaving streaks of makeup on the tattered bathrobe.

She led him into the living room and collapsed into her Queen Anne chair. Then she began to sob uncontrollably.

"I'm sorry to be like this with you. I'm sorry you have to see me like this." She thought back eleven years to the last time he saw her in such a state. On that day, she had trembled as much as she did today, the tears streaming over her husband's flag-draped coffin with the same intensity that they now flowed onto her bathrobe lapel.

He stood next to her chair and placed his hand on her shoulders. "Abigail, are you okay?"

She didn't respond.

He knelt beside her and placed his hands on both sides of her face, tilting her head gently to raise her eyes toward his. "Abigail. Abby, what is wrong?"

She closed her eyes and allowed herself to focus on the warmth of his hands against her face. For years, she had lived a life largely devoid of such human contact. Feeling it at this moment made her realize how deeply she had missed it.

As much as she prayed this day would never come to pass, it was here. There was no denying that fact, no turning back the hands of time. The only comfort she felt came from the thought that if she was going to display this degree of weakness and ask for some much-needed help, there was no one better to do that with than this kindhearted man.

She spoke in a whisper, the strength of her voice drained by the fit of sobs that had just subsided. "There is something I have never told you," she began. "It's about the day that Hal died."

"Abby, what the hell is going on?" The tension was evident in his tone.

"I know this is coming out of nowhere. I'm sorry. Let me try to explain."

She reached into the pocket of her bathrobe and pulled out a vial of pills. Unscrewing the top, she extracted two of the tablets and tossed them into her mouth, grimacing as she forced herself to swallow them dry.

"Okay, here's the story."

For the next ten minutes, she told him everything that she had never told him before, the burdens on her heart lightening with each disclosure. He played the role of priest to her penitent, accepting her confession without comment, occasionally nodding to offer encouragement or squeezing her hand in support. As she unfurled memory after memory, her tale twisted forward to the events of the past week, ending with the story of the note found on her doorstep and its final extortive demand.

When Abigail was at last silent, Terry began to speak. He was calm, almost clinical, in his approach. After asking her a series of questions about the events of the past eleven years, he came to the present day. "Do you have the note?"

"I gave it to Ted."

He frowned. "What about the envelope? Where did that go?"

"I assume I threw it out." She paused, thinking back to the events of a week ago. "No, no, wait." She forced herself out of her chair and looked across the room, mentally retracing the steps she'd taken several mornings before. Eyeing something just beyond the living room doorway, her memory locked into place. "The sideboard—right over there," she exclaimed, pointing into the dining room. "I tucked it into the top drawer." She stood up from her chair.

He grabbed her wrist. "Stay right here, Abigail," he commanded. The softness in his voice was gone. He was back on duty. "Don't go near that envelope."

He then added one further request. "Do you have a Ziploc bag?"

# CHAPTER 58

As his office printer hummed to life and began spitting out a draft of the last will and testament of Maxwell Paulson, Jack stretched both arms above his head and let out an audible yawn. Looking at the clock on his telephone, he saw that it was past nine. He had rarely been in his office this late.

With the Paulsons' estate planning done for the night, Jack turned to the last task on his day's agenda. Stepping into the hallway, he was greeted with silence. While the litigation department on the floor above was likely still humming with activity, the estate planning and tax lawyers on the forty-fourth floor had all packed it in for the night. Walking down the hall, Jack marched past three darkened doorways and turned into the fourth. The motion-activated lights turned on automatically as he entered Deb's office. He took a deep breath and looked around.

She was nothing if not organized. Colored folders were piled in neat stacks on her desk and credenza, the client names printed in perfect block letters on the folder tabs. Her bookshelves were arranged with similar care, current and past volumes of the Internal Revenue Code and Regulations placed in perfect numerical order. In sharp contrast to the image presented by his cluttered office, her workspace projected an aura of discipline.

He crossed the room and sat in her chair. Spinning gently from side to side, he rubbed his hands along the smooth leather arms and surveyed the office from this perspective. Although he was sitting calmly, his pulse began to race. He was wrong to be here. He was violating an unspoken trust.

But he couldn't help himself. Despite his vow to the contrary, he still spent way too many hours thinking about Deb, too many silent moments trying to figure out what really made her tick. And since she was at the theater with her mother, it was time to figure it out.

He again scanned the room. In addition to being well organized, her workspace was strangely devoid of anything personal—no knick-knacks, no photos. *Kind of like Deb herself*, he mused—a polished exterior with something hidden within. If so, where did she keep her secrets?

He flung open the top desk drawer. His heartbeat quickened as he peered inside, even though he saw only the usual assemblage of paper clips and pens. He should leave now. This was so wrong. But he couldn't stop.

He closed the top drawer and slid open the middle one. He felt guilty as he looked at her hairbrush and toothbrush, a feeling that only intensified as he spotted a bottle of perfume, a tube of lipstick, and several bottles of prescription medication. The guilt didn't stop him from rolling the prescription vials over, so he could read the labels.

*Ah, so that's it.* He had long wondered how her mood could swing from high to low so quickly. He now had his answers—Ritalin and Ativan, the dynamic duo behind her personality. He snapped a photo of the labels then rolled the bottles back into place and completed his mental inventory: some gum, a dog-eared romance novel, dental floss, toothpaste, and a box of mints.

He took out the bottle of perfume and placed the top against his nose. As he inhaled the scent of lemons and spice, he could picture her as if she were sitting in front of him, her dark hair cascading down her neck to the top of her silk blouse, her full red lips breaking into a lusty, mischievous smile.

He replaced the perfume and slid the drawer shut. *Enough. I should go home.* But he didn't. His curiosity overcoming his guilt, he slid open the large bottom drawer, full of files. He scanned the tabs. Here was everything one would expect to see in a lawyer's personal file drawer: an alphabetically arranged array of private information ranging from dental and disability at the front to pay stubs and taxes at the rear.

*What am I doing?* The guilt had come back with a vengeance. He eased the chair back from the desk and was about to shut the bottom drawer when he spotted one folder out of place behind the rest. He felt a lump in his throat as he saw the handwritten letters on the folder's tab: *personal.*

Jack snatched the folder and set it on the desk in front of him. He slid forward and jerked open the file to reveal a stack of letters, printed emails and photographs. His breath quickening, he pushed aside the letters and emails and took the small collection of pictures into his hands. Deb had marked the back of every photo with its date and location, and flipping through them provided him with a guided tour of select highlights of her life. He found a photo from a college formal, a tuxedo-clad frat boy pressed close against her plunging black gown. He found another from her first year of law school, a dozen girls posing in a darkened bar, each with a lemon wedge in one hand and a shot glass in the other. He worked through the stack, following her from year to year and place to place. She was smiling in nearly all of the photos, laughing in a few. In every one, she seemed youthful and happy, always surrounded by others. He had rarely seen her that way.

After staring at the faces for a moment, he concluded that the last picture in the pile was Deb and her father standing on a wide expanse of sandy beach. She appeared to be about eighteen or nineteen years old, wearing a red Cornell T-shirt over a black bathing suit. She was around the age she'd been when he saw her across a Cambridge street—the moment their lives had converged for the first time. Captivated by that thought, he lingered on this photo longer than the rest, staring longingly at her face before allowing his gaze to drift down her tanned, toned legs to the crystal-blue water lapping at her toenails. At the bottom of the photo, he noticed the telltale bumps of handwriting on the back.

After making a final lingering pass up and down her legs, he flipped over the photo to see what was written there.

Although his heart had been racing since the moment he set foot in her office, his pulse surged to a new high. The words identified the location of the sandy beach beneath her gorgeous legs: *Grand Cayman, spring break.*

His stomach clenched, and he suddenly felt warm. He looked at the photo again and heard Deb's words of a few weeks earlier echoing through his head. "I've never been there," she had insisted when they spoke about the Caymans. "I've never been south of Florida."

His gut cinched tighter as he heard one other voice echoing through his mind. "Just keep your eyes and ears open," Joe Andrews had said. "You know what I'm looking for."

*No way,* he thought. *It can't be.*

He snapped a picture of the front and back of the photo and hurriedly slipped everything back into Deb's desk.

*Just a coincidence,* he tried to convince himself. *Just another coincidence.*

# CHAPTER 59

Jack stepped inside the back door and quietly placed his keys and cell phone on the counter. From the silence and darkness of the house, he knew that Amanda was already fast asleep. But he wasn't quite ready to join her.

Seeing the picture of Deb in Grand Cayman had thrown him for a loop. Even after a crosstown walk and a long train ride, he was still completely wired. She had lied straight to his face. *Why? And what else has she lied about?*

He picked up his cell phone and for the third time in the past hour scrolled through his list of contacts to find Joe's number. This time he actually placed the call, and the sleepy federal agent was soon on the line.

"What's up, bud? It's kinda late."

"I know. I'm sorry, this probably could have waited for morning."

"Technically it *is* morning," Joe countered with an audible yawn. "So why am I no longer sleeping?"

"It's just that I saw something I can't figure out." Jack paused, unsure of how exactly to explain to a federal agent that he had just rifled through a colleague's desk. "It's probably nothing, but I—"

"Let's go, bud. Just tell me what's up so that we can all get back to sleep. Start with the short version."

"Okay, sorry. I saw an old picture of Deb in Grand Cayman."

"Where exactly did you see that?" Joe sounded more perturbed than intrigued. "If you were sharing photos at one of your lunch dates, I'm going to have to beat you."

"What?" Jack's jaw tensed. "What... what the hell are you talking about?"

191

"Forget it. Back to Deb. What's the issue?"

"I told you," Jack replied, a hint of anger coming over him, "I saw an old picture of her in Grand Cayman. She was on college spring break, standing on a beach next to her dad."

"And?"

"Okay, so maybe it's no big deal, but she once clearly told me that she'd never been there. She lied. No doubt."

"And?" Joe sounded completely bored.

"And I thought you should know. Grand Cayman, right? You told me to keep my eyes open, and I'm keeping my eyes open. Deb's been to Grand Cayman."

"Oh okay. Thanks. But plenty of college students spend spring break in the islands, and that doesn't make them criminals. Maybe she had a romp on the beach that's none of your business."

"I know, but she lied about it. Doesn't that make it suspicious?"

"Not to me. She lies about *everything*. Trust me, I know. Pretty girl, but she's got one foot out of bounds. Stay away from her, forget the photo, and go to sleep."

"Gee, thanks, Dad, for the life advice."

"Just trust me, that photo has nothing to do with Parker. Not relevant."

The "just trust me" line pissed Jack off every time he heard it. "Okay, Agent Andrews, I'm so sorry I bothered you."

"Don't be a jerk. And don't be sorry. I did ask you to keep your eyes open. But Deb's travels aren't the issue."

"Yes, sir. Have a good night," Jack said coldly.

"You too."

After the line went dead, Jack walked into the living room. He flopped on the sofa and turned on the television, feverishly flipping from channel to channel. After spending an hour watching football highlights, he stripped down to his boxers and T-shirt, stumbled into the bedroom, and lay down beside a sleeping Amanda. Still unable to sleep, he watched her face in the semidarkness and listened to the soft rhythm of her breathing.

He listened as Amanda breathed in and then back out. So calm. So peaceful. There was something so comforting about being in this simple bedroom with this woman he knew so well. Right now, there was no place he would rather be.

# CHAPTER 60

Terry O'Reilly was intimately familiar with the FBI's Integrated Automated Fingerprint Identification System, a national computer registry that holds fingerprint and background data on nearly a third of all Americans. The fingerprints of every intern and employee who had set foot in Abigail's apartment were run through the system, a generally uneventful process punctuated with the occasional discovery of an undisclosed criminal conviction or an immigration violation. So it was hardly noteworthy when Terry appeared at the New York City FBI office and handed Agent Cedric Davis a box of doughnuts and a Ziploc bag containing a torn envelope.

"Run out of fingerprint cards?" Davis asked with a chuckle as he lifted the plastic bag by the corner and placed it on his desk.

"Something like that. Do you mind checking for latents?"

"Not at all, but first I need to check something else out." Davis opened the box of doughnuts and peered inside. He selected a chocolate-frosted one covered with orange sprinkles. "Is it Halloween already?" he asked as he gulped down the first mouthful of orange and brown, using the back of his hand to wipe a stray sprinkle from his chin.

"A few days early. But at least you know they're fresh."

Davis nodded as he took another large bite of doughnut and took a sip of coffee from the mug on his desk. "Mm-*hmm*," he said with dramatic flair. "Now that is one fine doughnut. But get these things out of here before I eat them all. Drop 'em at the front desk on your way out."

Terry obliged by picking up the box and heading back in the direction from which he had come. A few other agents descended upon him as he went, reaching into the box for their own piece of his largesse. He

194

was glad for their interest. He never knew when he would next need their help.

When the crowd dispersed, only three doughnuts remained in the box. Terry proceeded to carry those to the reception desk, where he imagined they would be gone within a matter of minutes. "Thanks for the doughnuts," Davis yelled out to him. "I'll call you about the prints."

# CHAPTER 61

At three in the morning, a nearby clap of thunder woke Deb with a jolt. Her T-shirt and pillowcase were moist with sweat, the product of both the overzealous radiator in her bedroom and the intense nightmare from which she had just awoken. She had been dreaming about her father. It was a nightmare she had suffered through many times in the years since his unexpected death.

Professor Alan Miller had died as he'd lived, sitting at his desk at Harvard Law School, a thick law book clutched in his hand. There was nothing in his medical history to suggest that an aneurysm would strike him down at age fifty-five. But it had. In an instant, he was gone.

After he died, Deb was shocked to realize how much she missed him. Because of her sense of loss, and because of her constant desire to confront those things she hated most, she had volunteered to clean out his office at Harvard Law. For her, this meant entering the lion's den—returning to the place that embodied everything that her father had done wrong, everything that had hurt her. She would loathe every minute spent in that office. Being there would reopen a lifetime of old wounds. That was why she had to do it.

She had made the right choice. Working though her father's files took her on a journey she needed to take—a voyeuristic trip through the life of which she had desperately tried to be a more important part but somehow never could. Spending that one weekend clearing out his office, she learned more about her dead father than she had in all the years before.

Much of what she saw in his office confirmed what she had always thought of him—that he was a calculating publicity seeker obsessed with acclaim and awards. His desk was overflowing with letters admiring his work and certificates marking his many accomplishments. Yet included among those prized possessions was nearly every handwritten birthday card she had ever sent him. This treasure trove of cards spanned the full range from childhood scribbles to adolescent poems. Flipping through them, she finally realized the depth of what she had lost. She cried for her father for the first time since his death.

As that weekend progressed, she discovered that her father's office contained far more than award letters and childhood drawings. In particular, he had left two file cabinets chock-full of proverbial dirty underwear—files filled with notes and secrets that he had undoubtedly wanted to take to his grave.

Many of those secrets would have destroyed his legacy: love letters from women not his wife, photos from trips taken without his family, drafts of whole sections of his most famous law-review articles written entirely in others' handwriting. Armed with a paper shredder and a box of black garbage bags, the loyal daughter made sure all of those secrets died with her father. For nearly two full days, she shredded file after file, forever silencing the demons contained therein. All except for one, that is. One precious secret was spared this fate.

A lone manila folder tucked away at the back of a file drawer had turned out to be the most valuable possession in Alan Miller's office. Drawn to it by the famous name written on the folder's tab, Deb became nearly breathless when she read the scribbled notes contained inside. Reading through a sheaf of paper torn from a yellow legal pad, she learned what had really happened on that horrible birthday when she'd sat in the Faculty Club, waiting for the father who never came. She learned exactly why he had left her alone and where he had been. And she learned something far more important as well.

She learned how Harold Walker had died.

# CHAPTER 62

Terry O'Reilly was stirring some cream and sugar into a cup of coffee when his cell phone began to vibrate in his pocket. Quickly snapping the lid back on his cup, he lifted it off the counter with one hand while he dug in his pocket with the other. He placed his phone against his ear. "O'Reilly here."

"Top o' the morning to you," said Cedric Davis in a faux Irish brogue.

"Hi there, Cedric. Good morning to you too." Pushing the door open with his elbow, Terry exited the Starbucks and managed to reach the sidewalk without dropping either his coffee or his phone. "Find anything for me?"

"Don't I always?" Davis then reported step-by-step how an FBI technician used a brand-new type of iodine mist to detect the fingerprints on the envelope Terry had given him.

"Come on, Cedric, this isn't a courtroom. Just cut to the chase."

"Very well, old man. We got two hits. One is the doorman, retired NYPD."

"And two?"

"Two is a Jacob Edward Collins. Prints on file from a job at the Massachusetts Supreme Court. No arrests, no other hits. That what you were looking for?"

He could feel his jaw muscles pulse as they tensed. "Jacob Edward Collins?"

"Yep, that's the guy. Registry says he also goes by Jack."

"Thanks, Cedric. I owe you one," Terry said brusquely. "I'll check back with you later," he added then ended the call.

He placed the cup of coffee down by his feet and dialed another call. His heart pounded as he counted the rings. Three... Four... At five, he heard David Dalton's voice. "What's up, Terry?"

"What have you found out about our friend?"

"Well, good fucking morning to you too. I'm doing just great today, thanks for asking."

"Sorry, no time for chitchat."

"Well, let me at least wrap a towel around my nuts then. A guy can't even shower in peace with you around." After a moment of rustling sounds, Dalton continued. "I got nothing for you, my friend. The guy is squeaky clean. Doesn't even surf porn. Seriously, nothing on his computer at all. I mean, who doesn't surf porn?"

"Actually, I don't."

"You serious? Then you're missing out. I like the girl-on-girl shit the best. Way better than the stuff back in the Combat Zone, and it's delivered right to your living room."

"I'll have to try it sometime," Terry said dryly. "But listen, I just got a troubling report from Cedric Davis."

"Good old Cedric. How's that character doing? He got a file on your boy?"

"Yeah, he matched some prints for me. Our guy has been causing a lot of trouble for a special person."

"Seriously? So that's what's got you all grumpy."

"Yeah, it's a problem."

"Whatcha want me to do about it? Maybe pay him a little visit? Hopefully I catch another show from the little lady."

"What the hell are you talking about?" he asked. Clearly, Dalton had raided one too many crack houses for his own good.

"Nothing, brother. It's all good."

"Okay, then. So sit tight a while longer. I don't need you to do anything *yet*."

"Got it. You know where to find me when it's time."

"I'll let you know. But be ready. It could be soon."

# NOVEMBER

# CHAPTER 63

As an alumna of NYU law school, Deb had lifetime privileges to use the law library. However, using them required her to sign in and out, a paper trail that she would rather avoid. Fortunately, she still knew her way around her alma mater and was young enough to look like she belonged there. As a result, a confident walk and warm smile were all she needed to get past the security guard at the school's main entrance on Washington Square South and into the library's main reading room.

Under a beat-up Yankees cap and in her oldest pair of jeans, she fit in perfectly with the crowd of over-caffeinated NYU students spending this November night mastering the intricacies of such scintillating subjects as torts and commercial law. She had been in their place less than a decade earlier. If her experience was any indication, few of them would remember much of what they were trying to learn this evening. And none would ever recall seeing her as she approached one of the library computer terminals and sat in the wooden chair in front of it.

She looked around the room and caught sight of a shoeless blonde curled up in an oversized leather chair, a pair of designer loafers placed neatly on the floor in front of her. She had sat behind a girl just like that in first-year Property, dumb as could be but so very pleased with her five-hundred-dollar shoes. Daddy's little girl, no doubt. She wouldn't last one week at a place like R&H.

After a few more minutes of people watching, Deb turned to the task at hand. She opened an internet browser and connected to the website of the First Bank of Nevis. Sitting in anonymity among the bleary-eyed future lawyers, she typed in the account number and password for Ted Parker's newest account. As she pressed Enter and waited for the screen to refresh, she felt her chest twinge—a momentary pang of insecurity. Was greed getting the most of her? Was she turning a good thing into a disaster?

She sucked in a deep breath and let her doubts fade away. She was only doing what she needed to do. Abigail was getting sicker by the day. She had tortured the old lady enough. It was time for it all to come to an end. She'd promised as much in the letter she dropped on Abigail's doorstep some ten days ago. This was the end of her penitence, the time for Ted Parker to send his final fax.

The computer monitor flickered, and she clicked on the tab marked *Account balance*. Her breath caught as she waited for the figure of ten million dollars to appear, then her stomach dropped when she saw a zero. She refreshed the screen, but the zero still stared back at her.

*What the hell?* She logged out and back in. The zero reappeared.

She turned off the computer, slid the mouse across the tabletop, and stormed out of the library.

Her body tensed with rage as she stepped out into the night air. *Those idiots are messing with the wrong person.*

# CHAPTER 64

It was Friday. Abigail and Ted sat alone at their usual table in the Harvard Club. Plates of muffins and bagels had come and gone. Abigail had drained her third mimosa. A lively conversation had yielded to silent reflection.

"I need to head to the airport pretty soon," Ted said. "Thanks for meeting me early today."

Lost in her own thoughts, Abigail heard the words but said nothing in reply. Instead, she took a sip of cappuccino and looked up at the portrait of Senator Harold Walker. Staring at his strong features and graying hair, she drifted off to memories of the past. Finally, she looked back at Ted. "He was a good man," she said.

"I've met few finer," Ted replied. He reached across the table and gently placed his palm on the back of her hand. Although he was clearly trying to comfort her, his touch provided little solace. Instead, just over eleven years after the senator's death, his widow sat beneath his portrait and silently wallowed in the anguish of her life's most fateful day.

She hadn't heard him coming up the stairs. She didn't know he was there until the door flew open, and he was standing in the doorway. She would always remember how the changing look in his eyes reflected his changing emotions—shifting in an instant from concerned to horrified to furious. She would be forever haunted by the image of his wide eyes as he discovered her betrayal.

Until that moment, she had justified her affair as her way of dealing with the loneliness of his long absences. She knew on one level she was being monumentally selfish. But on another she could cast it as a giving gesture. The alternative would have been for her to make greater demands on her husband—to tell him he needed to spend more time at

203

home, to tell him that she feared the silence of an empty home almost as much as she feared her always-looming death. Yet such demands, however justified, would have stifled his career. On one level, she had done it all for him.

But she never had a chance to say all of that. She never had a chance to tell him how sorry she was. And neither had Ted. No chance to explain, as if he ever could, how his naked body lying on top of hers, his back glistening with the sweat of their passion, was not the deepest-possible betrayal of the man who had helped build his entire career.

There was no time for explaining that day. Just time for screaming and sirens and wailing and guilt.

She kept her gaze on the tablecloth as she spoke to her former lover. "We killed him, you and I. I've never been able to forget that—not even for an instant."

"We didn't *kill* him," Ted replied sharply.

She knew that in a technical sense, he was right. In the eyes of the law, there was no crime committed that day. Just a tragic accident. She had been told as much by one of the finest legal minds in American criminal law, Professor Alan Miller. For as a hysterical Abigail called 9-1-1, an equally frantic Ted called his old professor for advice. Professor Miller dropped everything to come to the aid of his former student's famous client, meeting her at the hospital just minutes after the ambulance arrived there.

"No, we didn't kill him," Ted repeated. "It wasn't our fault."

"Not our fault, eh? Keep telling yourself that, dear. Maybe one day you'll even believe it. But *I* will always know the truth."

Her eyes left the tablecloth as she looked up at the portrait of her husband and continued in a whisper, "And so will he."

AS TED AND ABIGAIL stepped out of the Harvard Club, a taxi pulled up to the curb in front of them. The door popped open from inside.

Ted took a step back and allowed the occupant to step onto the pavement.

"Thanks, pal," said the heavyset man in a rumpled dark suit. He juggled an oversized cup of coffee in one hand and a brown paper bag in the other. "Guess I need an extra hand."

"No problem," Ted replied. "After you, Abby," he said as he held the door open for his companion. "I'll drop you off on the way to LaGuardia."

Ted noticed that the man had paused mid-sidewalk and was intently looking back at them.

"Can I help you? You seem a bit lost."

"Um, no," the man replied. He brought the coffee cup to his lips and took a large swallow then wiped his ragged mustache with the back of his hand. "I'm all set."

# CHAPTER 65

"Happy anniversary, Amanda." Jack smiled as he moved his empty plate aside and slid a box across the linen tablecloth.

The only thing more dramatic than the jewelry they sold at Peter Suchy Jewelers was the way the salespeople wrapped the store's gift boxes. A kaleidoscope of colored paper and ribbons surrounded the small white box. She gently peeled it all away and peered inside.

"Oh God, it's gorgeous." She wrapped the vintage 1940s bracelet around her wrist and leaned across the table to kiss her husband. "I love it. It's beautiful."

"So are you," he replied without missing a beat.

"Can I ask you something?" Amanda's voice quivered as she spoke.

"Of course. What's up?"

"Should we take a vacation this winter?"

"Funny you should mention that." He reached into his jacket pocket and pulled out a photo of the Four Seasons in Nevis. He handed it to her, watching her eyes dance across the picture as she struggled to figure out what it meant. "I'm thinking Nevis in February," he blurted, almost involuntarily. "The Four Seasons. An ocean-view room. Are you free?"

"Absolutely. I'd love nothing more." A tear formed in the corner of her right eye and rolled down her cheek.

"Are you crying?"

"Happy tears." She sniffled and pressed her napkin against her face. "But can I ask another question?" she asked, even more timidly than before.

"Sure."

"Should we talk about *her*?"

He felt a heaviness in his gut. "Sure, I guess."

206

Amanda looked straight at him. "Are you having an affair?" she asked before looking down at the tablecloth.

"Oh God, of course not."

"Of course not?" she asked, briefly looking up.

"Amanda, it was one stupid kiss, that's all. One stupid kiss, and I was an idiot for letting it happen. I'm not having an *affair* with her. We're barely even still friends."

"Really?"

"Really. She's a lying backstabber. Nothing would ever have happened if it weren't for..."

"For what?"

He took a deep breath. "Nothing. It's silly."

She glared at him. "For what?" she repeated, much firmer than before.

"It turns out that Deb and I almost met back at Harvard. I missed her by an instant. And then, all these years later, there she is. So that messed with me a bit. What was I supposed to make of that?"

Amanda rolled her wineglass in her hand, her eyes following the ruby-colored shadows as they cascaded across the table.

"That's a crazy coincidence. Kind of like sitting next to someone in a bar."

"That's not quite the same."

"Why not?" she asked, her eyes now staring right at his. They burned with intensity, but her tone was kinder than he deserved. "Because you actually did that? So no wondering about how it could have turned out?"

"It's just—"

"It's just what? So, let's say you met her. Then what? You guys get married and live happily ever after? Or maybe you date for a while, break up, and in the meantime a certain girl from Holy Cross ends up with that blond hunk roommate of yours. And now I'm married to a congressman."

"You're too smart for him," Jack chided, trying to lighten the mood.

"A guy with his dimples doesn't need to be smart."

Jack felt his body tense with jealousy as he imagined Amanda on Scott Mitchell's arm. "Okay, good point," he conceded meekly.

"Glad you agree, because I'm right on this. You know what else? I'm thinking that New York was one big mistake. Lots of money but lots of trouble. If they come as a package, we don't need 'em."

"I'm not so sure. Stamford still seems like the minor leagues. A little firm just plugging along. I can do so much more."

"Yes, you can," she agreed unflinchingly. "And you proved that to yourself. Now comes the bigger question: can't you do 'so much more' while surrounded by people who genuinely care about you? You don't have to be the next Ted Parker, sitting behind a fancy desk in a big New York City office. I'd rather you be a normal person."

"Ted's normal," he protested.

"You think?"

"Actually, no." He sighed. "Truth be told, he may be a criminal."

"You serious?" Her eyes lit up.

"Actually, I am. That's a big part of why I've been so tense lately. I can't figure out what mess I walked into."

"So let me see if I have this right. Ted's a criminal and his right-hand woman is a lying whore. That about sum it up?"

"Quite well, actually."

"So what happens to their clients if you walk out the door?"

"Huh?"

"Their *clients*," she repeated, her eyes sparkling.

"They stay at R&H, I guess. I mean it's not like the world knows what really goes on at that place..." He paused, distracted by Amanda's broadening smile.

"So maybe..." he continued.

"So maybe," his wife parroted before completing his sentence for him, "you need to show the world the truth."

# CHAPTER 66

Deb's Sunday mornings with Ben always included breakfast at the Avon Diner, the self-proclaimed home of the best French toast in all of Hartford County. She sat in the passenger seat as the car turned west onto Route 44 and headed from Simsbury toward Avon. As they crossed the town line, she slid slightly closer to him and placed her hand on the inside of his leg. "You know that your father is incredibly proud of you, right?"

"Huh? I know nothing of the kind."

"Come on, seriously." She stroked his leg. "He couldn't be more proud."

"Let's not go there this morning." His eyes never left the road as he spoke. "I'm the son of the great Ted Parker. I work at a two-bit trust company in a third-rate city. I'm not sure that's exactly the stuff of father-son legends. Can't we just get some breakfast?"

"You think your dad wants you to be just like him?" she pressed. "You think he feels he's done everything exactly right? You know your dad a lot better than I do, but I don't think so."

Ben said nothing in reply. If he was thinking about anything other than the road in front of him, it was not evident from his lifeless expression. This was probably the wrong time for this conversation, but she had few other options. Sundays always passed quickly, and soon enough she would be on an Amtrak heading back to New York City. She needed to know what Ben knew about the bank account in Nevis. And she needed to know soon.

She tried a new approach. "I heard something at work."

He glanced over at her. "Huh?"

"I don't want to meddle in your business. I never have, and I really don't want to, but there is something I need to ask you." She paused, feigning reluctance to continue this conversation. "Is anything going on with Abigail Walker?" She edged away from him as she spoke, expecting him to go ballistic. The two of them had a clear rule: no talk about clients. Sure, they often nibbled around the edges of that restriction. They would have little to say to each other had they not, for their best stories all had some connection to the eccentric clients they served. Yet, unlike most of their casual conversational references to work, Deb's last question was far more direct and pointed than it should have been.

"I'm not going there," he replied, surprisingly calmly.

"I'm sorry to push you on this, but she's your father's most important client. He wants you handling her account for a reason and—"

He slapped his palm on the steering wheel. Ballistic had arrived. "Damn it. He wants me handling her account because the *National Enquirer* hasn't figured out where Hartford is. That's it. Let's drop it. I mean it." His knuckles turned white as he tightened his grip on the wheel.

"Not true. Not true," she muttered just loudly enough for him to hear.

He said nothing in response. She could feel the heat radiating off his reddened face. His eyes were fixed on the road as he slowed to a stop at a red light.

"Can I ask you just one more question?" she asked sheepishly. "Promise me you'll answer it. And promise me also that you'll forget I ever asked it."

"Fine."

"You promise?"

"Yeah, whatever, I promise."

"Did you father ever say anything to you about a bank account in Nevis?"

She watched his face intently but saw no reaction.

"Nevis, the island? I know he and Suzy have been to the Four Seasons a bunch of times. Beyond that, he's never mentioned it."

Deb had known Ben long enough to know he wasn't being coy. He had no clue about Nevis. The account at the First Bank of Nevis was empty because he hadn't funded it. And if he hadn't funded it, that could only mean one thing—Ted had never asked him to.

She didn't know whether to be confused or furious. In reality, she was both. But she also knew that now was not the time to yield to either emotion. She had work to do. And her first task was to recover from her impulsively foolish choice of having this conversation. "Hmmm. I'll have to ask Jack what he was talking about," she said, missing no opportunity to once again drag that name into the mix. "I guess I have it wrong. Perhaps it's a different client. Boy, that was stupid."

"Don't sweat it. But really, let's drop this whole thing."

She placed her hand back on his leg and slid it slowly upward. "Fair enough. Do you know what I'm thinking about now?"

"Not a clue."

"French toast. Hot, steaming plates of French toast."

"Now that's something I know a lot about," Ben said as the car picked up speed.

# CHAPTER 67

Deb stood between two bookshelves at the back of the R&H library, a room in which she rarely even ventured. This had once been a bustling research center. Now it was a glorified warehouse for materials too old, or too esoteric, to be on Westlaw. She pulled a dusty treatise off the shelf and flipped through the index, trying to find the century-old law that governed a client's trust account. She paused as she heard two men step into the room.

"So what's the big secret?" She recognized Clay Warren's voice.

"Did you hear they passed her over?" Steve Oswald replied in his distinctive whine as the door shut with a thud.

"I know. Billed more hours than any associate in firm history and gets nothing to show for it. That's nuts."

"Well, *she's* nuts—we both know that part." Both of them laughed.

"Yeah, plus I've always wondered about those hours. She must bill for all her smoking breaks."

"Wouldn't surprise me. At least the firm did right by some of the others. I was especially glad to see two women in M&A."

"Yeah, but nothing in T&E? I can't imagine Parker couldn't get it done. It should have been a slam dunk."

"You didn't hear?"

"Hear *what*?"

"The best part. Parker didn't go to bat for her. When Deb came up for a vote, he did nothing to help her. Sat there mute. Didn't say a single word."

"That can't be?"

"Mary Vincent told me herself. Thought you and I deserved to know."

"Wow. *Seriously?* I never saw that one coming. Maybe Parker has some integrity after all. That woman's got some freaky power over him, but at the end of the day, he did what's right by the firm. You have to give him credit for that."

"Yeah, true enough. Can you imagine her as a *partner*? She already acts like she runs the firm. And, as we both know, she's a crappy lawyer anyway. Sure she's smart, but she's way too aggressive."

"That's for sure."

"Okay, so that's the news for today. I need to get some documents out but had to share this with you."

"Thanks for that. Made my day."

"And hey, this all stays between us, right? Mary will be pissed if this goes beyond us."

"Of course. Who am I going to tell? Deb?"

"Oh man, she would freak. Totally freak."

"I'd pay to see that."

"No, you wouldn't."

After another round of laughter, the door opened and shut.

Deb stood in silence, sucking in deep breaths, trying as hard as she could to suppress her rising tears. *What a bastard Ted was. Backstabbing, ungrateful piece of crap.* She had never felt more betrayed. Given her history, that was saying an awful lot.

She held herself together as best she could as she left the library and walked quickly past a line of secretarial desks. Tears started to flow uncontrollably as she stepped into her office and slammed the door behind her. Her heart pounded mercilessly. Her lungs struggled to capture enough air. She grabbed a bottle of Ativan out of her desk drawer and placed two of the tablets under her tongue. Her pounding heart began to slow, her feelings of fury slowly yielding to a more controlled sadness. She pressed a tissue against her eyes and thought about the conversation she had just overheard.

The petty barbs didn't bother her. These morons could call her whatever names they wanted. They could call her stupid, they could question her talents. She was twice the lawyer that either of them was, and they damn well knew it. Nobody gave a crap what they thought, and that certainly included her.

But the partnership vote was another matter entirely. She pictured Ted sitting in that fancy conference room, saying nothing on her behalf. He was a superstar of the firm. He controlled its most famous clients, generating more revenue than just about anyone else. And if Mary Vincent or any of those other losers said a single negative thing about her, he could have jumped to her defense. He should have had her back. But he didn't. He hung her out.

She thought back to their meeting in his office, where he blathered on about poor economics and firm politics. He had fought for her but lost, he'd said. *Bullshit. It was all bullshit.*

She was done. She had long known that she needed to get away from this place where she had already wasted far too much of her life. But now she was finally ready. It was time to dump Ted and make a new life—a fresh start. But she was going to do that on her terms, not theirs.

Despite her rising anger, her breathing had become regular and slow, her heart back to its regular beat. The Ativan was doing its job, calming her down. But she didn't want to be calm. She wanted war.

*How dare they? Screw all of them.*

She grabbed her coat and flung open her office door. A minute later, she was in the elevator, heading for the street.

# CHAPTER 68

S carcely a second after a waitress in black pants and a red polo shirt placed two steaming plates of eggs, bacon, hash browns, and toast on the dingy Formica countertop, Bob Masterson grabbed his fork and shoveled a pile of scrambled eggs into his mouth. Washing it down with a gulp of coffee, he addressed his dining companion.

"I'm telling you," Bob said while reloading his fork, "this is the best breakfast in New York City."

"I hope you're right," Joe Andrews replied. He took his first tentative forkful off his heaping plate. As he swallowed, he politely nodded in assent. "I might just have to agree."

"Bet there's no place like this in DC."

"Come down sometime and see," Joe offered as he subtly used a wad of paper napkins to blot the grease off his hash browns.

"Deal."

After three months of working with Bob, Joe felt genuine sorrow knowing that this would be their last breakfast together, at least for now. He was getting ready to head back to DC to resume his permanent assignment in the nation's capital. Bob was staying in New York, continuing work on the dozens of files he had largely ignored during their pursuit of Ted Parker.

Although Joe didn't taste anything particularly spectacular about the food, it was great to eat a greasy breakfast with Bob. Tucked away in this small diner, he felt far more alive than he ever had sitting behind a desk in Washington—less like a bureaucrat and more like a cop. And through his whole life, from elementary school through law school, that was all he had ever wanted to be.

Now that cop sat in a New York City diner, eating a breakfast of eggs and bacon as he prepared to leave the city that had been home for the past twelve weeks. In many ways, Bob Masterson was right when he advertised this meal as the best breakfast in New York City. It wasn't the eggs or the bacon that would make this a memorable morning. It was the companionship, the camaraderie.

Special Agent Joseph Andrews was about to leave New York City in bitter disappointment. But thanks to the kindness of his new friend Bob, he would do so with a full belly and an equally full heart.

# CHAPTER 69

J ack sat at his desk, the contents of Michael Putnam's voluminous files spread in front of him. The documents that R&H had drafted years earlier had withstood the test of time. Jack's minor update had taken just a few minutes' work. *The firm won't get rich off this one,* he thought.

*I wonder?* He sifted through the stack of files and pulled out the one marked Billing. He flipped through the large piles of bills and mentally tallied the total for the past two years of legal research and tax filings until he was over two hundred thousand dollars. *Wow, Ted sure knows how to bill.*

He then flipped through the internal time reports used to generate the bills until something caught his eye. *Deb? What does she have to do with tax returns?* He pulled out the next report and saw the same thing. Five hours of her time charged to *tax-return review* in one month. Another five in the next. A stream of sixty hours a year Jack was quite certain she never worked.

Jack set the time reports next to the actual bills and compared them. *Unbelievable. Totally unbelievable.*

He grabbed the phone and called Steve Oswald's office.

"Hey, Jack. What's up?"

"A quick question for you: has Deb Miller ever worked on Michael Putnam's 1041s?"

"Nope. Clay and I coordinate them all. Parker's the billing partner, but the tax group does the work."

"You sure?"

"Yeah, positive. Why, what's up?"

"Swing by my office, and I'll show you. I think I've just figured out how Deb bills all those hours."

"I'll be there in five minutes."

"Great. And when you get here, I have something else to talk about."

———— ◉ ————

THREE HOURS LATER, long after Clay Warren had joined them, Jack and Steve finished their conversation. A stack of billing files was heaped on the corner of Jack's desk. In a half dozen of them, the client had been repeatedly billed for Deb Miller's *tax-return review*, even though she never worked on the matter.

"You guys are welcome to think about it more," Jack offered as he stood from his desk and began loading the files onto a cart.

"No reason," Clay said. "I've heard enough."

"Me too," Steve agreed.

Jack pressed his hands into his stomach, trying to loosen the cramp in his gut. Then he patted the pile of fresh photocopies in the middle of his desk. "Once we hand these over, there's no turning back."

"Yeah, but we have no other choice," Steve responded. "Call your friend."

# CHAPTER 70

Susan Parker shot her husband a disapproving glance as he slipped out of bed, his cell phone pressed against his ear. As he stepped onto the cold marble floor of the master bathroom and shut the door behind him, he was equally annoyed. He could count on one hand the number of times Deb had called him at home. He could count on one finger the number of times she had done so while so obviously impaired.

"You suck, Ted. You totally suck."

He had heard a lot worse language in his three decades as a New York City lawyer. But he'd never been spoken to that way by one of his associates, especially not at almost midnight. Yet despite his anger, his first response, as it so often was with her, was to try to defuse the situation. "Okay, perhaps we should just talk in the morning."

"No, we shouldn't. There's nothing more to say."

"Look, would you like to tell me why you're so upset, or should we just get off the phone?" The pitch of his voice rose as he spoke. He felt like he was speaking to a small child, trying to defuse a temper tantrum. "I don't know why you're so angry."

"You know *exactly* why I'm so angry. You do. Yes, you do."

He wasn't sure if she was sobbing or laughing on the other end of the line. It sounded like a blend of both. She sniffled audibly and then launched another verbal salvo. "I used to love you. I used to worship you. But you totally sold me out."

He tried to interrupt her but couldn't get a word in edgewise as she continued to ramble on. "You have disappointed me," she said. "You have disappointed me so very much."

"Look, it's very late," he interjected, a bit more sternly than before. "I'm sorry for whatever has you so upset. But I don't think this is the time or the way to talk about it. Let's talk tomorrow, okay? First thing. I'm sure we can figure it out."

She said nothing in response for what seemed like an eternity. *What the hell is going on with her?* He had dealt with her moodiness and petulance before. But he had never heard her like this. Never so completely unwound, so clearly spiraling out of control.

After a few more moments of blessed silence, she was back at it. "You have disappointed me, oh great Ted Parker," she hissed through the phone. "The great Ted Parker. Ha! Well, know what? I hate being disappointed. And I hate you."

With that, the line went silent.

---

AFTER THROWING HER cell phone on her bed, Deb paced from one side of her bedroom to the other. She wasn't the least bit tired. She had spent the whole evening working herself into a frenzy about what she had overheard in the R&H library. Her decision to chase six shots of tequila with a line of cocaine at a bar on MacDougal Street had served only to increase her level of hostility.

The coke still had her pretty wired, and the telephone battle with Ted had done nothing to calm her down. As she continued to retrace the same path back and forth across her bedroom rug, pure hatred pumped through her veins. She wanted revenge, the taste of blood.

And then, as if by divine inspiration, a plan came to her.

Tomorrow, she had the incredibly good fortune of having her annual appointment with her gynecologist. She didn't generally relish the thought of a pap smear and another lecture about safe sex. However, on this day, it represented the best stroke of luck she could ever hope for. Everyone knew about her appointment. Jack had already agreed to arrive early to cover for her. *It's perfect.*

She sat on the edge of her bed and opened her laptop. She cackled as she pounded away at the keyboard, basking in the brilliance of her plan and relishing the pain she was about to cause.

When the typing was finished, she sent a single page to her printer and looked at the clock. It was just past midnight. This new day would be the best of her entire life.

# CHAPTER 71

A t precisely 7:39 a.m., Deb let out an audible yawn as she entered the lobby of 1593 Broadway. She was operating on scarcely four hours of sleep after her tequila- and cocaine-fueled bender. Plus, it was more than an hour before she normally arrived for work. Exactly as expected, she recognized no one as she strode across the largely desolate lobby. There was one notable exception: Bert.

Albert Cranshaw, as he was formally known, was pushing seventy, an employee of 1593 Broadway since the day it was built and the first face Deb saw every morning as she stepped into the building's marble-covered lobby. When he first started working in the building, he was little more than a janitor, spending his days cleaning the lobby floor, polishing brass, and keeping a general eye on the place. However, the owners of 1593 Broadway had long since installed an elaborate new security system in the main lobby, directing all those entering the building through a group of turnstiles, and requiring every employee entering or leaving the building to swipe an electronic ID card. Visitors didn't have those ID cards, and that was where Bert fit in. He was the keeper of the visitor log and manned the desk sitting next to the one narrow passageway into the lobby not blocked by a turnstile. If anyone without an ID card needed to gain access to 1593 Broadway, he would need to speak to Bert.

The elderly Bert wasn't perfect for the job. He had no police background, and he was not in particularly robust physical shape. His memory for names and details, too, was patchy at best. A terrorist intent on infiltrating 1593 Broadway could be in the building's penthouse before Bert realized what had happened. But Bert was charming and cheerful. His grandfatherly demeanor drew attention away from the fact that sitting just beyond him was an armed security guard monitoring a bank of high-tech surveillance cameras.

"Good morning, sweetheart," Bert said with a smile as he saw Deb approach. "How are you today?"

She sighed. "Harassed and frazzled. I have a doctor's appointment and left the paperwork and my ID upstairs. I just need to grab them and then run back out."

"Of course," he said.

She strode through the unguarded passageway and toward the elevators. The other security guard said nothing as she passed by him as well.

"You're the best, Bert," she shouted back over her shoulder. "I'll see you in a minute."

Upon reaching the elevators, she pushed the up button, which illuminated for only an instant before the elevator doors opened in front of her. She stepped inside and pushed forty-three. Then, as an afterthought, she pushed the buttons for forty-four and, selected at random, twenty-nine. She didn't think there could possibly be any logs of where individual elevators had gone but wanted to cover her every track just in case.

Talking to Bert had been one necessary exception in her effort to arrive undetected, but by the end of the day he would probably forget having seen her. Plus, if anyone tried to figure out when she'd arrived for work that day, they wouldn't ask senile old Bert. They would check the electronic records generated by her identification card. And that card remained where it had been all morning, carefully tucked away in the handbag now hanging off her right shoulder.

After the doors opened and closed on floor twenty-nine without incident, the elevator arrived at the forty-third floor. Located just below the main entrance to R&H, this floor housed some smaller associate and paralegal offices, a makeshift kitchen, and the firm's administrative heart: rooms devoted to telecommunications, photocopying, mail, and files.

In contrast to the lushly appointed hallway and grand reception area that greeted those arriving at the main floor above, the forty-third floor offered no such trappings. This was a place where work was done, not one where impressions were made. Accordingly, the doors were made of dinged metal rather than polished mahogany. Industrial-strength locks replaced ornate brass doorknobs. A paper sign taped crookedly on one door identified the delivery entrance, while the remaining doors on the floor were unmarked and completely nondescript.

Only those who had worked at R&H for some time would know that one of those unmarked doors opened into a dark hallway near a rarely used section of the file room. Amid the high-tech security of 1593 Broadway, this door had been left vulnerable, protected solely by a single-cylinder lock—the original one installed when R&H had first moved its offices to the building. Neither security cameras nor an electronic keypad recorded who entered or exited through it.

Years ago, Deb had been given a copy of the key to that door by a member of the mailroom staff. "Great way to sneak back in after a smoke," he had told her, and she'd used it for that purpose many times before.

She slid the key into the old lock, turned it, and pulled open the heavy door. As she walked down the silent hallway beyond, she felt the tension rising through her body. *Please, nobody be down here this early*, she prayed. If she did bump into anyone, it would not be the end of the world. She would say she was fetching an old file, an innocuous task that would have brought an associate to this part of the hallway. Yet, as much as she had prepared herself for that possibility, it never came to pass. There were no unexpected encounters. Indeed, there were no signs of life.

Silently, she slipped to the back of the records room, soon reaching an area with a photocopier and an old fax machine. Nobody used this space much anymore. The scope and pace of modern legal work had become such that only a few of the firm's records were actually kept on-site at 1593 Broadway. Most were now housed in a high-tech warehouse on the outskirts of Newark. And when those files needed to be copied or distributed, the task would fall to that facility's four employees and their six industrial-sized photocopiers. The little fax machine in front of her was a relic from an earlier time. Yet it was perfectly suited for this morning's task.

She pulled a single page of paper from her handbag and slid it into the fax machine. After dialing a telephone number she knew by heart, she pushed the green button marked *send* and listened as the fax dialed the number and transmitted its data. Soon, the small LCD screen flashed two magic letters: OK.

Her mission accomplished, she slipped the paper back in her handbag then retraced her steps in silence and semidarkness to the waiting elevator car. She looked at her watch. It was still well before eight, early enough that her odds of meeting anyone on the way out were slim but not quite none. As the elevator made its way back downward toward the lobby, she watched with anticipation as the numbers on the elevator's display panel counted down from forty-three to one.

It felt like an eternity before she arrived back in the lobby and, involuntarily holding her breath, waited for the elevator to open. The brass doors slid apart to reveal just three waiting passengers, none of whom worked at R&H. Avoiding eye contact as best she could, Deb slipped between them to cross the lobby and leave through the same visitors' passageway where she'd entered a few moments before.

"Bert, you're a lifesaver," she gushed as she strode back past him. "I'll see you later on."

She quickly reached the revolving doors at the far end of the lobby. After spinning through them and stepping into the brisk November air, she turned westward on 47th Street, heading away from the throng of morning commuters. Glancing back over her shoulder, she spotted an approaching taxi and raised her hand to hail it.

Ten minutes later, the taxi dropped her at the elegant Upper West Side brownstone housing the office of her gynecologist, Dr. Kimberly Thomas, a woman who, if history was any guide, had delivered a baby in the wee hours of this morning and was already running more than an hour behind schedule. And so when Deb arrived at 8:05 a.m. for her seven-thirty appointment, she joined the other women in Thomas's waiting room, reading magazines, tapping at their phones, and making occasional comments about how much they loved this doctor even though she always ran late.

After a few minutes, another woman stepped into the crowded waiting room and sat down next to Deb. "It's packed in here," she observed. "How long have you been waiting?"

Deb looked at her watch, pretending to be calculating the exact answer. "It's been almost an hour."

---

AT 8:22, DEB PUT DOWN her magazine, pulled her cell phone out of her purse, and dialed Jack's office.

"How is it being in charge over there?"

He laughed. "I've needed an extra cup of coffee this morning, but everything is under control."

"How early did you get in?"

"Around seven thirty. A little early for my taste, but I was able to get everything done for the Taylors without any distractions. It's sure quiet around here in the mornings."

"I wouldn't know. I'm not exactly an early riser myself."

"Good point," he conceded.

"Well, thanks again for covering for me," she said. "I really appreciate it. I've been stuck here for an hour and haven't gotten anywhere."

"Don't worry about it. I'll handle anything that comes up."

"Super. Thanks. Hey, is Ted in a good mood?"

"I don't know. I haven't seen him yet."

"Haven't seen him yet? You didn't show up that early to not get the benefit of a little face time. Go down the hall and see him."

"Okay, maybe I will."

"Not *maybe*. You *have* to go see him. Tell him I called to say I'm running later than I expected. Ask him if you need to help prep for any of his morning meetings. I know the Williamses are coming in at ten."

"Okay, I can do that."

"You're the best. I need to run, though."

She slipped her phone back into her handbag and grabbed the magazine back off the table. As she mindlessly flipped through the pages, she chuckled as she imagined Jack striding into Ted's office to announce his early arrival. *What a moron.*

# CHAPTER 72

While Rosa was in the kitchen, fixing tea and breakfast, Abigail sat in the dining room and read the *New York Times*. The mayor had given a speech the prior evening, setting out an ambitious agenda for the city both he and Abigail called home.

As Abigail read through the details of the mayor's proposals to improve the city's worst public schools, Rosa stepped into the room with a steaming cup of Earl Grey.

"I think I'll take this into my office," Abigail said. "The morning light is lovely this time of year."

She stood from the table and took the cup of tea from Rosa's hand. Inhaling the scent of spicy orange, she crossed into the small office in the next room and headed toward the antique writing desk tucked beneath the window. Along the way, she paused in front of a larger desk buried under stacks of correspondence. Perched on the corner of that desk was a multifunction printer, a single piece of paper sticking out of the top. She grabbed the sheet of paper and began to read.

A moment later, her teacup crashed against the floor. As she reread the contents of the faxed page, her entire body began to quake. Her tormentor was back. And he was angry. She had defied him, failed to meet his latest demands. And, as the last line of the fax perplexingly added, she had done something more. *You have disappointed me*, it read, *and I hate being disappointed*.

Abigail was terrified, but also furious. This was all Ted's fault. *He* was the one who said to ignore that last letter. *He* said, "So let's just stop." She snatched a telephone off the table and dialed the number she dialed in every moment of fear or fury. As the phone rang in Ted's office, her eyes continued darting across the faxed page.

Suddenly she noticed something that sent a wave of nausea flowing through her body—the small capital letters on the fax header. She felt her stomach tense as her hands began trembling even more violently than before. "Oh my God," she said aloud even though there was no one in the room to hear her. "That simply can't be."

She continued muttering to herself as she reread the words printed in block letters on the fax's top corner. *Reynolds & Harris.* Not possible. But it was. The words were crystal clear. The fax had come from R&H.

She disconnected the call to Ted and frantically dialed a different number. "Terry," she cried, "I need you. I need you *now*."

"What's wrong?" he asked with obvious alarm.

She didn't immediately reply. She was still staring at the header on the fax, trying to figure out its significance. Had her tormenter slipped up by revealing his location in that way? Or was it intentional, the ultimate sign of hubris? Either thought filled her with dread. "I just received a very troubling fax from R&H."

"Troubling how?"

"I'll explain it all when you get here. Just please come quickly. I need you. I really do."

# CHAPTER 73

Whenever he ate lunch at Hunan Palace, Jack never had to wait more than five minutes to be served. Today was no exception. It had been just over five minutes since he and Deb had ordered their lunch, and steaming plates of chicken and broccoli and shrimp lo mein had already magically appeared on the white tablecloth in front of them.

He snagged a piece of chicken between his chopsticks and looked across the table at her. So much had changed since the first time they shared lunch in this restaurant. The spell had been broken. He had finally come to see her many darker attributes. Crass. Unpredictable. Monumentally self-absorbed.

He doubted whether anything she did was genuine. But there was one lie in particular that had continued to gnaw at him—one last puzzle he needed to solve.

"Remember how you talked me into that Nevis trip?" he asked casually.

"Kind of," she replied without taking her eyes off her shrimp.

"I forgot why we picked that place."

"I think it was a toss-up between there and Detroit." She plucked another shrimp from the plateful of steaming noodles. "I think you were leaning toward Detroit for its weather."

"Really, be serious."

"Serious about what?" She lowered her chopsticks toward her plate and nudged a rogue slice of carrot toward the edge. "I said you should go away in the winter, and somehow we got talking about Nevis," she said, nonchalantly twisting some lo mein. "Ted has been there and loves it. Not sure there's more to it than that."

"Plus, you've been there too, right?"

She looked up at him, her lips pressed together tensely. "Nope. Never been there. I told you, I've never been south of Florida." She looked back at her food.

"Not even the Caymans?"

She slammed her chopsticks on the tablecloth and stared at him, nostrils flaring. "What's with the inquest?"

"It's not an inquest. I'm just trying to have a conversation." He fumbled with a piece of broccoli. "Friends have conversations," he said as he dropped the vegetable casually into his mouth.

"Well, it's bizarre. Let's just change the subject."

"Well, have you?"

"Jesus, what's with you today? Show up early one morning, and you're all cranky? What the hell do you care about my travel history?" She snatched her chopsticks off the table and looked back at her plate. "Mind your own business."

"Just curious, that's all."

"Just annoying is more like it."

After an awkward pause, he deliberately softened his tone. "You're so fun to get upset," he said, forcing himself to chuckle. "You got so serious on me. 'What's with the inquest?'" he parroted. "I think *you're* the one who needs more sleep."

"Oh come on, I wasn't being serious."

"Oh yes, you were. Like I touched some kind of nerve. It was just an innocent question—I'm still thinking about my vacation plans. Not sure I picked the right island."

"God, so *that's* it! You really can't make a decision, can you? You're pathetic. Just go to Nevis. Have a great time. Send me a postcard. But just drop it now, okay?"

"Absolutely." Jack picked at his food for a moment, his body tensing as he brooded about all that had happened in his three months at R&H. *Just drop it, eh?* "You're a piece of work."

"Now what are you talking about?" Her cheeks were reddening once again.

"I don't ever know what you're really thinking. I don't even know if we were ever really friends. Were we?"

"Of course we were friends." She reached across the table and patted his hand. "We *are* friends. I adore you."

"As much as you adore Steve Oswald, or even more?"

She snapped upright as she yanked her hand away from his. "Seriously, what the hell has gotten into you today?"

"Spring break. Spring break, you liar. You have been to Grand Cayman, and I damn well know it."

"What the hell? How do you—"

"You mentioned it one night at dinner. You were pretty drunk, like usual. Guess you don't remember it."

"You are full of crap." The flush of redness moved up from her cheeks to the tips of her ears. "Who told you about that?"

"So you admit it?"

"Tell me who told you that. Right now." Her shoulders heaved up and down as she breathed, her eyes locked on his in fury.

He felt a tinge of panic in his gut. It felt good to turn the tables on her, but her rising anger was intimidating, and his confidence was fading fast. "It doesn't matter."

Her entire face was now the color of raw meat. Her jaw muscles pulsed as she spoke. "It *does* matter. Tell me the truth right now. Who told you about that trip?"

"I just guessed." He could hear the quiver of panic in his own voice.

"You're a liar."

"Maybe I am," he said, boldly leaning toward her. "Fits right in around here."

She slid her chair back from the table and stood. "You're a fucking liar," she boomed, her voice attracting stares from throughout the restaurant. "I hope you enjoyed working at R&H. Time to go crawling back to Daddy."

———●———

AS HE STEPPED OUTSIDE, Jack dialed Amanda's number.

"Everything okay?" she asked, a shrill hint of nervousness evident in her voice. "You never call me during the day."

"Yeah, yeah. Sorry to scare you, but I think I might have just gotten myself fired."

"Seriously?"

"Maybe. I just lost my cool with Deb. Not exactly the way you and I planned it, but I have to admit it felt awfully good."

"Good for you," she said. "And what about Joe?"

"Gave him everything this morning."

"Then get the hell out of there before everything blows up."

# CHAPTER 74

Ted looked up from his desk just as Deb sat down across from him. "I assume you're here to apologize," he said. "That phone call last night was way over the line."

"He needs to go! Right now. I'm so done with him!" She sniffled as she rubbed her nose with the back of her hand.

"Excuse me?"

"Jack is a total jerk. I want him gone."

"Look, I don't know what—"

"I want him gone. Now!"

Ted had spent way too many years working his way up the R&H hierarchy to be spoken to this way by an associate. Twice in one day was twice more than he could handle. "How dare you come in here and act like this! Since when do you make hiring decisions?"

"Since right now." She was as intense as he had ever seen her, her lips quivering with anger. "You're going to fire him. He needs to go."

"Look, Deb, I'm about out of patience with you. You need to pull it back together, okay?"

"No, not okay." She sniffled again. "Not okay at all, asshole."

"*Get out!* Now get yourself out of here before someone says something they will really regret."

"Regret, huh? You know what, Ted? You're such an idiot. You should know better than to mess with me, and you've done it way too much lately."

"What the hell is wrong with you?"

"You are. You sit behind your fancy desk and act like you're in charge of me. But you're not. And the sooner you accept that, the better off you will be."

"Not one more word." He raised a pointed finger in her direction. "Get out!"

"Oh my." She laughed maniacally. "You are so scary." She stood and placed her hands on the top of his desk, facing him eye to eye from just inches away. "Now, I'm going away for the weekend, and you're going to do what I asked. *Or else.*"

"Get out of here!" he said, standing from his chair. "This craziness is going to be very hard to forgive."

"Oh yes, some things are hard to forgive," she said as she lifted her palms from his desk and stood upright. "And you of all people should know that."

———————

TERRY O'REILLY WAS thirty blocks uptown, having an equally intense conversation with David Dalton.

"Bastard," Dalton said. "Greedy bastard."

"Sick bastard, if you ask me," Terry replied. "He's tortured the woman for years."

"So what we gonna do about it?"

Terry could hear the pounding of his own pulse echoing through his ears. This was a decisive moment in both his life and his career. For some two decades, he had served the Walker family. Yet, despite his best efforts, Abigail had always turned to others in her moments of greatest crisis. This morning, all of that had changed. "I need you," she had finally admitted. He was finally in command.

"Remember Ricky Moore?"

"Ah, good old Ricky," Dalton said, recognizing the name of the Dorchester robber Terry had gunned down in a darkened alley. "You sure? Didn't think the old lady would go for that kind of shit."

"I didn't either, but I spoke to her this morning. She said it herself—'Get rid of him.'"

Terry watched as Dalton rubbed his hands across his stubble, a gleam evident in his eyes. Dalton had always loved this kind of darkness. Terry had not. Yet he was sure he had made the right call. This was his shining moment.

"Haven't gone hunting in a while," Dalton said. "It should be fun." He rubbed his hands together. "So, when?"

Terry didn't hesitate. "As soon as you can."

# CHAPTER 75

A dejected Joe Andrews slumped in the passenger seat of a government-issued Ford as it headed east toward LaGuardia airport. The sunlit morning had turned into a dreary evening, the increasing darkness providing a suitable metaphor for his experience over the last few months. The journey to New York that had begun with such promise nearly three months earlier was now ending in complete disappointment. In about an hour, he would be on a Delta Shuttle flight to Washington. When his flight lifted off and entered a blackening sky, his investigation of Ted Parker would come to its official end.

Not even Jack's evidence of billing fraud had earned Joe the benefit of more time to pursue Ted Parker. "Hand everything over to Masterson, and let him finish this off," Special Agent Sanford had ordered him. "You've done good work here, but they need you back in DC."

Ted Parker might yet come to justice. But the glory would not be Joe's.

As the Ford emerged from the Midtown Tunnel and onto the Long Island Expressway, a light spattering of rain hit the front windshield. Sitting in silence, Joe stared into the side mirror and watched New York City fade into the background. He imagined that off in the distance behind him, Bob Masterson was back at the Harvard Club, dismantling the surveillance operation he had helped to set up three months before.

"We'll get him for you," the driver said. "Don't worry about it."

Joe stared out the window at the gray sky. "I hope you do."

# CHAPTER 76

Abigail sat in her usual seat at the Harvard Club, her first two glasses of wine long since finished. She hadn't told Ted why she had summoned him to dinner. Now that he had finally arrived, it was time for him to find out.

"You can't control your own people," Abigail snapped as soon as Ted sat down. "For years you have tried to control every aspect of my life, and you can't even keep your own house in order."

"What are you talking about?"

"I'm talking about this." She tossed the sheet of paper across the table.

His eyes scanned the sheet. "When did you receive this? Why didn't you call me?"

"I got it this morning. You see where it came from, don't you? You see the words at the top of the page?"

"I think we should cancel this dinner."

"You led him right to me. How could you be such a fool?"

"What the hell are you talking about? Who is *he*?"

"Jack Collins, you fool. Oh Lord, do not play dumb with me. You brought the devil right to me. You invited him into my very home."

"What? Oh no, you have it all wrong. We—"

"Wrong? The only thing I have done *wrong* has been to let you always make my decisions for me. Today I solved my own problems."

"Look, Abigail, you really need to listen to me."

"I need to do nothing of the sort. I spoke with Terry. It's over. He will do what he needs to do."

"'*Do what he needs to do?*' What the hell does that mean?"

"I have done what I should have done four years ago."

"You don't know what you're doing."

"Yes, I do. For once, I do."

"No, you don't." Ted pounded his fist on the table. "Listen to me. *I* know what's going on here. And you're wrong. *You* haven't disappointed anyone. *I* have. Deb told me so just last night, using precisely the same words."

"I'm not sure I'm following this."

"It's Deb," Ted said emphatically. "Deb Miller. It's been her all along."

"Impossible. It can't be."

"Yes, it's her. I always had a suspicion, but now I'm certain."

"Oh no. Terry..."

"Terry what?"

"We have to stop him." She snapped up from her chair, knocking her wineglass off the table as she did so.

"Abby, where are you going? What's going on?"

"My God. Oh my God," she replied as her breath left her. "They are going... going to kill him."

"What the hell is going on?" Ted asked, his voice booming.

As Abigail noticed a tuxedo storming toward her, she kept tapping at her phone. "Oh, Terry, Terry. Please, no."

"Mrs. Walker, I'm so sorry, but there are no phones in the dining room," the maître d' said breathlessly as he arrived. "May I escort you to the lobby?"

She bolted out of the dining room, continuing to fumble with the phone as she went. Suddenly someone grabbed her shoulder and spun her around. She turned to face a burly man, his ragged mustache glistening with sweat.

"FBI," he said as he wrapped a meaty hand around her wrist and took an audible gasp of air. "Please stay right there, Mrs. Walker."

# CHAPTER 77

Jack's wool overcoat hung from a brass hook in the 46th Street entryway to Farrell's Pub, his cell phone tucked in the side pocket. Twenty feet away, he stood at the bar with six of R&H's tax lawyers, each of them already having consumed a few pints of Guinness to celebrate Clay Warren's thirty-fifth birthday.

"To the best friend a guy could have," Steve Oswald slurred as he raised yet another beer.

The group clinked glasses and downed large swallows of the black lager.

"You guys are awesome," Clay said loudly, trying to be heard amid the din. "Even you, Collins. You're not bad for a straight guy from Connecticut."

Glasses clinked again and pointed in Jack's direction as everyone had a good chuckle at his expense. He didn't mind the attention. Tonight he felt welcomed and included, one of the few times at R&H he had ever felt that way. No hidden agendas. No ulterior motives. Simply a good time.

Jack drained his last sip of Guinness and placed the empty glass on the bar.

"You good for another?" Steve asked.

"I shouldn't."

Steve rolled his eyes at him. "Come on..."

"All right, one more. Although I'm already past my limit."

"Good, we have a lot to celebrate."

"We sure do," Jack agreed.

The bartender slid another Guinness across the counter.

"Cheers," Jack said, holding his glass out toward Steve.

"Right back at you." Steve banged his glass into Jack's, sending warm suds onto both of their hands.

Jack passed his glass to his dry hand and shook the beer off the other. "Hey, can I ask you something kinda crazy?" he asked sheepishly.

"Sure thing."

"Know anything about Atlantic Coast Bank? Anything related to Ted?"

"Atlantic Coast? Is that our new bank?"

"No. It's a bank in the Caymans."

"Nah, never heard of it."

"Well, there's one thing we didn't talk about the other night. There's something going on in the Caymans with Ted and Abigail. She's sending money to his offshore account."

"In the *Caymans*? That's not right."

"I know, yet another wrong thing going on at R&H. I probably should have filled you in earlier, but—"

"No, I'm telling you, that's *not right*. Wrong place, Jack. Ted would *never* put money in the Caymans, especially if he was doing something shifty. We all researched it once."

"*We?*"

"Yeah, Ted, Deb, and I. Years ago, for one of the Orion Financial guys. If I can remember his name, I'll have the file pulled for you. He ended up using the Cook Islands. Much more privacy. The guy wanted Caymans, but Ted talked him out of it."

The back of Jack's throat tightened. "Talked him out of it? Why?"

"For good reason. The Caymans share way too much information with the Feds. Ted told the guy to pick someplace more private. He was pretty funny about it too. 'If you're going to open an account in the Caymans, put my ex-wife's name on it,' Ted told him. 'Let the IRS try to deal with her.'" Steve laughed heartily as he threw back another gulp of beer.

Thoughts began to race through Jack's head. He pictured the photo of Deb in the Caymans. He thought back to all her lies. The room swirled around him as his heart began to pound. *Oh my God,* he thought. *She set Ted up.*

He slammed his glass back onto the bar and fought back the urge to vomit. "Oh no," he muttered as the taste of burnt Guinness filled his mouth. "I have to go."

"You okay?" Steve asked.

"No, not at all," he replied then bolted toward the door.

# CHAPTER 78

Joe Andrews lifted his cell phone from the console between the Ford's front seats and saw Bob Masterson's number on the display. "What's up, Bob?"

"Your friend is in serious trouble."

Less than a minute later, the Ford was heading in the opposite direction on the Long Island Expressway, its flashing blue lights clearing a path westward through the evening traffic.

"Goddamn it," Joe yelled as he frantically dialed Jack's number. "Come on, bud, pick up. Pick up the fucking phone."

Jack failed to answer one call and then another. The air in the Ford grew warm and musty as Joe nervously passed his cell phone from hand to hand, contemplating his next move. The same questions kept cycling through his mind. Where was Jack? Why hadn't he answered his phone? Was he even still alive?

Momentarily relieved when his phone rang, his heart sank again when he realized it was only Bob Masterson. "Give me good news, Bob."

Bob largely complied, detailing how he had rapidly taken control of the unfolding crisis. A team of New York City police were camped out in the lobby of 1593 Broadway. Another team was on its way to Deb's apartment. Stamford police were with a very nervous Amanda Collins, and the MTA police were keeping a lookout at Grand Central Terminal.

"Nice work," Joe said. But there was one glaring omission. "Where's Jack?"

"We don't know."

As the car weaved its way through traffic, Joe tugged on his seat belt to be sure it was tight. Desperate to think of someone else who might know Jack's whereabouts, he ticked through a mental list of all the people he knew to be associated with him. Obviously, if Amanda knew where he was, she would have told the uniforms at her house. He sure as hell couldn't ask Miller or Parker. And then, as if divinely inspired, he remembered a name buried deep within the files he had boxed up earlier that morning. "Claire Reed," he barked. "Parker's secretary. Her name is Claire Reed. Track her down. Now!"

"I'm on it," Bob said. "Give me five minutes."

"Make it two."

Two minutes later, Bob was back on the line. "Farrells," he said. "It's a pub on 46th. In Hell's Kitchen."

"West 46thStreet!" Joe yelled to the driver before turning his attention back to the phone. "Bob, get in touch with someone at that bar. Make sure Jack doesn't leave."

# CHAPTER 79

Jack dashed out of Farrell's and into the November night, fumbling with his overcoat as he went. He was dressed entirely wrong for what had turned out to be a warm and rainy evening. His overcoat was too heavy. He carried no umbrella. He would be soaked from his hair down to his wingtips by the time he finished the crosstown walk to Grand Central.

As drops of rain splattered around him, he glanced over his shoulder down 46th Street, hoping to catch a lucky glimpse of a passing cab. But no luck. So he began the trudge eastward toward Times Square, the rain beginning to dampen his hair and coat.

He walked briskly down the slick sidewalk and fumbled in his pocket for his cell phone. Another wave of tension surged through him as he looked at the display. *What the hell?* He had missed a dozen phone calls and a stream of text messages longer than he had ever seen. Scrolling through them, his heart pounded as he read one dire warning after another, one phrase repeated more than any other: *You're in danger.*

He heard a faint sound behind him as he lowered the phone from his ear. He snapped his head toward it. Squinting into the misty darkness, he saw a set of headlights approaching from a block behind him. *Please be a taxi,* he hoped. *Oh please.*

He forced his trembling hands to dial Amanda's number without taking his eyes off the approaching headlights. The two white circles grew slowly brighter as the car inched toward him, his breathing becoming calmer as they approached. Then they flickered from view, momentarily blocked by a faint shape, a shade darker than the darkness that surrounded it. As Jack made out the blurred outline of a human figure crossing the street, he lost his grip on the phone, and it tumbled to the street.

Jack's pulse pounded as he saw the moving shadow heading straight toward him. He turned around and started to briskly walk away.

"Hold on a second," a deep voice called from behind him.

But Jack didn't comply. Instead, he put his head down and ran as if he were back on the Stamford High track team, hurtling forward as if his life depended on it.

# CHAPTER 80

Deb sat on the windowsill of her fourth-floor walk-up, her feet resting on a wooden kitchen chair. She took a long drag on her cigarette and leaned her head out the window, a smattering of rain hitting her face as she exhaled. Looking down at an unusually quiet Minetta Lane, she watched the cascading raindrops glistening in the street lights below.

Flashing red lights flickered across her view as a police car zipped down MacDougal Street. Moments later, another appeared on Minetta, stopping directly in front of her building. She heard a car door slam and then another. She felt her stomach tense. *Not possible,* she thought. *No way.*

Soon came a pounding on her door. "NYPD," a gruff voice shouted. "Open up."

Deb bolted from her perch. Pressing her hands against the cold metal door, she looked through the peephole. She saw the distorted image of a police officer, one hand pressed against the door and the other down at his side. Another cop stood well behind.

She scurried back across the apartment, stopping on her way at the kitchen table. She snatched a small plate off the table and held it just below the table's edge, using it to catch the stray flakes of cocaine she swept away with her palm. She put the plate in the kitchen sink and rinsed it in a stream of warm water.

Another pounding rattled her apartment door, this time sounding more urgent than before. "NYPD. Police. Open the door."

She dashed back to the window and stuck her head outside. A line of red lights now flickered in the rainy street. Another car door slammed.

She stuck one leg out the window and straddled the sill, her bare foot rubbing against the roughness of the building's façade. She pressed the cigarette into the wet brick and let it slip from her fingers.

The door rumbled another time. "NYPD. Open the door."

She could safely ignore them. They probably didn't have a warrant. *At least not yet.*

She leaned farther out the window as raindrops splashed off her face. The stillness below had completely yielded to the sounds of car doors and police radios. Flickering red lights bounced off everything in sight. A dozen onlookers now milled around, their faces shielded by baseball caps and hoods.

Her heart raced within her chest as she gasped for air. *How? Where did I go wrong?*

She leaned back inside and grabbed her phone off the small kitchen counter. Without looking at the screen, she dialed Ted's number.

After three rings, he picked up. "Er, Deb," he said, sounding unusually stilted. "Um. Where are you?"

"I'm at the office, in the library. I had a ton of work to finish."

"At the office? Really?"

"Did you ever care about me?"

"Look this isn't the time. You need to—"

"It's *exactly* the time. Did you ever care about me?"

"Please, let's not do this now. You just need to—"

"I need to know. Did I ever really matter to you?"

"This isn't the time."

"Answer me, damn it!" she wailed as she stuck her head back out the window, a stream of tears joining the raindrops pouring down her face. "Just answer me."

"Of course I cared," he said. "I still do," he added, sounding as heartfelt as she had ever heard him.

"Then just tell me you're sorry." She could taste the saltiness of her tears.

"Oh, I am. I'm sorry for *everything*. I know I let you down."

"I forgive you." She tossed the phone back into the apartment. "I forgive you," she repeated into thin air.

She braced her hands on the inside of the window and leaned farther into the darkness, the cold rain spraying her steadily as it slicked her shirt against her chest. Suddenly she was back on her uncle's sailboat, tacking through a windswept Caribbean. She could picture her father at the tiller as she sat in the bow, her wet hair dangling toward the clear blue water.

"Hey, you up there," someone yelled from the street. She turned over her shoulder to see the beam of a flashlight shining up at her. "What the hell are you doing?"

She said nothing as she turned away from the light and leaned ever backward, the rain hitting her like a fierce sea spray. She closed her eyes and thought of warmth and sunshine, taking herself back to a happier time and place. She began laughing with joy as the rain pelted her face.

"I've missed you, Daddy," she mumbled skyward as she suddenly began to sob. "I'm sorry I made such a mess."

"Hey, you," the voice again called from below, "get back inside."

But she paid no attention. Instead, she leaned farther and farther backward into the driving rain. Then she slid her hands off the window frame and tumbled into the night.

# CHAPTER 81

The steady rain plastered Jack's hair against his scalp as streams of water ran into his eyes. He swiped his hair aside without slowing down as he hurtled eastward. His lungs burned with every stride. *Just another block,* he said to himself. Soon he would reach the theaters and the bustling streets beyond. *There have to be people up ahead.*

"Come on, Jack," yelled the man from behind him, his halting voice making clear that he was as winded as Jack. "Stop, and let's talk."

*He knows my name.* The thought jolted Jack like a cattle prod, and he surged faster toward the lights in the distance. But the rush of adrenaline proved short-lived. As he passed more empty doorsteps, he felt his stride shortening, his progress growing increasingly labored. He could hear the footsteps behind him growing louder as his pursuer drew closer. He scanned the sidewalk in front of him as he sucked in a deep breath. His legs felt heavy. He was nearly done.

A few doorways in front of him, he saw a swath of light cascading out a storefront. On the sidewalk, a small metal stand displayed a menu. Finally, an open restaurant. A safe haven. He was just five strides from the doorway. Then four. Then three.

He felt a sharp tug on his collar. "Your wallet," yelled a gruff voice behind him. "Gimme your wallet."

Jack tried to pull away, but his feet slipped backward as an unseen hand tugged at him and twisted him around. As he began to spin, Jack eyed the menu stand. *Am I close enough to reach it?*

"Gimme your wallet," the voice boomed again, this time close enough that Jack could smell it. Scotch and cigarettes. "I'm done fooling around."

*Me too,* Jack thought, as he lunged forward and grabbed the menu stand. He wrapped his hands around the slick metal post as he snapped around to face his attacker, swinging the sign as hard as he could. He heard the whooshing sound of metal pushing through air and then felt the impact as he connected just below the man's chin.

The dark figure stumbled backward. A faint popping sound echoed through the street, intermixed with the sound of a shattering window across the block. A gun tumbled to the sidewalk, the matte metal rattling as it slid on the pavement and skittered over the curb.

Jack swung the metal stand a second time. This time the man saw it coming. He turned away from the incoming blow, and it glanced off his shoulder. He stepped forward and grabbed Jack's overcoat with one hand as he swung forward with the other.

Jack turned away from the punch, but it still hit its mark. He felt a sharp sting in his cheek, followed by a spreading warmth. Ignoring the pain, he stepped forward and seized the man's left arm with both of his. He stared into small dark eyes as he tussled with his foe.

"You're a dead man," the man taunted. "Dead."

Jack couldn't break the man's grip on his collar. The wet wool dug deeper and deeper into his neck. To relieve the pressure, Jack stepped forward, his body pushing into the other man's. "Help," Jack yelled as loud as his burning lungs would allow. "Help!"

He gasped for air. He was completely spent. Like a prizefighter one punch from being knocked out, he pressed in toward his foe, trying to prevent him from delivering the fatal blow. The man's stubble scratched at Jack's skin as their faces pressed together. "Nobody's gonna help you." He jammed a palm under Jack's jaw and knocked it upward. "Nobody."

Jack could feel death encircling him. His legs trembled as the pressure on his jaw forced his head up and back. He pulled downward on the man's sleeves, trying to loosen his grip.

Then over the man's shoulder, Jack saw headlights hurtling toward them. Flashing blue lights reflected off the windows on both sides of the street. *Oh thank God.* He just needed to hold on for a minute longer. He felt a sharp pain in his gut as a knee hit him from below, followed by another whack on the bottom of his jaw. His teeth crunched together as he tasted his own blood. The air left his lungs. He lost his grip on the man and tumbled backward, hitting the wet sidewalk with a splash.

Jack scrambled to his feet as he saw the dark figure reaching down for the gun. "I told you nobody was coming for you," he said as he palmed the pistol. "Man, I love this shit," he added through laughter. He turned his head slightly toward the right as he spoke.

*Yeah, he's hearing it now.* The unmistakable roar of a car engine grew louder and louder as it hurtled toward them.

Suddenly the street was bathed in white light. Jack lifted a hand to shield his eyes from the blinding rays as tires screeched on wet pavement. The car slid to a halt, both doors opening at once as shouting voices emerged from behind them.

"FBI! Freeze!" bellowed one voice. "FBI! Drop your weapon!" yelled the other. Amid the storm of words, he recognized a familiar accent and heard one order above all the others. "Get down, Jack! Get the fuck down!"

Jack threw himself into the rain-slicked street, in the process shredding his pants and the palms of both hands. As his face pressed against the wet pavement, he heard a pair of gunshots.

———◉———

JOE'S BULLETS BOTH hit the mark, and the hooded man dropped to the sidewalk with a thud. Joe moved out from behind the protection of the Ford's doors, his weapon at the ready until after he had kicked the Glock away from David Dalton's lifeless body. Joe then headed straight for Jack.

Jack was a total mess. Blood streamed from both hands. His right pants leg was in tatters, his overcoat soaked in rainwater and blood. Joe helped him to his feet, catching him when he started to slump back to the pavement. As a cacophony of sirens approached from all directions, Jack leaned his head into Joe's shoulder.

"Who the hell was that?" Jack mumbled.

"Good question, bud," Joe replied, wrapping his hand around the back of Jack's wet hair. "Where the hell do I begin?"

# CHAPTER 82

"I wasn't sleeping," Jack insisted, snapping to attention as the silver Ford turned onto Oak Street in Stamford and arrived in front of a nondescript blue colonial. Looking at his watch, he saw it was well past midnight.

"More like passed out," Joe said. "I could use some of what that paramedic gave you."

After exiting the car, Jack and Joe walked together toward the house's rear door. Joe wrapped his arm around his companion's shoulders as the two men headed up the slate walkway. Neither man said a thing. For his part, Jack was too exhausted to speak. Plus, he needed no words to express what he was feeling. The past evening's events had once again affirmed what he had long known to be true: he never had a better friend than Joe Andrews, even before Joe saved his life.

Stepping off the slate pathway and onto the concrete stoop, they stopped in front of Jack's kitchen door. The two men embraced as Jack said simply, "Thanks." A lot was packaged into that single word. *Thanks for driving me home. Thanks for finding me tonight. Thanks for being a good friend. And, by the way, thanks for saving my life.*

Before Jack could even pull his keys out of his pocket, Amanda flung open the door, wrapped her arms around her husband and kissed him on the side of his face that wasn't bandaged. "I love you," was all she managed to say, and all she needed to, before she burst into tears.

After a full minute of holding her husband so tightly he could barely breathe, she released him and hugged Joe, planting a kiss on his cheek as well. "Thanks, Joey. I love you too."

"I love you too," he replied.

After another round of kisses and handshakes, the federal agent stepped back onto the slate path. "I still have a long night ahead of me," he explained. "A pile of paperwork like you won't believe, and at some point I'm supposed to head back to DC. For some reason, I missed my flight tonight," he added, smiling.

A few minutes later, Jack and Amanda stood at their living-room window, holding hands and watching as the sedan disappeared into the black mist of the Connecticut night. As the car faded from view, Jack shuddered as he thought about the events of the past several hours. Had Joe arrived just an instant later, things might have ended so very differently. Jack might never have made it home. Amanda might have been planning a funeral. His parents, for the second time, might be mourning life's greatest loss. In a single instant, the span of one heart-beat, everything could have changed.

It was a fitting, and fortunate, end to a journey that had begun with a similar instant. Eleven years earlier, while Jack stood at a Cambridge crosswalk, an equally fateful moment had changed the arc of so many lives. As an ambulance raced past Jack, the dying senator inside uttered his life's final words. In that instant, Deb and Jack just missed meet-ing. In that instant, Abigail and Ted's adultery altered both of their lives and ended the senator's. In that instant, Professor Alan Miller made the choice to serve a famous client and ignore his only daughter. All of their lives had once converged in a single moment, in a single place just out-side Harvard Yard. Long after the fact, they had remained bound to-gether by that fleeting encounter.

The consequences were not over for Ted and Abigail. Those two could expect to pay a price for the course of events they'd set into mo-tion on that October morning. Criminal investigations would follow. A media frenzy would ensue. The taint of scandal would follow them to their graves. Terry O'Reilly would face a similar fate, his devotion to the Walkers having first defined and then ultimately destroyed his life.

But for Jack, things were different. His demons had faded into silence, taking with them his gnawing doubts about the paths he had chosen and those he had not. After all these years, he had finally learned an elusive truth: fate had been kind to him.

He took Amanda's hand in his and stepped away from the window.

"Hey, I've been thinking about that Nevis trip," he said as he led her down the hallway toward their bedroom.

"And?"

"I'm thinking I can't wait until February to see you in a bikini. Any chance you can go next week?"

"Hmmm, I don't know. Are you sure you can get a week off from that fancy job of yours?"

He laughed. "I would think Ted has bigger problems than my vacation schedule."

"You think?"

"Pretty sure. And so what if he fires me? Saves me the trouble of quitting."

He felt her clutch his arm firmly as they reached their bedroom. "Okay," she said. "Let's get out of town. But first, let's go to bed."

"Great idea. I'm exhausted."

She pulled him forward into the blackened room and leaned her body into his.

"I said *bed*, Jack," she whispered into his ear before kissing him passionately. "I said nothing about sleep."

As she fumbled with the buttons on his shirt, he thought back to the moment he'd first seen her. He pictured her youthful face across that crowded bar, her blond hair tucked neatly under a baseball cap, as she fiddled with one of her dangling pearl earrings as she spoke. Had he missed her by a second, he thought, his life would have turned out so very different, so much worse.

"What are you thinking about?" she whispered as she slid his shirt off his shoulders.

"You," he replied truthfully. "Only you."

He closed his eyes and felt the warmth of her hands swirling across his back, their motion like leaves fluttering in the breeze. For a moment, he could picture himself back at Harvard, walking through Cambridge Common on a sunlit spring morning. Emerald-green maples arched above him as he strode boldly through the middle of the park and reached the asphalt beyond. Crossing the street, he glanced at the brick apartment building he walked past every day. The place was silent. The sidewalk was empty.

Without breaking stride, he continued on toward Cabot House. He lifted his face toward a deep-blue sky and basked in the warm sunshine. The brick apartments slipped into the distance behind him.

And he never looked back.

# EPILOGUE

J ack rested his feet on his battered oak desk and looked at the clock. It was nearly nine. Almost time for a new beginning.

Although nearly a year had passed, it seemed like just yesterday that he'd sat at this same desk, holding back tears as he looked at the man sitting across from him and said the hardest words a son can ever say. "Dad, I have to leave."

At first, Gene Collins had said nothing in response. He had spent nearly four decades building the law firm that bore his name and the name of his father. Never once before that moment had Jack given him any hint that he would chart a different course. And yet there was nothing ambiguous about what he had just said. "You want to try New York?" his father had asked him solemnly. "Is that what you want?"

"I do. I really do," Jack had said, staring down at the surface of his desk.

"Well, then, I've got some ideas." Like his son, Gene Collins had taken the safe road home to his father's law firm. Like his son, his classmates had not. Indeed, many of Gene's law-school friends occupied offices spread among the top floors of New York's tallest skyscrapers. And their phone numbers were all in the top drawer of his desk.

"I'll make some calls," father had said to son. "I'm sure we'll find you something."

Jack's eyes misted over as he thought about just how much he was asking his father to do. He had buried a daughter. He had spent months recovering from heart surgery. And now his son was abandoning him.

"I love you, Dad. I'm sorry." As the emotions poured out of him, he had said both sentences at almost the same time.

Gene Collins wasn't one to gush. That had always been his wife's job. But as he headed back to his office and placed telephone calls to nearly two dozen contacts in New York City, his actions spoke louder than words. They said, "I love you too."

Jack would always remember the events that began on that spring day. He would remember his joy when his father told him that Daniel Reynolds thought there might be an opening at his storied New York City firm. He would remember his excitement when Ted Parker extended his handshake and an offer to join his elite practice. He would also remember everything that happened thereafter—the silent struggles ending with a very public scandal and the heartache as he came to understand all the events that had transpired around him. As excited as he had been the day he decided to join R&H, he was even more excited to return to Collins & Collins.

"Hey, Jack," Claire Reed called gently from his office doorway. "He's here."

"Okay," he replied, jumping to attention. "Can you let Clay and Steve know?"

"Already have."

Jack took a deep breath then grabbed his suit jacket off the back of his door. After putting it on, he rubbed his hands down the front to press away any wrinkles. "How do I look?"

"Like the most famous lawyer in Connecticut," Claire said, plucking a loose thread off his lapel. "In other words, pretty darn good."

A minute later, he walked into the conference room and extended his hand to the waiting guest. "Welcome to Collins, Warren, and Oswald," he said warmly.

Michael Putnam shook his hand firmly. "Good to see you, Jack. Glad you're officially up and running."

"We sure are. And all your files have come over from R&H, so you're officially a client."

"Excellent."

"I figured that Steve and Clay would go over partnership taxes first, and then we can talk trusts and estate planning. Make sense?"

"Completely," he said. "Oh, I brought you a little something," he added, handing Jack an envelope. "Consider it an advance against my bills."

Jack opened the envelope and looked at the check inside. One hundred thousand dollars. *Not a bad first day.*

"And we need to talk office space too," he continued. "That spot is opening up in Six Greenwich Point. Killer views across the Sound to Long Island. And I know a guy who can cut you a deal on rent."

"Yes, we'll talk about it. But for now, I'm glad to be here for a while."

"I bet you are."

Steve and Clay stepped into the conference room, each of them toting a stack of files.

"The cavalry has arrived," Jack said as his partners set the files on the table. "The best tax lawyers within fifty miles."

"Plus, neither of us is under indictment," Steve added.

Clay and Steve took turns shaking their client's hand and then invited him to sit at the table.

"Call me when you're ready for my part," Jack said. "Thank you again, Michael," he added as he tucked the envelope into his jacket pocket. "I can't say that enough. We really appreciate all you have done."

Jack stepped out of the conference room and walked over to the hallway window. As he stared out into the brilliant morning, he was joined by a tall blonde, a steaming cup of coffee outstretched before her.

"Nice day, huh?" Amanda asked.

He took the coffee in one hand and pulled her body tight with the other.

"Yeah, it's an awesome day," he replied as he took a sip from the cup. "Even better now that you're here."

He interlaced his fingers with hers as together they stared out into the new day, into their new future.

In the sunlight, Jack spotted the first white blossoms of spring shimmering on the pear tree below. Things had looked so much more impressive from the forty-fourth floor. And yet the view from his office had never been better.

# ACKNOWLEDGEMENTS

I started this novel longer ago than I care to admit, inspired to do so by a conversation that I can scarcely remember. As I have taken that long journey from first idea to published work, I owe a debt of gratitude to those who so willingly offered encouragement and shared their time and insight.

A number of published authors were very kind to this newbie. Thank you, Ian Ayres, Robert Bailey, Bill Brazell, John Dobbyn, James Grippando, Sarah Darer Littman, Brad Meltzer, Sheryn MacMunn, Jonathan Putnam, and Mary Simses for taking time away from your own writing to help nudge mine along.

I've learned that writing law review articles and novels demand very different skills sets. I was professionally trained for the former, but not the latter. Fortuitously, the experts stepped in along the way. Thank you, Jessica Anderegg, Darlene Gardner, Debra Ginsberg, and Maya Meyers for your brilliant editorial work, for finally teaching me how to show and not tell, and for pruning back so many sentences choked with excessive, unnecessary, and repetitive adjectives.

For all the amazing work behind the scenes, thank you to Lynn McNamee, Erica Lucke Dean and everyone at Red Adept Publishing. Thank you also to my mentor, Jennifer Klepper, and my amazing fellow authors at Red Adept for all the support and guidance.

Even though my parents, Ed and Gert, and my sister, Amy, had no choice but to read the early drafts, I'm still grateful they did. I'm also thankful for the dear friends who volunteered to read drafts and offer sage advice. Thank you, Andrea Cohen, Jennifer Warner Cooper, Alison Creed, Todd Thomas, and Michele Walters for your friendship and your generosity.

In a class by herself among my beta readers is my wife, Alexandra. I'm quite certain she's read this book as many times as I have, finding something worth changing with every pass. I've appreciated all your thoughtful advice, even if I initially resisted every word of it.

Last, but most certainly not least, thank you to my super agent, Liza Fleissig, as well as Ginger Harris-Dontzin and the rest of the team at the Liza Royce Agency. Liza was the second agent I queried about this novel, and also the fifty-second. I'm so glad we finally inked the deal. This book, and its author, are much the better due to Liza's vision, enthusiasm, and tireless efforts on our behalf.

# About the Author

Jeff Cooper is a law professor, lawyer, former Presidential candidate, and published author of both fiction and nonfiction. A graduate of Harvard College, Yale Law School and New York University School of Law, he spent much of his career working in the law firms and trust banks fictionalized in his novels.

His nonfiction writing has been published in Law Journals across the country, excerpted in prominent legal casebooks and treatises, and reprinted both in the U.S. and abroad. His debut novel was a finalist for The Daphne du Maurier Award for Excellence in Mystery/Suspense.

Jeff was born and raised in New York and now lives in Greenwich, Connecticut, where he has served as an elected member of the Representative Town Meeting, a Justice of the Peace and a Director of several non-profit organizations. He is married with three children. When he's not teaching or writing, he can be found on the golf course.

Read more at www.jeffcooperauthor.com.

# About the Publisher

**Dear Reader,**

**We hope you enjoyed this book. Please consider leaving a review on your favorite book site.**

Visit https://RedAdeptPublishing.com to see our entire catalogue.

Don't forget to subscribe to our monthly newsletter to be notified of future releases and special sales.